ADORED BY THE ARCHDUKE

Hawk Castle, Book 2
A Habsburg Historical Romance

by Lily Harlem

*"What Mars gives to others,
Venus delivers to Vienna."*

© Copyright 2024 by Lily Harlem
Text by Lily Harlem
Cover by Dar Albert

Dragonblade Publishing, Inc. is an imprint of Kathryn Le Veque Novels, Inc.
P.O. Box 23
Moreno Valley, CA 92556
ceo@dragonbladepublishing.com

Produced in the United States of America

First Edition July 2024
Trade Paperback Edition

Reproduction of any kind except where it pertains to short quotes in relation to advertising or promotion is strictly prohibited.

All Rights Reserved.

The characters and events portrayed in this book are fictitious. Any similarity to real persons, living or dead, is purely coincidental and not intended by the author.

ARE YOU SIGNED UP FOR DRAGONBLADE'S BLOG?

You'll get the latest news and information on exclusive giveaways, exclusive excerpts, coming releases, sales, free books, cover reveals and more.

Check out our complete list of authors, too!

No spam, no junk. That's a promise!

Sign Up Here
www.dragonbladepublishing.com

Dearest Reader;

Thank you for your support of a small press. At Dragonblade Publishing, we strive to bring you the highest quality Historical Romance from some of the best authors in the business. Without your support, there is no 'us', so we sincerely hope you adore these stories and find some new favorite authors along the way.

Happy Reading!

CEO, Dragonblade Publishing

Additional Dragonblade books by Author Lily Harlem

Hawk Castle Series
Loved by the Last Knight (Book 1)
Adored by the Archduke (Book 2)
Embraced by the Emperor (Book 3)

The Lyon's Den Series
Lyon at the Altar

Adored by the Archduke

Sent over land and sea to wed a man you've never met. Disaster…right?
Not when he turns out to be handsome, charming, and ambitious—and he drives you crazy with lust.

Joanna of Castile's life is changing forever. Swapping Spain for Flanders and leaving her family behind is her duty. As is marrying the Archduke of Austria, Philip the Handsome, who rules the Low Countries with skill despite his young age.

The moment their eyes meet, lightning strikes and powerful passions erupt. A joining like no other, a match made in heaven. Joanna basks in her good fortune and in her husband's seductive attentions.

But when life intrudes on their harmony—kings wage war, queens demand inquisitions, and heirs pass on their crowns—will Joanna be able to quash rumors about her state of mind? And will her husband ever be the true King of Castile?

More importantly, can Philip and Joanna's love survive all that is thrown at them? And can a future queen keep an archduke as truly hers and hers alone?

Notes from the Author

While writing HAWK CASTLE, I have truly let my imagination run wild and free to create a fun, romantic romp through history in the company of an eclectic bunch of vibrant, powerful, and passionate men and women.

In other words, while this story is inspired by long-ago characters and events, please don't quote HAWK CASTLE in your history thesis, as I can't be responsible for your grade!

By the way…

*Joanna of Castile was also known as 'Joanna the Mad,' but perhaps she was simply feisty, intelligent, and headstrong and when feeling betrayed or lonely could not contain her frustration, fury, and sadness.

**The relationship between Archduke Philip of the House of Habsburg and Joanna of Castile is documented in many ways, but what they all have in common is it was an intense firework display of love, lust, and fierce possession.

***The title "archduke" was created by the Habsburgs for themselves.

Chapter One

1496
Castile, Spain

"What are you reading now, Joanna? You always have your head in a book."

Joanna raised her eyebrow at her brother. "Listen to this." She held the book a little higher and cleared her throat.

"Go on, then," John said, flicking at a fly. "Keep reading." The meadow was alive with insects—butterflies, bees, and small, red beetles that headbutted into each other. "Though I should imagine you know Mother's gift from Columbus by heart, you've read it so often."

Joanna ignored him. "'They brought us parrots and balls of cotton and spears and many other things, which they exchanged for glass beads and hawks' bells.'" She paused. "I am not sure why he took hawks' bells."

John shrugged.

Joanna went on. "'They willingly traded everything they owned. They were well-built, with good bodies and handsome features. They do not bear arms, and do not know them, for I showed them a sword, they took it by the edge and cut themselves out of ignorance.'" She held up her hand. "Imagine that. Cutting yourself on a sword because you have never seen one and know not of its danger."

"Imagine." He plucked a long, dry blade of grass and chewed

on the end. He lay back on the grass and closed his eyes.

"'They have no iron,'" she continued. "'They would make fine servants. With fifty men, we could subjugate them all and make them do whatever we want.'"

"Mother would never allow it," John said.

"I agree. She has told Columbus that any people he discovers are Spanish subjects and cannot be enslaved." She sighed and shook her head. "She also means to ensure they are all Catholic, or converted to Catholicism."

"Be careful of your tone, Joanna."

"Why must I?"

"You know why. Our parents are pious monarchs. They plan to spread the word of God and His salvation through Jesus Christ throughout the new world. Any sign of heresy, no matter how slight, will not be good for you. Look what happened to the Moors."

"Indeed." She closed the book, lay down beside her brother, and squinted up at a cloud shaped like a horse's head moving from east to west in a deep-blue sky. "And look what happened to us."

"What do you mean?"

"We have had to pray and live by God's rules every day since we were born."

"Seriously." He turned to his side. "Do not let our parents hear you speak this way. I fear for you if you do. You will be strung up with weights on your feet and flogged."

She raised her arms over her head and pointed her toes. "The spring sunshine is lovely today."

"We should have gone hunting." He lay back down.

"I felt like being lazy." Joanna had taken a long ride the day before, on her favorite mare, Gianna, and now she was tired. It had been a wonderful ride accompanied by her groomsman, Raul. She'd spotted a fish eagle and a herd of wild boar.

A sudden commotion behind them had John sitting bolt upright. "What the...?"

"I have been looking everywhere for you." Catherine's head appeared above the long grass. She'd abandoned her headwear and would no doubt be scolded by Beatriz for it. But she did look lovely with her long, strawberry-blonde curls flowing out behind her. "Why do you always hide from me?"

"We do not," John said, flopping back down. "We were simply resting. Or trying to."

"I want to rest with you." Catherine pouted and placed her hands on her hips.

"You'd be bored," Joanna said. "We're not nearly as interesting as playing on your clavichord."

"That is *really* boring." Catherine dropped to her knees with a dramatic huff.

"Oh, come now." Joanna reached for her younger sister and hugged her close, tickling her ribs as she did so. "You love the clavichord even more than learning numbers."

Catherine giggled and squirmed, her small limbs slippery. "I do not love, either. Get off me. Get off me."

"You don't mean that." Joanna kissed Catherine's temple and held her tighter.

Catherine squealed then laughed harder. A skylark took to the air, twittering above them.

"Stop it. You are disturbing the peace," John said sternly.

Joanna stopped tickling her sister but kept her held in a hug.

"You are always so bossy, John," Catherine said, catching her breath.

"That is because one day, I will be King of Asturias. Therefore, I must practice being stern and commanding."

"Maybe you should practice your law and languages with as much conviction," Joanna said.

"I have done my lessons with De Miranda this week."

"To his satisfaction?" Joanna asked, pulling a face at Catherine.

Catherine giggled then sat up and held out her finger, clearly hoping a small, blue butterfly that was fluttering nearby would land on it.

"He was as satisfied as he is with your studies," John said, "if not more so."

Joanna said nothing. John wasn't as committed to his education as she was to her own. Perhaps she was blessed that she found it effortless to remember history, heraldry, and philosophy. Mathematics and languages came easily, as did reciting poetry and playing musical instruments.

Catherine stood, her summer gown creased now and her cheeks pink. She followed the butterfly toward an ancient olive tree.

"Do you ever wonder what they will be like?" Joanna asked, keeping watch on her little sister.

"Who?"

"You know who."

"Our betrothed?" John sat and flicked away the strand of grass he'd been chewing. "Yes, of course I do."

"And do you wish that you could choose your own wife? Rather than our parents choosing for you?"

"What kind of question is that?"

"A simple one."

"It is not a simple one. We are the children of Ferdinand II of Aragon and Isabella I of Castile, which makes our matrimonial choices of great import. Whom we marry won't just affect our lives, but that of the new Kingdom of Spain."

Joanna was quiet.

"And you should not complain," John went on. "For it is peasants who choose their spouses. We are royalty."

"I wish I were a peasant." She sighed dramatically and folded her arms.

"What has gotten into you today?" He reached for her hand and tugged it from the crook of her elbow. "You concern me so with the way you speak. If it were to fall on anyone's ears but mine, then…" He frowned.

Joanna studied her brother. His auburn hair was already

lightening in the spring sun and his brown eyes were lined with black lashes. He had a sprinkle of freckles on his nose and cheeks that would become more noticeable over the summer months.

For a moment, she compared his eyes to Raul's. They were similar, though Raul's were darker, like shiny hazelnuts, and he looked at her with an intensity that made her think he could see into her royal soul. "Nothing has gotten into me," she said, turning away.

"There is something. Please. I beg you. Tell me."

"It's just…" She bit on her bottom lip.

"Joanna."

"I heard Father talking."

"And?"

"France's grip on Naples is tightening. The French king also has his sights set on Granada."

"King Charles is a greedy man."

"Who is taking what he wants." She touched her brother's cheek. "And the rest of Europe will not watch on without action."

"I can tell your mind is busy." He narrowed his eyes at her. "Go on."

"We are of age now, our parents have been reaching out to secure our marriages, and I feel the announcement is drawing close."

"You do?"

"Yes. We must align ourselves with border allies to defeat France. Grow in territory and in power. We need the support of Rome."

"You are wise, sister of mine," he said. "To think of such things." He laughed. "Perhaps you should be king and not I."

She also laughed, the tension suddenly lifting from her. "I am far too pretty to be king, though I dare say I could rule with the skill of any man."

"I will have to write to you, when you are married in a distant land, and ask for your consultation."

"You will have forgotten all about me."

"No." His smile dropped. "Please don't think that. You are my sister, my friend, and dear to my heart. I will never forget about you and will always pray for your health and happiness."

"As I will yours." She squeezed his hand.

"I'm hungry." Catherine was beside them again. "Have you got any bread?"

"No." Joanna stood. "But we'll get you some, and some olives and jam too." She held out her hand and Catherine slipped her small one into it. "Come on, John, back to the castle."

"And, no doubt, extra lessons in canon and civil law."

"You love it, really." She linked her arm with his and they made their way up the meadow.

Beatriz was waiting for them, the silvery embroidery on her long, stiff, blue gown glinting in the sunshine. "Children," she said, plucking a fluffy grass seed from Catherine's hair. "You must make haste. Your parents are waiting for you."

"They are?" Joanna said. "Why? What has happened?"

"A letter has arrived and—" She shook her head. "I cannot say more. It is for the king and queen to discuss with you and I know nothing of it, not really."

Joanna gave her brother a lingering look.

"Do you think it could be…?" He held out his palms. "What we were just speaking of?"

"Maybe it was God's way of telling us first." She touched the cross that hung around her neck. "Making our paths easier."

"I don't know what you are talking about." Beatriz tutted. "But you must go and smarten yourselves up before being presented to your parents. Come. Come. This way." She held out her arms and seemed to herd them toward their bedchambers. "Maria is already preparing."

"Can I have some bread and olives?" Catherine asked. "While you brush my hair?"

"Yes, they, too, are awaiting you. Quickly now. And whatever have you done with your hair, child? And once again, your headdress is gone."

ONE HOUR LATER, Joanna stood in a line with her siblings in the Great Hall. Her mother and father—perched on ornate, golden chairs—wore jeweled crowns and red robes. Behind them, an intricate tapestry held the Trastámara family crest and due to the high windows that let in little light, the room was aglow with candles.

A heavy, serious atmosphere hung like a dense fog weighing everything down.

"Where is Isabella?" John whispered out of the corner of his mouth.

"Our grieving sister… is in her room starving herself, I should think." Joanna frowned, but the truth was she worried for their older sister, who had lost her young, Portuguese husband in a riding accident.

"Finally, you are here." The queen's voice filled the room.

"We are sorry to keep you waiting." John dipped his head and kissed the back of his mother's hand. He then stood beside Joanna so that all four children were in a line of age order. John, Joanna, Maria, and then Catherine, the youngest.

Joanna resisted the urge to fidget. The sheer number of nobles and priests standing around told her something momentous was about to be announced. It reminded her of when her older sister, Isabella, had been informed of her marriage to Prince Alfonso of Portugal. She'd left Castile not long after.

Her father, Ferdinand, held out his palms and raised his eyes heavenward. "God has spoken to us in the form of a letter, and now we know what we must do to defend Christendom and Spain."

The children were all quiet, even Catherine, who had a tendency to interrupt serious matters with tales of rabbits, foxes, and birds.

Joanna's heart rate picked up when De Leon, her father's

elderly head bishop, stepped forward with a tightly rolled scroll held in the grip of his gnarled fingers.

"This," Ferdinand said, holding up the scroll that had just been passed to him, "is the final piece of the puzzle." He looked at each of his children in turn. "Do you want to know what puzzle?"

It seemed to be a rhetorical question, so Joanna stayed quiet.

Catherine, after a heartbeat, said, "I like puzzles. Beatriz and I, we did a—"

"Quiet, my love," the queen said, touching her finger to her lips. "This is important, for all of you. You must listen closely."

Catherine reached for her sister Maria's hand.

"This letter is from the Holy Roman Emperor, Maximilian of Austria." The king pursed his lips, as though waiting for his words to sink into everyone's minds. "And completes our plans for your marriages." He looked at each child in turn.

Joanna wanted to glance at John but forced herself to stare straight ahead. Her marriage was not as important as his. The best Joanna could hope for was not to have to travel too far—for she would go and live in her husband's land—and that he would be tolerable in conversation and not as ugly as an old toad.

"My only son, my heir, John, Prince of Asturias," the king said, "your match has been agreed upon, much to our satisfaction." He looked at his wife with a smile then turned back to John. "You will marry the Archduchess Margaret of Austria. Daughter of Archduke Maximilian and Duchess Mary of Burgundy."

"Thank you, Father," John said with a bob of his head and showing no emotion at all.

"And Joanna." The king tipped his head and studied Joanna.

She held his eye contact. She wanted him to know she trusted his judgement and that her loyalty was to him alongside Aragon, Castile, and all of Spain.

"Maximilian has given his blessing that you will marry his son, Archduke Philip of Austria and ruler of Burgundian possessions under the guardianship of his father."

Although she managed to maintain her grace on the outside, Joanna's mind was spinning and her heart thudding. "I trust in God and you, wise King, that the match to Archduke Philip of Austria will be all that it should be." She bobbed her head low.

She'd heard of the archduke in the Low Countries—of course she had. King Charles had been squeezing into that territory for some time and did have possession of Burgundy.

If it were her in charge, she'd oust King Charles and not allow anyone to elbow their way into her lands. Perhaps when Philip inherited truly from his father, that was what his plan would be.

"Maria, my dear Maria. You are but a child." Ferdinand interrupted Joanna's thoughts. "Thomas of Scotland will be a good match when you are of age."

"Thank you, Father." Maria clasped her hands beneath her chin and looked down at the stone floor.

"And our littlest, sweetest, though probably noisiest daughter, Catherine." Ferdinand raised his eyebrows at Catherine, a smile playing on his lips.

"I try not to be noisy," Catherine said, her high-pitched, childish voice singing around the room like a songbird. "But I will try harder to be quiet."

"Enjoy childhood while you can." The queen smiled indulgently. "As long as you complete your lessons, your father and I have no problem with you enjoying yourselves. My angel"—she pointed at John—"is a good example to you younger children. Work hard and God will deliver for you. John has become everything we hoped he would."

"Yes, Mother," Catherine said, her pretty face set seriously. "I will."

"So Catherine of Aragon," Ferdinand said, indicating a nearby courtier to bring a tray of wine closer. He took a goblet. "You will marry at the earliest time that is respectable, Arthur Tudor, Prince of Wales."

"The Prince of Wales," little Catherine repeated. "Where is Wales?"

"It is next to England and governed by England," the queen said. "You will have much power when he becomes king and you will become Queen of England and its possessions."

Catherine's eyes widened. "I'll be a queen? Like you, Mother?"

"Yes. And I am sure you will make an excellent queen." Isabella swung her gaze over her children. "You will all make excellent spouses and rulers." She pressed her hand to her chest, over the rich, blue gown that was fitted close and right up to her neck. "I know that in my heart because God tells me so."

Chapter Two

1496
Coudenberg Palace
Flanders

"Thomas, I refuse to let you beat me," Philip said with a frown as he plucked another arrow from his quiver.

"So cheat." Thomas laughed, his dark eyes sparkling with mirth. "If you can figure out a way how to."

Philip didn't answer his chancellor and friend. Instead, he lined up the tip of the arrow with the highest point on the target, pulled back the bowstring, let out a long, slow, steadying breath, and fired.

The arrow flew through the air, the blue kingfisher feather at its tail glinting in the sunlight. And then it hit, right in the middle of the red target.

"Yes!" Philip punched the air. "That's how you do it."

"Well done. You have excellent aim." Thomas squeezed his shoulder. "And even more so when you think you might lose." He chuckled.

"I am not in the habit of losing."

"A trait you have surely gotten from your father."

"My mother too." He glanced out at the soft, low hills that surrounded Coudenberg Palace. Trees dotted the landscape in copses and as single splashes of green. Philip hoped the fine weather would hold and summer would stretch on. He didn't enjoy the winter. Long, dark nights and so many pickles, his guts started to ache.

"Another round?" Thomas asked.

"Sure. If you don't mind losing again." Philip gestured to a courtier who was standing as straight as a pike and holding a brass tray full of wine goblets.

The courtier stepped up quickly and Philip took a drink.

"Has my sister returned from her ride?" Philip asked the man.

"I believe so, Your Grace."

"Good." Philip sipped his dark wine. He had received a scroll that morning by envoy, from Germany, and it was addressed to them both with instructions to open it together.

Why his father liked to befuddle him this way, Philip had no idea. It wasn't as if they were close. Maximilian had left Philip to rule the Low Countries and surrounding territories when he'd been fifteen years old and now, at eighteen, Philip knew full well he was doing a good job and was beloved by the people. The Estates General and government met regularly and peace and economic development were their main focus—with Philip's guidance, of course.

Meaning Philip had plenty of time for archery, hunting, tennis, and stick fighting. Life was meant to be lived, was it not?

"Could you tell my sister to join me in the Aula Magna," he directed at the courtier.

"Yes, Your Grace."

He finished his wine and set it back on the tray. "I will be there shortly."

The courtier dipped his head politely then stepped aside to speak to another uniformed member of palace staff.

"You didn't open the scroll from your father yet?" Thomas asked, walking back toward him with a quiver of arrows plucked from the target.

"No, the King of the Romans asked me not to."

"And you did as you were told?" Thomas laughed.

"It seemed respectful, all things considered."

"I commend you, as will God." Thomas paused. "What do you think the scroll contains?"

"Details about strengthening his borders and increasing his power, no doubt."

"You know him well."

For a moment, Philip was quiet. He would have liked to have known his father better. Perhaps he would, in adulthood. But it was hard to predict how with Maximilian's vast territories and ever-increasing duties now that Philip's grandfather had died.

"I shall go first," Philip said, taking an arrow from Thomas. "And the breeze has picked up. Let us see who has prowess of the bow and arrow now."

They fired several arrows, each an excellent shot and hitting the target. Then, when the sun went behind a cloud, Philip's stomach grumbled and his impatience grew to know what was in the scroll from Maximilian. "Come, we will return to the palace."

Thomas nodded and handed his bow to a courtier. "Would you like me to accompany you or do you wish for a private consultation with your sister?"

"I think private might be for the best." Philip knew how his sister hated to have to hide her feelings. She'd always been that way. Wanting to appear dignified and graceful took its toll on occasion and he cherished the fact that he was one of the few people on God's good Earth with whom she could truly relax. "I will fill you in on the details later."

"Very good, Your Grace."

Philip squeezed Thomas's shoulder. "And I thank you, Thomas, as always, for your friendship and advice."

"It's is my privilege." He pressed his hand over his heart.

When Philip arrived back at the palace, he found his sister, Margaret, waiting for him. The scroll was on the long banqueting table that spanned the length of the vast ornate Aula Magna. Sun shone in from the huge, westerly windows, creating large, golden rectangles on the stone floor. The fires were lit, crackling away in their huge inglenooks, despite the warm day.

"It is from Father," Margaret said, pointing at the red, wax seal on the scroll.

"You are very perceptive." Philip grinned and kissed her cheek.

"I try to be." She picked up the scroll. "I am surprised you waited for me before opening it."

"It came with instructions for us to open it together."

"You don't always follow instructions, Philip." She laughed.

"I do when it's my father instructing." He reached for a slice of pork pie and took a bite.

"Shall I do the honors?"

He nodded.

As her elegant fingers cracked the seal then unraveled the tightly coiled paper, Philip had a strange sense of calm. He suddenly knew what the letter held. It came to him as sure as he knew he loved his lands and his people.

It would be concerning his and Margaret's betrothals.

"It is dated two weeks previously." Margaret held the scroll aloft and several curls of red wax fell to the floor.

Philip stood beside her and they read together in silence.

Archduke Philip and Archduchess Margaret, my beloved children, I pray this letter finds you in good health and prosperous.

I will get straight to the matter at hand and inform you that I have decided upon your marriages. It has taken some time to come to the arrangements, but I trust you will find them pleasing for our kingdom and the House of Habsburg.

Philip, you will wed Princess Joanna of Castile, daughter of King Ferdinand II of Aragon and Queen Isabella of Castile.

Margaret, you will wed Prince John of Castile, son of King Ferdinand II of Aragon and Queen Isabella of Castile.

The Spanish kingdoms are on the rise and share our abhorrence of King Charles of France's reign. Your unions with the Trastámara family will strengthen our borders and bring us greater powers. And it is these powers, ultimately, that will defeat the Turks and protect Christendom. It is a great service to God that you wed to my choosing.

The proxy wedding will take place on the last day of June. After this, Princess Joanna will travel to Flanders, and upon her safe arrival, Margaret will travel to Castile.

It is my hope to attend both weddings, but I cannot make promises, as I am inundated with matters that demand my constant attention.

Be well and safe, my children.

Your father, Maximilian of Austria, King of the Romans

"It is decided, then," Philip said, taking a step back and staring out of the window at the blue sky. A single, white cloud, shaped like a dog, slid from left to right. "Our spouses have been agreed upon once and for all."

"I wonder what they are like." Margaret poured wine into two goblets and sat at the bench. She took a deep slug.

"He will not come to the weddings," Philip said, also picking up a drink.

"He might. He hasn't promised, but he might come. Here at least, to Coudenberg. It is not such a journey from Germany as Castile."

"He won't. He didn't come to my inauguration, if you remember." Philip shrugged then sipped his wine.

Margaret said nothing. She'd known their father's absence had hurt Philip.

"And we are to marry a brother and sister," Philip went on. "I hadn't even considered that a possibility."

"You are lucky. I wish I were to stay here."

"Why?" Philip asked.

"This is home. Spain is a strange land with strange ways and they do not speak my language." She pulled a face. "I will be an outsider."

"You will be queen one day. That is not being an outsider."

Margaret was quiet for a moment. "I will pray that by then, I have learned their ways and their tongue."

"I know you will dazzle them, dear sister." He stepped up to her and squeezed her hand. "But I will miss you every day."

"As I you."

"Perhaps you could stay a while, after Joanna arrives. There is no need to rush if all is well and the fleet don't mind waiting at port. Joanna can teach you a few Spanish words and tell you a little about her brother so your journey isn't full of worries about his disposition."

"I'm not worried about his disposition." Margaret paused. "Or at least I wasn't until you put the thought into my mind that he might be unpleasant of nature."

Philip laughed. "I am sorry, I did not mean to. I, too, wonder what my wife will be like."

"Just as Father and Mother must have thought the same before they met," Margaret said. "They had a proxy marriage before Father's long journey to Ghent."

"And that marriage turned out pretty well." Philip didn't dwell on thoughts of his parents meeting. Instead, he looked to his own future. His father was right. Marriage into the Trastámara family would be advantageous. It would give the Habsburgs more power in European court, a court that was progressive and wealthy and good to have on one's side.

"I think I will go for a walk," Margaret said, standing. "Around the rose gardens."

"Would you like me to accompany you?" He set down his drink.

"I thank you, dear, kind brother, but no. I wish to be in my own thoughts."

"I understand. It is big news."

She kissed his cheek and smiled, though it didn't reach her eyes.

"Do not be sad," he said softly. "Be optimistic and have faith in God."

"I am grateful that my faith is strong." She turned and left the room, her soft footsteps fading as she went through the large doorway.

Philip pushed his hand through his hair. It instantly flopped back around his face.

Joanna of Castile.

He knew nothing of her, yet she was to become the woman he knew most about. She was to become the mother of his children, his heirs. She would be the companion at his side through good and bad and as age crept up with its gray hairs and sagging skin.

"Your Grace."

Philip's attention was caught by Thomas.

"Come in," Philip said, waving his arm. "I have news."

"And is it as you expected?" Thomas asked, striding alongside the table, the short sword at his belt shifting with each step.

"It is news of my sister's and my intended." Philip helped himself to more wine, then passed the jug to Philip.

"And...?" Thomas raised his eyebrows and took the jug.

"And as you would expect from an astute man such as my father, the marriages are strategic and well thought through."

"You keep me in suspense." Thomas studied Philip, jug aloft.

"For that, I apologize. I just have an inkling that my betrothed, Joanna of Castile, may cause me some problems with Charles."

"The King of France?"

"The very same." Philip sat and crossed his legs, bobbing his foot so the toe of his boot stabbed the air. "As you know, my father hates Charles with a passion, yet I—"

"Have formed a tenuous friendship with him."

"It suits me. Keeping an enemy close means I can predict his actions and so far, they have been benevolent—to us, at least."

"You are a very wise ruler." Thomas inclined his head.

Philip huffed. Sometimes he felt like he and Charles had a friendship akin to a lion and a lamb, he being the lamb, because France had great armies and a far reach. But Philip intended to change that. He would, one day, be the one with the large army and the highest influence. "You see, Thomas," he said, thinking aloud, "Joanna's father, King Ferdinand, has no good words to say about King Charles. He hates him and his ambitions for Naples and Grenada."

"And King Ferdinand will soon be your father in the name of marital law, with whom you should align." Thomas poured a drink and sipped. "It is definitely a conflict. Charles will not be pleased about the marriage, and neither will King Ferdinand when he discovers your friendship with Charles."

"A conflict I must navigate." Philip rubbed his clean-shaven chin. "Though I don't doubt that I will be able to do so with charm and flattery."

Thomas chuckled. "Traits you have in bucketfuls."

"You are generous with your flattery." Philip smiled. Yes. Marrying into Spain would be advantageous. He could see that. He was surprised at himself for not predicting it as his father's choice. As long as he could keep everyone's interests aligned with his, and Ferdinand and Charles appeased, there would be no great problem. Hopefully.

"Joanna is not heir to the Spanish throne, is she?" Thomas asked.

"No, had she been the sole child, like my mother, she would have been an even better match for me, but…"

"But what?"

"My sister, Margaret, will be Queen of Asturias, the combined territories, when she marries Joanna's older brother, John, and he inherits."

"Ah, so you will always have a sympathetic ear in the Spanish kingdom." Thomas nodded, the cogs of his mind clearly turning. "When John is king and your sister his queen."

"Exactly."

"It is a good match all around," Thomas said, sitting opposite Philip. "Our borders will be strengthened, no matter what Charles's reaction proves to be."

"And the Habsburg bloodline will move south, enriching our

family's influence for years to come."

"Indeed." Thomas chinked his goblet to Philip's. "Let us send prayers that Joanna of Castile has a safe journey here and is of sound mind and pretty face."

Philip drank deeply. It was too much to hope that he'd be physically attracted to a woman he was marrying to gain power and influence...wasn't it?

Chapter Three

Castile
Spain

Joanna held her small, gold cross between her thumb and index finger and stared out of the window at the stable yard.

Raul was brushing her horse, his movements efficient yet tender as he flicked the brush over Gianna's gray coat. Small, wispy strands of hair caught on the breeze, floating up and off. Every few minutes, Raul would pause to pet Gianna's neck or muzzle and speak soothingly to her.

It was clear he adored Gianna as much as the horse adored him.

Joanna's mind wandered, as it often did, to how it would feel to have Raul concentrate all that attention and care upon her. To know the heat of his work-worn hands on her bare flesh. To learn the shape of his broad shoulders, long, lean back, and taut buttocks with her palms. It was a desire she had to keep buried deep.

Soon she would leave for Flanders and he would be in her life no longer. Her fantasies of his tan skin sweat-slicked against hers would be forever locked away. And the flash in his eyes, when he stood close to her, smiled at her, would be a memory that would likely fade over time.

She sighed and resisted the temptation to stamp her foot as frustration welled. If only she could know what the archduke was like… perhaps leaving Raul would be easier if she did.

The temptation to run away with Raul, run like the wind, to a faraway place where she could live a simple peasant life by day and lie with the man of her dreams all night was almost too much to resist.

But resist she must. Her love for kingdom and country had to come first. She'd been brought up to believe that as a true fact. She would not let her parents or her people down.

At that moment, Raul paused brushing Gianna's tail and looked up at the window.

Joanna caught her breath and dropped the cross so it hung around her neck once more. She didn't step back into the shadows. It was too late. Raul already knew she'd been watching him.

And it was her right to, if it pleased her. She was a princess and this was her castle.

He tipped his head, the sunlight glinting off his black-as-night hair, and his mouth tipped into his usual easy smile. It was as if seeing her studying him had pleased him immensely.

She swallowed tightly and her heart did a strange flip as heat went through her body.

A sudden idea came to her and she rushed to her bedchamber, gown held an inch above her ankles for speed of movement. Once there, she flipped open the lid on a mother-of-pearl jewelry box and plucked from within it a small cameo set in a gothic, silver design. It contained the image of a young woman—*her* image—in profile and wearing a rolled headdress.

Quickly, she tucked it into her pocket. Within minutes, she was descending the stone steps that would lead her out into the stable yard.

Once there, she paused, blinking in the bright sunshine. The yard was quiet. A cat slunk between two piles of hay, no doubt on the lookout for mice and rats, and a wiry-haired dog slept in the shade beside an empty food bowl.

Raul stopped what he was doing and turned to her. "Your

Highness."

"It is midday, but still you work," Joanna said, walking toward him and checking for stray hairs that may have sprung free from her blue, velvet headdress.

"A horse cannot brush itself." He patted Gianna's neck.

"That is true." She came to a halt at his side.

"Do you wish to ride, Your Highness?" Raul said. "I could fetch her saddle."

"No, it is too hot." Joanna wrapped her hand around the brooch in her pocket. "That is not what I wish for at all."

Raul appeared to hold in words as he studied her.

Joanna caught her breath. Was he about to tell her how he'd also been having thoughts about them running away together? How perfect their life could be if only they were far from here.

"What can I help you with? I am at your service." His dark eyes studied her face and his eyebrows pulled low.

"I should like to brush my horse." She held out her free hand.

"But that is not a task for... Of course, Your Highness." He gave her the brush.

"Show me how." She set the brush on Gianna's rump.

"Just go with the direction of hair," Raul said. For a moment, his hand hovered over hers, then he rested it down, covering her knuckles and his long fingers aligning with hers. "Like this. Slow and gentle."

Joanna's heart stuttered and every hair on her neck stood on end at the feel of his body heat, his breath...his whispered words. He shouldn't have been so near to her. He shouldn't have been touching his young mistress, but he was.

Flouting all the rules had never been so exciting.

"Caress her, show her you care," he said softly as he steered the brush downward. "She will become almost trance-like, bewitched by touch."

Joanna bit down on her bottom lip, thoroughly bewitched herself and imagining Raul was talking about her that way. Or was he? Heat grew between her legs and her nipples tingled. She had the sudden urge to rid herself of her clothes. To demand that Raul do the same. Her stomach clenched and she locked her knees to stay upright.

She'd never been so close to a man this way. A man she dreamt of, thought of, whose name was on the tip of her tongue in the dead of night when her fingers slipped between her legs.

"She is enjoying your attention," Raul said, his voice barely a whisper now. "For she feels connected to you above all others."

"Is that true?" Joanna let her hand be guided by his.

"It is a truth I know in the bottom of my heart."

"What else do you know in your heart?"

He stilled with his hand covering hers and his chest touching her back. She could hear and feel his breathing.

"Raul? I demand you answer me." Her heart pounded. She was staring at the brush resting on Gianna's coat but barely seeing it.

"I cannot answer you, Joanna."

She turned, forcing him to release her. When she looked up she was surprised by how close they were.

It was quite improper, as was the use of her name so casually. She didn't care.

"Raul. What else do you know in your heart?" She studied his lips, soft and plump, perfect for kissing. Black stubble grew on his chin and cheeks and she was sure it would scratch her delicate flesh should he come any closer and press his mouth to hers.

"I can never tell you, for it can never be," he said.

"What can never be?"

"You know what I speak of." His lips tightened and he shook his head. "I cannot give you what you need, Your Highness. I am not the one for you, no matter how much you are the one for me."

She swallowed tightly. "But surely, it goes both ways, I—"

"No." He touched his finger to her lips. "I also love Spain, and the people of my country. You owe them a duty that I cannot distract you from."

"Not even for one—?"

"Do not dangle temptation before me. I am a mere mortal." He stepped back. "I beg you, Princess. Do not tempt me."

"Am I so easy to resist?" She placed her hands on her hips. "Look at me. Am I so easy to resist? Tell me."

Taking a deep breath, he looked her up and down. "Truth be told, it's the hardest thing I've ever done." He took another step backward, as though needing to put distance between them. "I must go now."

"Go?"

His jaw tensed and his fists formed tight, round balls. "Yes." He turned and took several fast paces toward the barn.

"Wait." She reached for the brooch again. "Raul, wait. I command you."

He stopped but didn't turn.

"I want you to have this." She rushed to his side and held out the cameo.

"I cannot take anything from you." He didn't even look at the delicate piece of jewelry.

"A parting gift for my head groom. You have served me and Gianna well for a long time." She paused. "Good work should be rewarded. Here, take it."

To her relief, he did, then lifted it up to examine the image. "It is you."

"Yes."

He frowned. "They will say I have stolen it."

"It is a gift. From me to you." She curled his fingers around it. "But keep it close to your body, your heart. Keep it hidden if you must. For I leave soon and we will never see each other again."

He closed his eyes, his long, dark lashes forming small shadows on his cheeks.

"And when you think of me," she said softly, "know that I think of you too."

"You are generous of spirit." He opened his eyes again. "To say such a thing."

"What do you mean?"

"You will be with your new husband, a powerful, influential man with whom you will fall in love and to whom you will give many children."

"And you will be with your wife, Raul. She will be sweet as honey, pretty of face, and willing to please."

"I will never marry." He slipped the brooch into the chest pocket on his sleeveless tunic. "For my heart has already been stolen. It will never belong to another. Not now. How could it?" His eyes flashed, as though they were filled with moisture. His voice was tight.

Joanna felt like a dagger had landed in her chest. It stole her breath and her lower eyelids prickled. "Raul," she managed.

"Be happy, my beautiful princess. That is all I ask of you. Be happy." He stepped around her, then with his head bent, he marched to the barn and was swallowed by the shadows.

Her throat was constricted with emotion and she dashed at a tear that had spilled.

"Joanna."

Her mother's sharp voice was like a sudden, unexpected slap to the face. She set back her shoulders and blinked rapidly.

"What on Earth is going on?" Queen Isabella hurried over the yard, not her usual domain, with her skirt held safe from straw and dust. "I just saw you talking to that stableboy and—"

"Is it not permitted for me to ask about the health of my horse?"

Isabella frowned, two neat lines slicing over her brow. "That is perfectly acceptable." She searched Joanna's face as though hunting for secrets. "But from what I saw…"

"What did you see, Mother?"

Isabella's face darkened. "You leave tomorrow, my child, a virgin bride for Archduke Philip of the House of Habsburg. Do not make me doubt your unsullied state."

"Mother!"

"The archduke demands an immaculate bride, as does his

father, the King of the Romans."

"And I am as such."

Isabella nodded and reached for the cross at her neck. "Only you and God know the truth and I hope it is so."

"Mother." Joanna reached for Isabella's hand. "How could you doubt me? You of all people. You know I am a good and pious Catholic who reveres the word of God."

Isabella sighed. "I just want the best for you. For all of us. Life is hard enough without being foolish and following one's heart."

Joanna was quiet, knowing that was exactly what she'd been thinking of doing. Following her heart. Following Raul to wherever he suggested they go.

"Remember Helen of Troy, Guinevere, Sappho—all women who followed their hearts and in doing so, it led to their demises. Each and every one of them." Isabella tapped her temple. "We must follow this, our brains, and you have an especially quick one, my love. Do not let those rushing thoughts lead you down the wrong path. The path to an eternity of burning in hell."

"There are no such immoral thoughts, Mother, you must believe me." She pulled in a deep breath, wishing her heart would stop racing. "I have no intention of going to hell, only to Flanders to marry the man you wish for me."

"Good." Isabella nodded. "Because it *is* what we wish for you. And for you to produce heirs."

"I will do my best, Mother." She nodded at the doorway into the castle. "Shall we get out of the sun?"

"Yes."

They made their way over the stable yard, Gianna munching on her hay and watching them lazily. "Can I ask you something, Mother?"

"Of course."

"What do you think he is like? Philip."

"I have heard he is very handsome. Strong jawed, broad shouldered, and with steely, gray-blue eyes and hair the color of sunshine."

"You have heard all of this?" A sudden thrill Joanna hadn't been expecting gripped her. "From whom?"

"It is a common knowledge. Unsurprising, given who his parents are."

"He is handsome," Joanna repeated. "That is good. And his nature?"

"It is reported that he is an excellent horseman, hunter, and fighter, again like his father, and he also has a charming way about him, particularly when it comes to politics." She paused. "And women."

"Women?"

"Some men are good at charming women and they like to put it into practice. Take your father, for example."

"Father? Yes, I suppose he is good at charming people." Joanna thought of the way the king could command respect and simultaneously change the mood of a room, steering people in the direction he wanted their thoughts to go and orchestrating moods and emotions. "I am pleased if the archduke turns out to be also charming."

Isabella huffed slightly.

"What is that noise for?" Joanna asked.

"Charming is not always the blessing you think it is."

"Why ever not?" Joanna stopped and turned to her mother.

Isabella sighed. "A charming and handsome man is likely to have a queue of women waiting to get into his bed."

"What? No. A husband wouldn't do that. Father wouldn't and I'd forbid Philip to, I—"

"My love, you have much to learn as a wife." Isabella took Joanna's hands in hers. "Men like to have many lovers. A woman can take only one, but a man…"

"No." Joanna shook her head. "That's preposterous. God would frown severely on such a sin."

"It is not a sin in the eyes of many."

"It is in *my* eyes." Joanna clenched her jaw so tightly, she feared for her teeth. "I will not allow my husband, even if he does turn out to be as ugly as an old toad, to have other women in his bed. He is mine, and mine alone."

Isabella sighed again. "I hope it is not a conversation you ever have to have with him. The ones I have had with your father on the subject have been some of the hardest of my life."

"Father has taken lovers?"

"Yes." She held up her finger. "But we will talk no more of it." Isabella closed her eyes and sighed. She turned away.

Joanna's heart twisted to think of the pain her mother must have been in knowing her husband had other women in his bed. How she hadn't scratched out their eyes, sliced off their hair, burnt them with hot pokers, she didn't know. If she were staying in court long enough to pluck up the courage, she would tell her father that it was unbecoming of a king and dishonorable of a husband to commit adultery.

She would pray for them both.

"Beatriz has nearly finished your packing," Isabella said, the shake gone from her voice. "You should oversee the cases before they are put on a cart and sent to the port."

"Er, yes, I will. Thank you."

Isabella smiled.

Joanna gave into a sudden urge to hug her mother. "I will miss you, dreadfully."

"As I you." Isabella held her close and stroked her hair. "In your marriage hope for friendship and easily borne sons, nothing more, then if you get more, it will be a bonus, my dear daughter."

Chapter Four

Port of Laredo, Castile

THE GANGPLANK LEADING onto the *Julia* was the first step into Joanna's new life.

The towering galleon, constructed of oak, had several decks and a squared-off raised stern. A long row of heavy cannons pointed their black muzzles through round gun ports, their wooden coverings propped open.

Colossal weathered ropes held the white sails tightly to the seemingly endless rise of masts. Atop the tallest mast, above the crow's nest, a large flag flapped lazily in the breeze—the flag of Castile and Aragon, four red, horizontal lines on a yellow background. Anyone approaching would be in no doubt where the ship called home. They would also do well to approach with caution if not a friend of Spain.

All around was hustle and bustle. Barrels, chests, and boxes were being loaded onto the deck. Chickens squawked in pens. A skinny, ginger cat scampered past, head down, and overhead gulls screeched and swooped.

"Your Highness," Beatriz said at Joanna's side. "Are you quite all right?"

"Yes. Yes." Joanna nodded. "I just didn't think it would be so big."

"I suppose it is better than being too small." Beatriz let out a tight laugh.

"Are you nervous about the voyage?" Joanna asked.

"Apprehensive. The ocean is deep. I cannot swim."

"Let's hope it doesn't come to that." Joanna suppressed a shudder. The journey would take many weeks and she hoped the weather and the water would be kind.

She was a tangle of emotions. So much so her skin prickled and her heartstrings were tugging her back to Castile. Saying goodbye to her parents and siblings had been harder than she'd ever imagined. It was only now, not being with them, leaving them for the longest time, that she realized she'd perhaps taken them for granted. John and Isabella had been her best friends for so long, Maria and Catherine delights to be around with their childish inquisitiveness and wonder in all things new.

And now…now she wondered if she'd even be able to carry on breathing without them.

She dashed at a tear, not wanting to appear weak. She was a monarch, after all, and God's strength was within her.

"Your Highness, we are ready for you to board." The ship's captain stood before her. His round face was lined by the weather the way the ship's ropes were, and his gray hair thin and wind-blown. He wore a black blazer, black pants, and black boots. The only color on him was a red scarf knotted at his neck.

"Thank you, Captain Alonzo," Joanna said, gathering her gown. "I trust all is well with the *Julia*." She nodded at the ship.

"She is a fine vessel. Solid and seaworthy. No shipworm, I can assure you."

"Shipworm?" Beatriz asked, pressing her hand to her chest. "What in God's name is that?"

The captain chuckled. "Nothing you need to alarm yourself with, madam, for there is none."

"That is a relief." Beatriz fanned her face. "I do not wish to sail with worms or any type of pestilence, come to that."

"You will be comfortable, I can assure you." The captain smiled. "A home from home. Come, let me show you to your cabin."

For a moment, Joanna hesitated, absorbing the solidity of the ground beneath her feet. The hardness pressing onto her soles. Spain. Her home. Her land. Her love.

"Princess?" Beatriz said, gently touching the small of Joanna's back. "Are you ready?"

"Yes. I am ready." She pulled in a deep breath and stepped onto the gangplank. She walked up it steadily and holding the hand rope. She hoped the ship would be stable underfoot. Already, her stomach felt queasy.

"This way," the captain said. "Don't trip on those." He pointed to a box of cannonballs.

"Oh." Joanna dodged them.

"And watch out for these *pequeños cabrones*." He pointed to a gull. "They will take any food out of your hand and they will dirty your silk gowns with their shit."

"Duly noted." Joanna frowned at the huge bird who was studying her with beady, black eyes.

"Now here, be careful." The captain led them through a doorway and down a dimly lit narrow corridor. "If you have candles lit, they must always be in storm jars. The last thing we want is a fire on a wooden boat. Water all around does not mean we won't burn."

"Yes, of course. That makes sense." Joanna nodded.

He stopped at a doorway with brass hinges and handle. "The crew is under strict instructions that this is a female-only area. We have four maids on board who will deliver your meals and clean."

"Yes, the king and queen were very specific about that." Beatriz raised her chin. "The princess is to have a restful journey in the company of women only."

"And it is what she shall have." The captain smiled at Joanna. "Though do remember I am at your service. I will serve you in any way I can."

"I would like to be kept updated, daily, as to our progress," Joanna said. "I am a great admirer of Columbus and his explorations. I wish also to chart our progress on a map."

"You can read a map?"

"Naturally." She frowned at him.

He inclined his head. "I will not only ensure you are updated, I will do it personally and give you a nautical map so that you may study the route at your pleasure."

Joanna smiled. "Why thank you. I would enjoy that very much."

"It should be a reasonably smooth ride," he said. "Though the Bay of Biscay can be somewhat wild."

"'Wild'?" Beatriz repeated with a grimace. "I knew we should have gone by land."

"And been at the mercy of King Charles? I think not." Joanna shook her head. "It would please him very much to see me dead before I can marry the archduke. It would stop an alliance that is sure to vex him in years to come."

"You will be quite safe with me, I promise you," Captain Alonzo said. "Remember that even when the ship lurches."

Beatriz paled. "Lurches…but I—"

"The sailors say there are three types of people," he went on, "the living, the dead, and the seasick. It is not pleasant, but it will pass…eventually."

"Seasickness," Joanna said, reaching for her cross. "Oh, dear."

"I do not like the sound of it." Beatriz frowned. "Her Highness is of a delicate disposition, like every princess and bride-to-be and—"

"Ah, now, let us get on with the task at hand. Take a look at your cabin." The captain smiled and opened the door. "Not as big as a castle but hopefully suitable for our voyage."

Joanna stepped into the cabin and her eyes widened. It was indeed much bigger and much grander than she'd imagined. The paneled walls gleamed. The small-paned windows let in a good amount of light and were strung with red, velvet curtains.

There were two beds, one a four-poster with red canopy and swags, and the other a smaller one with red coverlets. A large desk was set with books and a tray holding wine and goblets. A screen covered in images of exotic birds half-hid a bathtub and chamber pot.

In the corner her chests had been neatly stacked ready for unpacking into wardrobes set into the wall.

"It is perfectly adequate. Thank you, Captain." Joanna smiled at him then walked inside, over a red oriental rug, and set her fan upon the table. "And thank you also for your service. I will be thankful to both God and your skill and expertise when we reach our destination."

He smiled and puffed up his chest. "It is an honor to be at your service, Your Highness. And please, make yourself comfortable. I shall have Cook send in food shortly, for it is best to eat before we set sail."

"We are leaving soon?"

"The sooner, the better."

And with that, he was gone.

"What do you think?" Beatriz asked, pouring wine into two goblets.

"If it were to stay unmoving, I'd say it was perfect," Joanna said. "But the way everything seems to be anchored down..." She pushed at the lamp on the table, which didn't move, owing to some screws pinning it in place. "Reminds me that we are going to be rocked back and forth."

"It is summer. Perhaps the weather will be kind. We should pray for that." Beatriz passed her a drink. "You rest up. I will unpack your things."

"Thank you. Can you set out my books? On the shelf there, please."

"Of course, Your Highness."

FOUR WEEKS LATER, Joanna hung on to the post at the end of the bed and clutched her stomach. There was nothing left inside of her to come up. For two days solid, the wind had lashed the ship from every angle like a dragon huffing and puffing. The ocean boiled beneath them and sent sharp fingers crashing up to the windows. The cabin floor had become liquid, or so it seemed, sliding underfoot, dipping and rising as though navigating mountains and valleys.

"Oh, Joanna." Beatriz gasped, her formalities having slipped. "Please, what can I do to help you?"

"Nothing, my friend. You are in as terrible a state as I." She heaved then groaned. Was it better to lie on the bed in this condition and be tossed around, or hang on to the post and stagger but at least be upright? She had no idea.

"How long will this hellish storm last?" Beatriz was curled up on her bed, knees hugged in tight as she gripped the headboard. "It is as if the devil himself is stirring up the ocean and the *Julia* with it."

"It is evil, that is for sure." Joanna screwed her eyes up tight. She tried to think of the pleasant meadows of home. Gianna's sweet horse face. The sound of her sisters' laughter. The elegant painting in the library of a Spanish landscape she adored so. But nothing could take her mind from the dreadful sickness that plagued her. Not even conjuring up Raul's smiling face and soulful eyes. It was as if the seawater itself rushed through her veins, tightening her guts and stealing her vision.

The nausea was unrelenting. Having stolen her ability to eat, it now was taking her limbs and making them weak and shaky. A cold sweat peppered her skin, sternum, armpits, and back.

The ship lurched then fell. A book slid from the desk and clattered to the floor.

"Please, you should lie down." Beatriz went to move, as if to help her.

"No. No, please stay there. I can do it."

She lurched to the bed, falling onto it, and was instantly rolled to her stomach. She groaned and grasped the bedding. It smelled of ginger, a tonic Cook had sent up to her that had spilled.

"All we can do is pray," Joanna mumbled. "Pray that this is soon over or we die and are put out of our misery."

AFTER EIGHT WEEKS at sea, the *Julia* finally docked in the Port of Ghent. Joanna stood on deck with her headdress attached firmly and looked at her new lands. They were flat and sprawling, the buildings squat with tiled, orange roofs. There were lots of little clouds in the sky, flung like dandelion seeds over the blue expanse. Somewhere beneath them, the archduke waited.

The port, like the one she'd left in Spain, was a hive of activity. Wares and containers being loaded and unloaded, including her chests, which were being stacked onto a cart. She studied the mass of people, looking for her betrothed, even though his face was only a conjured image in her mind.

"Could I have the honor of escorting you off the ship?" Captain Alonzo asked.

"Thank you." She slipped her hand into the crook of his elbow. She'd become fond of the captain during their time together, despite the miserable two weeks off the coast of France. He was jolly and intelligent and also fair with his crew, from what she had seen. He was thoughtful of the needs of the women on board, which she appreciated. Especially when she knew for some of the sailors, they brought bad luck.

He led her across the decking, Beatriz following, and then assisted her onto the gangplank. When she reached the bottom, with the captain close behind, she was greeted with a familiar face.

"Lord Belmonte," she said, smiling warmly. "I was not expecting you here."

The nobleman stood before her wearing leather boots, suede breeches, and short-sleeved chain armor over a black tunic. A large, steel sword hung from his belt, along with a dagger. Around his neck was a rosary. He had a silvery scar on his cheek, slicing from just below his right eye to the curve of his mouth, and his dark hair was overly long, flaring out at his ears and nape.

Behind him stood two helmeted knights. Their Milanese full body armor shone in the sunlight. They too had swords and daggers and also a shield bearing the Trastámara crest. They stood with feet hip width apart, chins tilted, as if prepared for battle at any moment.

"Princess," Lord Belmonte said, "I am here at the request of your parents, and at your service." Belmonte dipped his head.

"At my parents' request?"

"They wish for you to have protection in a new court in a strange land."

Her heart squeezed. How thoughtful of her parents to send Belmonte and knights. Over the last weeks, she'd felt like a fragile fledgling leaving the nest alone, yet here was protection and support in the form of an old and dear friend.

She took his hand. "It is so good to see you. I had no idea you were in Flanders."

"It is a dangerous journey by land, but I made it some time ago." He gently squeezed her fingers.

"No matter the danger, it must be better than by sea." She looked at Captain Alonzo. "No offense, Captain, but you know the Bay of Biscay did not suit my constitution."

"It will never be so bad for you again," he said. "The first time at sea is the worst."

"First and last." At one point, she hadn't thought either she or Beatriz would ever smile again, they'd felt so wretched.

He chuckled. "I will leave you now and will pray for your health and happiness."

"I bid you farewell, Captain, and a good and well-earned rest here before your return journey. May God watch over you and all the souls who sail with you." She smiled at him then looked at Belmonte again. "Tell me, is my future husband here?"

"I believe he is waiting for you at Coudenberg Palace."

"Oh." She frowned. "I had presumed he'd be eager to greet me."

"My guess is he is a busy man." Belmonte gestured to a red carriage with large, wooden wheels and charged with four bay horses. "He has sent this for you and your ladies. Come, let us get on our way."

"Yes, thank you." She bristled, irritated that the archduke hadn't made the journey to the port.

"Perhaps he is hoping for a more private meeting in more congenial surroundings," Beatriz said, obviously sensing Joanna's frustration.

"Mm."

The interior of the carriage was plush and comfortable and Joanna stared at the passing countryside as they rattled toward the palace—her new home.

"I do still think that it is odd," she said to Beatriz. "That he wasn't there to meet me. The grand wedding ceremony is tomorrow. This is all the time we have to get to know one another before standing at the altar."

"You are already married by proxy."

"You make excuses for a man you do not know?" Joanna frowned.

"I know he is a man with great responsibility." Beatriz nodded at the window. "Land to rule over, people to govern. Perhaps he is ensuring there will be no pressing matters upon your arrival at the palace. So he can give you his full attention between now and the ceremony."

"I appreciate you trying to reassure me." Joanna tried to beat down the disappointment that she wasn't now traveling with Philip. After her long and arduous journey, surely, it was the least he could have done—to meet her as she'd stepped onto dry land.

Finally, the stunning sweep of flat landscape gave rise to the hill Coudenberg Palace was situated upon.

Beatriz leaned forward. "It is indeed a palace. I am not sure I could count all of those windows and chimney stacks."

"It will catch the wind," Joanna said. "The only hill on this flat land."

"Flat land that may well flood. It is sensible to be on higher ground, is it not?"

Joanna didn't answer. The carriage rattled past a herd of small, speckled deer and a copse of swaying, silver birches. Her knights traveled directly behind her on their horses and Lord Belmonte was in front. The rest of her entourage was responsible for the carts and mules that had been unloaded from the ship or gathered from the port.

Eventually, they came to a stop beside a sprawling flight of stone steps that led to the palace entrance. Great, gray urns held tall, trimmed bay trees and a red rug had been placed on the ground for her to step upon.

She studied the waiting group through the window of the carriage, searching for the archduke's mop of blond hair and his steely-blue eyes.

But she saw no such figure and when Belmonte opened the carriage door, the knights on either side of him, she pouted and stepped down. "This is Coudenberg Palace, is it not?"

"Yes, Your Highness," Belmonte said.

"So why is it merely courtiers here? Does my husband not wish to meet me even now?"

"I have come in his place and bring his sincere apologies." A woman stepped forward. Her sky-blue dress fitted her neatly, the waist nipped in and the neckline trimmed with lace. Her headdress was tall and a golden veil hung from the tip, sparkling in the sunlight. Her pretty features were petite, her mouth like a rosebud.

"And you are?" Joanna asked, looking her up and down.

"Margaret of Austria. Daughter of Maximilian, King of the Romans, and Mary, Duchess of Burgundy."

"Margaret," Joanna repeated, her perusal of her intensifying. "The archduke's sister."

"Yes." Margaret stepped forward and kissed Joanna's cheeks, first the left and then the right and then the left again. "My brother sends his regrets. He will be here shortly. I hope I do not disappoint you too much."

"I was rather hoping to see him at the port, at the very least upon my arrival here."

"My brother is a man of his own mind." Margaret smiled. "But I can assure you he is very keen to make your acquaintance. Shall we?" She nodded at the steps.

"Yes, of course."

Margaret glanced at Belmonte and then settled her attention on the two knights.

The knights clasped the grips of their swords. Energy and readiness came off them in waves. They didn't need to speak to harness attention.

"And these are?" Margaret asked, pausing.

Belmonte stepped forward. "Her Highness's personal protection on request of the king and queen, parents of the princess, duchess consort. You understand they are anxious. Their precious daughter is in another country, another court, one they do not know and its situation is in uncomfortably close proximity to their enemy."

"Very well." Margaret nodded, her lips tight. "Come, this way. I am sure you wish to freshen up after the journey."

"We were very comfortable on the boat, once out of the Bay of Biscay." Joanna walked up the steps, Margaret at her side, along with two skinny dogs with lanky legs, long noses, and whip-like tails.

"I have heard it is brutal." Margaret pulled a face. "A storm every day, even in the summer."

"You have heard right. I actually wished I would die at one point, the sickness was so extreme."

"How awful, but I'm so glad you didn't." Margaret smiled. "Or you would not be here at all."

Joanna liked her new sister almost instantly. She was warm

and had an openness about her. She was also wonderfully elegant and beautifully dressed. The material of her gown and veil were of the finest quality. Perhaps there would be opportunity for Joanna to have some court clothes of a similar ilk. Maybe that was what Philip would prefer. Her Spanish traditional clothes might be strange to him. Which would be a problem, as it was all she had with her.

"This way." Margaret led her into the palace.

Courtiers were lined up beside the door and bowed their heads as she and Margaret walked past.

"The staff will bring in your chests," Margaret said. "And I'm sure your lady's maid will take it from there."

"Yes, she will. Beatriz is very capable."

Margaret gestured to a wide staircase. "This way to your bedchamber. I have warm lavender water awaiting you."

"Thank you."

At the top of the stairs and out of the view of the courtiers, Margaret stopped. "I have to ask." She gripped Joanna's hands. "I can hold my tongue no longer. Please, tell me what John is like."

"John."

"Yes, your brother. He is all I think of. All I want to know of."

Joanna laughed at the earnestness in Margaret's voice. "I understand your situation perfectly, for it has been mine also for the longest time."

Margaret smiled. "Please, tell me what you can. Be truthful. I can take it."

"Do not fear." Joanna fell serious. "John has a handsome face." She paused and circled her nose. "Freckles here, in the summer."

Margaret giggled. "Tell me more."

"His hair is brown, his eyes blue, and he is strong. He likes to ride and hunt and stick fight."

"And his nature?"

Joanna smiled. "He is clever and honest and most of all, he is very kind. He will think you are beautiful, of that I am certain."

"He will?"

"Yes."

Margaret clasped her hands beneath her chin. "You paint a good picture of him in my mind. Surely, he has some faults."

Joanna nibbled on her bottom lip. "Perhaps one." She paused.

"Go on." Margaret swallowed.

"He is terribly spoiled by Mother. She calls him 'her angel.' Perhaps it is a son thing."

"Oh, dear." Margaret frowned.

"But it is not a terrible fault to be loved by one's mother, is it?"

Margaret looked away and reached for the cross at her neck. "Come, your bedchamber is just here."

After washing and sipping honeyed tea, Joanna made her way back down the wide staircase with Beatriz.

The two knights were close behind. They had waited outside her bedchamber door while she'd prepared. Big. Silent. Impenetrable.

"Ah, you are here," Belmonte said, looking up at her. "The archduke awaits you in the Aula Magna."

"Good. I have kept *him* waiting." She tipped her chin. "That is the very least I should do."

Lord Belmonte stepped close. He touched her cheek. "I have known you since you were a babe," he said quietly. "I wish only the best for you. Please remember that, whatever happens."

"You sound pessimistic about my future."

"On the contrary. I just wish you to know that my council will always be with your best interest at heart. My loyalty is to you and your family. This is a new land for me also. New people for me, like you, we have yet to know."

"I appreciate your allegiance. I really do." She smiled up at him. "You have reduced my longing for home considerably, Lord Belmonte. I will send my thanks to God."

"I am happy to be here." He stepped aside, his right arm outstretched toward the huge, wooden doors emblazoned with a golden eagle crest. "Now go and meet your husband."

CHAPTER FIVE

"SHE IS HERE?" Philip strode into the vast Aula Magna with Thomas close behind him. His dusty boots clipped on the floor. He was hot. He'd just ridden in from Ghent. He was also thirsty.

"Yes. She is," Margaret said.

A courtier poured him wine.

Philip took it. "And?" He gulped the drink back then studied his sister.

"I think you will agree it is a good match."

"Mm." Philip intended to decide that for himself.

"Apparently, she was not impressed," his grandmother, who was seated on a black chair and dressed, as usual, all in black, said, "that you were not here to greet her."

He frowned briefly then sent his scowl over the collection of nobles and courtiers who stood around the room. He didn't want to disrespect the dowager with his irritation. "It was for her benefit I wasn't here."

"Really?" the dowager said.

"Yes. I went to Ghent to source some local fabric. A gift for my bride."

"I am sure she will be very pleased," Margaret said. "Would you like me to bid her to enter?"

"Yes. Go ahead." Philip gestured for more wine, then took a seat on the big, golden chair at the head of the room. It was set up on a red-rugged platform and had a matching chair at its side. Behind it hung the Habsburg crest—a black, double-headed eagle—the golden embroidery sparkling in the sunshine streaming in through the vast windows.

Margaret waited a moment, as though checking her brother was truly ready for this momentous meeting, then turned and walked to the door.

The huge, long room was silent, except for her footsteps and the swish of her gown. Once at the door, she pulled it open, the hinge creaked and in the distance, a bird sung loudly.

Philip's heart raced, despite the fact he'd told himself it wouldn't. This marriage was a business arrangement. Heirs must be produced and Joanna of Castile had the necessary bloodline for those heirs. What did it matter if he liked her or not?

What did it matter if he *desired* her or not?

Margaret stepped back, leaving the door wide open.

In its frame stood a small figure flanked by two knights in full body armor and gripping long, polished swords.

Joanna. Finally. Here was his bride.

He stayed seated, glad to be, for a rush of anticipation and awe had poured into his veins and frozen him in the moment.

He took her in. Her floor-length gown was the color of fresh cream with the neckline and the long sleeves lustrous black. She wore a white headband with a black hood and escaping from it were long curls of pale hair.

She walked forward, slowly, with her chin held high and her arms at her sides. She stared straight ahead.

Straight at him.

His belly tightened and he pursed his lips. She was different to any other woman he'd ever met, he knew that instantly. She was regal, proud, and graceful. It was the way she moved, filled the space despite her delicate stature, and kept her attention firmly on him.

It was as if she saw no one else in the crowded room.

When she reached halfway she stopped, her entourage halting behind her.

Philip swallowed, his throat suddenly dry, then finished his wine and set it aside. He stood, unfolding to his full height. His long dagger hung from his belt and he straightened his scarlet tunic that was emblazoned with the Habsburg crest.

The room looked to him.

He raised his head, kept his expression neutral, and stepped down from the plinth. It was here he was close enough to make direct eye contact with Joanna.

And when he did his breath caught in his chest. For she held his gaze with confidence, something that was a rarity in anyone he met.

He liked it.

A lot.

Still, he didn't speak. Each step closer grew his curiosity and his intrigue.

When finally he was but four footsteps from her, he stopped. The tension in the room was knife-sharp, as if the nobles, along with his grandmother, sister, and Thomas had all held their breath.

But he didn't care.

Right now, there was only Joanna and him in the Aula Magna. Everyone else had ceased to exist.

Her skin was like the finest porcelain. Her small nose was straight and slightly upturned at the end, and her lips were the color of peony petals. Her hair, although it was pale, had a hint of strawberry running through its blonde strands.

He clenched his fists, resisting the urge to pull a curl into his finger and know its softness.

Dragging in a long breath, he studied her eyes again. They were dark brown—at odds with her paleness—and the color of his favorite bay horse.

She was staring at him unblinking, not giving away any of her emotions—a sealed scroll. A tight barrel. An enigma of the most enchanting kind.

A little thrown by her boldness—most people bowed to him—Philip pushed his hand through his hair and cleared his throat.

He stepped up close, so close that he could speak into her ear. "You are real?"

"What do your eyes tell you?" she whispered in reply.

"That you are beautiful." He looked into her face, so close now. "More beautiful than I could ever have imagined."

"And your ears?" She tipped her head slightly and swiped her small, pink tongue over her bottom lip. "What do they tell you?"

"My ears tell me your voice is a sweet as any songbird."

"And your nose?" She raised her eyebrows.

His heart was pounding, his senses alive. He dipped his head to the crook of her neck. A lock of her hair tickled his nose as he breathed deeply, filling his lungs with her. He repeated the action with his eyes closed. She smelled of lavender and sunshine, an intoxicating mix that did strange things to his belly. "My nose tells me you smell of everything I need."

A flash of gratification crossed her eyes. As if she'd achieved something she'd set out to. As if she'd won a game he hadn't known they'd been playing.

He didn't care. She *had* won him. He wanted to learn what every flash in her eyes meant. Each tilt of her head and curl of her lips. He wanted to know her.

His wife.

"So you believe I am real now?" she asked.

"I have thought of you for a long time." He stepped around her, studying her gown, her slender shoulders, and narrow back. It was all very pleasing. "Many images of your appearance came to my mind in that time."

"You prayed that I wasn't an old hag." She twisted her head and once again raised her eyebrows.

"As you likely prayed I wasn't an old toad." He smiled and stood before her.

She smiled too and it changed her face, softened it, made her even prettier, even more becoming. Not least because he saw the amusement dancing in her eyes. She was a woman with a sense of humor, and he'd wager, spirit.

"Perhaps I haven't decided if you are an old toad or not yet," she said.

For a moment, he was quiet, surprised by her words, then he chuckled. She did indeed have spirit. "I hope to convince you that I am not in the least bit like a toad." He knew he wasn't. He'd been told from a young age how handsome he was. And it wasn't just words; it was the way people, girls, studied him, reacted to him. He was thankful to God that his wife was the prettiest of all the women he'd ever known.

He looked up and over her shoulder, suddenly landing back in the room full of people. "Who are you?" he directed at the man standing between the two knights.

"Your Grace, I am Lord Belmonte of Aragon. Here at the behest of the King and Queen of Spain."

"And why are you here at their behest?" He frowned at the knights who didn't have Habsburg crests on their armor but were in his court.

"The princess's parents wish her to have some protection." Belmonte paused. "This is an unknown country and within a stone's throw of King Charles, their mortal enemy. I believe they sleep better in their beds knowing that she has loyal soldiers of Castile and Aragon watching over her."

Philip felt his breaths quicken with each word. Prickly heat traveled over his skin. "I will be her protector." He stabbed his thumb on his chest. "She is mine and as such, *my* responsibility." His voice rose. "No harm will come to the princess. Not one hair of her head."

"I believe you, Your Grace," Belmonte said. "But I ask you to respect the wishes of King Ferdinand and Queen Isabella. They do not know of you or this country. This has been a dealing with His Majesty Maximilian, also a man they do not know well."

"As I know not of their country. My much beloved sister will soon be traveling to—"

"And if you wish to send protection, that would be most welcome in Castile," Joanna said. "For anyone who loves a daughter or sister would wish for that. God would wish for that too."

Philip looked at Joanna. His jaw tightened. "You understand my frustration?"

"Of course. And maybe that you feel slighted too. But I beg you not to. I have made a long and arduous trip by sea—it is nice to see a face I have known since childhood. Lord Belmonte has been like an uncle to me."

Philip studied the older man again. Had he been placed as protector or spy? "And you mean to follow my wife everywhere?" He set his hands on his hips, the tip of his dagger angling forward when he touched the handle. "You and your knights?"

"The knights will be vigilant but silent at all times," Belmonte said. "Their job is to stop any physical harm befalling your wife, nothing more."

"And you?"

"I am here if Joanna needs me."

There was a collective intake of breaths. A few people shuffled.

"You dare to call my bride by her first name?" Philip raised his eyebrows.

"Forgive me." Belmonte dipped his head. "Please."

Philip frowned then drew his attention back to his betrothed. "You are safe here." He took her hand, raised it to his mouth, and kissed her knuckles. Her flesh was warm and soft and she tasted of petals and powder.

"I thank you," she said quietly. "But I also wish to be happy here, as well as safe."

He kept hold of her hand and stepped closer, so close, there was barely a hair's breadth between them. "I can make you happy." He looked into her dark eyes and whispered. "I can make you feel many things."

Her breath hitched and her pupils widened.

He touched his mouth to her ear and whispered, "Many wonderful, breath-stealing things that will have you begging for more."

"Why… I…?" She pressed her hand to her chest. "What an improper thing to say."

"But a truth." He enjoyed seeing the flush rising on her cheeks. "We are to share the same bed, are we not?"

She swallowed and nodded.

"And we are to create heirs. We should have some fun with that, don't you agree?"

"You speak of things that—"

"Starting this very night." Philip stepped back and clapped his hands. "Thomas. Get the bishop now," he shouted. "This marriage needs to be blessed immediately. I will not wait to make this woman mine."

Joanna gasped again.

"But, Your Grace, the wedding is tomorrow." Thomas stepped from the crowd. "It has all been planned."

"You think I don't know that?" Philip marched up to him. "Tomorrow is too long to wait. Get the bishop now. That is my order."

Thomas frowned, then dipped his head. "Yes, of course. Straightaway."

Philip spun around. "And everyone out. Out!" His skin itched to be alone with Joanna. It was a sudden and desperate need to speak to her without the judging, curious eyes all around.

"Your Grace," one of the noblemen, Samuel, said. "This is most untoward."

"You think I care?" Philip waved his arm through the air. "This is my palace and these are my lands and this is the woman to whom I am wed to by proxy. And I want this marriage blessed *now*. And I wish to be alone with her. *Now*." He spun around. "Out. Everyone. Now!" He pointed at Belmonte, the knights, and the woman supporting Joanna. "Including you. Get out."

The murmur of conversation rose as people moved. Margaret helped their grandmother to standing.

Philip stood with his hands on his hips before Joanna. He felt as if his heart were beating a new rhythm, one that was wild and exciting and urging him on.

She tilted her chin, her jaw tight and her chest rising and falling with her rapid breaths. The first rise of delicate flesh at her neckline caught his attention and sent a rush of interest to his groin.

He would say a hundred thankful prayers later. Because if ever a woman had stirred a need in him it was Joanna of Castile. And it was more than her sweet prettiness. It was something deeper—a bewitching, intoxicating, fascinating sensation that had gripped him in the most seductive of ways from the first moment he'd seen her.

Chapter Six

Joanna stared at her groom—a stranger but not. He was tall and handsome, good to look at, it was true, but she also longed to run her fingers through his blond hair and feel the touch of his lips on hers, know the shape of him without clothes on.

It was a need that was growing in her belly, expanding, gripping her, becoming her entirety.

Never in her dreams had she thought Philip of Habsburg would look this way, would *be* this way. Confident. Commanding. Alluring. Possessive. She wouldn't have dared to even hope.

But now, standing before her, in this room that was quickly vacating of all other people, she knew he had suddenly become her everything. Whether they had been matched or not, she would have wanted the archduke. She would not have been able to resist the way she had resisted Raul.

Philip was looking at her with his steel-blue eyes that blazed hot and passionate. And like her own, his breaths were coming fast, as though impatience and longing had gripped his chest.

Within a minute, the room quieted, and then the door shut with a resounding bang. Silence descended.

"It is quite improper," she said, "to be alone before our wedding has been blessed."

He didn't reply, just studied her closely.

She lifted her gown an inch and walked to the window, staring out at the vast expanse of greenery and the trees jabbing the sky in the distance. Her mind was spinning. What was happening to her?

Suddenly, she was aware of him behind her, close, his warm breath caressing her neck.

"I will not touch you," he said, "until we have been blessed by the bishop."

His nearness weakened her knees. She fought to remain still and dignified. "And you could not wait until tomorrow to touch me?"

"Could you, me?"

She didn't answer. Couldn't find the words.

"My beautiful Joanna, I have never set my eyes upon a woman so exquisite as you. My flesh longs for yours. My heart aches to be near to you, as near as a man and woman can be."

She closed her eyes and pulled in a deep breath. A quiver in her cunny had her pressing her thighs together.

"Each moment that we are not as one," he said, coming closer still but not actually touching her, "is a moment that pains me. Pains every inch of my body." He groaned softly, as though it did actually hurt him.

She turned and looked up into his face.

He looked down at her with an intensity that caught her breath. She took a step backward, her shoulders bumping into the coolness of the window. "Your need is—"

"Great. Yes. Isn't yours?" He dipped his head to hers.

She stared at his lips, slightly parted. Was he going to kiss her?

"We have waited so long," he murmured. "Years, months, weeks, days, and hours to be together. It has only ever been you and will only ever be you."

"Philip," she said, his name like a love potion spreading on her tongue. "My husband."

"Joanna. My wife."

She set her palm on his tunic, over the Habsburg crest. It was cool, though she was hot. Heat had spread right through her—her sternum, her breasts, her belly, and between her thighs. She wanted to know Philip without his tunic, without his breeches. She wanted him. All of him.

The way he wanted her…or so it seemed.

"You have enraptured me with the speed of an arrow," he said, his lips hovering over hers. "I will commit to you with my heart, my body, and my soul."

"As I will you." Lust was a new, almost violent sensation. She cared not for propriety, or God's will. "Kiss me."

His mouth twitched into a smile. "We should wait for the bishop."

"I care not for any of the ceremonies or blessings." She gripped his collar. "Kiss me. Now. I command it."

Suddenly, his arms locked around her, hauling her close.

She caught her breath and squeezed in close.

"If I start kissing you, I should warn you, I may not be able to stop."

"I will not want you to."

Bang. Bang. Bang.

Hard rapping on the door blasted around the room, echoing up to the high ceiling and down the stone walls. It was about as graceful as cannon fire.

Suddenly, he released her. His cheeks held a flash of red and he did not take his eyes from her. "Soon," he said. "Soon I will kiss you…everywhere."

Everywhere?

Joanna stepped away from him and straightened her gown. What had just come over her? It had been powerful and intense, all consuming. She'd been ready to strip him of his clothes and shed hers, to do all the things she'd thought of doing with a man right there on the floor, or over the long table, perhaps on the throne at the head of the room. She wouldn't have cared. She'd have done anything to have Philip join his body with hers and drive them both wild with pleasure.

A tall man with dark, curly hair strode in. Thomas, if she remembered his name correctly.

Behind him came a rotund bishop dressed in white robes and with a tall, red miter perched upon his head.

"Ah, good." Philip rubbed his hands together. "You are here, Bishop, and just in time, I would say."

Thomas held out his hands and shook his head, as if exasperated. "Shall I call everyone in?"

"No, no, no need for that." Philip gestured to the bishop. "If you could just give us God's blessing, quick as you can, that will be all."

"Your Grace, the ceremony is tomorrow, is it not?"

"We will still have the ceremony tomorrow so the masses can enjoy our union, but we wish to start our married life right away." He reached for Joanna's hand and knotted his fingers with hers. "In fact, I believe for the sake of my wife's reputation, it is of the utmost importance that we do."

"Her reputation?" The bishop raised his eyebrows at Joanna.

Joanna's cheeks heated further. Never had she been looked at this way by a man of the church. He was shocked, shocked by *her*. She studied her feet and bit on her bottom lip.

"Do I need to spell it out?" Philip asked. His voice held a sharper edge now.

"Well…I…" The bishop fiddled with the Bible he held, twirling the golden thread that hung from a bookmark. "It's very unusual and…"

"You see my wife standing before you," Philip said, leaning closer to him as if a conspirator.

"Yes."

"She is beautiful, is she not?"

The bishop nodded.

"She is so beautiful that I cannot wait another minute to claim her as my own. To bind our souls together for all of time. I wish to feel her body under mine, around mine. I wish for us to procreate as God intended, and I plan for that to happen soon…very soon."

"Never have I…" The bishop looked from Philip to Joanna

and back again. His red jowls wobbled.

"So, as I previously said, you should get on with it." Philip gestured to the Bible. "Or God, you, and Thomas here might find yourself bearing witness to the consummation itself, over the very solid table right in the center of this room."

"In the name of the Lord, what a thing to utter." The bishop kissed his rosary and then sent his eyes heavenward.

"I think you should just say the words, Bishop," Thomas said. "Before you and I regret it."

"Yes. Yes of course." The bishop opened his Bible.

Philip turned to Joanna and took her other hand. He smiled, his eyes softening but still brimming with desire.

Her heart did a leap of longing and happiness and she squeezed his fingers.

"Please repeat after me. I, Philip of Austria, Duke of Burgundy, take thee, Joanna of Castile, to be my wedded wife, to have and to hold from this day forward, for better, for worse; for richer, for poorer; for fairer or fouler; in sickness and in health; to love and to cherish; till death us depart, according to God's holy ordinance and thereunto I plight thee my troth."

Philip repeated the words. His voice sure and sound.

Joanna did the same with her own vows. The blessing wasn't how she'd imagined. Alone in a quiet room with just the bishop and one other man she didn't know. But she didn't care. It was the best thing that could have happened—the *only* thing that could have happened.

"I now pronounce you man and wife and your matrimony blessed by the Father, the Son, and the Holy Spirit." The bishop crossed himself. "May God be with you today and every day of your marriage."

"Excellent." Philip stepped up close, cupped Joanna's face, and pressed his lips to hers.

Joanna gripped his forearms and accepted her first kiss. It was sweet yet sure, exciting and full of delicious promise.

He moaned softly and pulled back. "We really should take

this somewhere more private."

She giggled, floating on happiness. "I do not know what you mean, husband." The disappointment of Philip not being at the port to greet her was long forgotten.

"You will."

A twinkle in his eye made her body tremble with longing.

"This way," he said, wrapping an arm around her waist. "I will show you."

They walked the length of the room and then the doors opened. Her two knights stood directly outside, behind them a swell of people.

The moment Philip and Joanna appeared between the knights, the crowd quieted.

"Noblemen and councilors." Philip held up his hand. "My wife and I are now blessed by God. Tomorrow, we will celebrate in style. We will feast and dance and enjoy excellent music as we celebrate our marriage."

Joanna studied the sea of faces. Surly-looking men she didn't know. For a moment, she felt small in this strange land with strangers, but then Philip slid his arm tighter around her waist and pulled her against the length of his body. "I am sure you will understand that my wife and I wish to…" He paused. "Wish to…" He paused some more. The crowd shifted uneasily. "Wish to get to know one another."

There was a collective exhalation.

"So if you will excuse us." He suddenly stooped and slipped one arm behind her legs and the other around her waist and scooped her up.

"Oh!" She clutched his shoulders, his body solid beneath his clothing.

He grinned at her. "Shall we?"

Before she could answer, he stepped forward.

The crowd parted. Murmurs of congratulations and good wishes followed them to the stairs.

As they climbed, she glanced over his shoulder. The knights

were close, their helmets shut as always and their hands on the grips of their swords. Their armor rattled softly as they took the steps.

"They will have to wait outside," Philip said without turning. "Like my father, I wish for a rule that I am the only man permitted inside my wife's bedchamber."

"I am sure that will be acceptable to them."

"As long as when you scream in pleasure"—he grinned—"they do not think I am murdering you and rush in, swords at the ready."

She gasped. "Philip, what a thing to say. I fear I have married a very bold man who cares not for propriety."

"I care very much for propriety," he said with a chuckle as they reached the top of the stairs. "That is why we have just had our marriage blessed before we spend the night together consummating it." He strode toward the room she'd used earlier to freshen up. "And, my sweet one, I thought you would have more questions about screaming with pleasure than propriety."

She swallowed, nerves suddenly gripping her. Perhaps she'd pushed that comment away on purpose. Was it really possible to scream with pleasure? "Doesn't one usually scream in pain?" She curled her toes in her shoes.

"Let's just say there are different types of screams, and I look forward to showing you exactly what they are."

They arrived at the bedchamber. Philip shoved the door open and stepped inside.

Her nerves doubled when she saw the large, four-poster bed she'd practically ignored earlier. It was dressed with heavy, blue-and-gold curtains and canopy. Two golden doves decorated the peak at the top. At the end was a plush long chair upholstered in sunshine yellow and with plumb-green cushions.

Her chests had been stacked in the corner. She doubted Beatriz had unpacked them yet.

Philip back-kicked the door and it shut with a slam. A sound that was very clear to everyone not to enter.

"I have thought of you for months," he said, "and now finally, we are alone in the bedchamber together."

He set her down, but the moment her feet touched the rugged floor, his mouth crushed against hers.

She clung to him and kissed him back. Her heart rate rocketed when her shoulders hit the wall and his solid body pressed against hers, toe to chest. Her headdress fell off, landing on the ground forgotten.

He groaned and slid one hand to her waist and the other into her hair. He delved his tongue to find hers.

She opened her eyes, the feel of his urgent, wet tongue a surprise and the taste of him dark, sweet, masculine—a flavor she could become drunk on.

"We will be very happy together," he said, kissing a trail across her cheek. "I can tell."

"Yes. Yes, we will." She lifted her right leg, needing to get closer despite the already possessive hold he had on her.

Her gown shifted and he took full advantage, reaching for it, rucking it up. Cool air washed over her legs and her cunny trembled. Her breasts were heavy, her nipples tight peaks poking at her gown.

He was kissing her again, desperately, his breaths coming as fast as hers. Excitement raced through her, anticipation like another living creature inside of her. She wasn't frightened of her first time, just desperate to know, to feel, to experience. Have it all. All of him.

And it certainly seemed like her new husband was up for the job of showing her everything she needed to know… and more.

Chapter Seven

"My love," Philip gasped. "You are making me crazy with desire. My mind, my body, my soul. I want you. From the moment I set eyes on you, I've wanted you."

"And I want you." She locked her hands around his neck and pulled him in for another kiss.

The next thing she knew, she was once again in the air. Their lips didn't part as he walked them to the bed, his arms locked around her buttocks and her feet dangling. Her shoes fell off, tapping to the rug.

And then he was laying her down on the soft blankets and covering her with his long, muscular body. Her head sunk into the pillow and she arched to meet his kisses.

It was then she felt it, the thick wedge of solid flesh behind his breeches. It pressed up against her groin, long and hard—demanding.

"Oh…" She pulled back and stared up at him.

"Now you have the proof of my need for you, my wife," he said, giving her a wickedly seductive smile.

"But…but…it is so big."

He raised his eyebrows. "You thought that I would be small?"

"I thought… I don't know what I thought."

He sat up so he was straddling her hips and took hold of the bow that held the neckline of her gown in place. "We will get to know each other's bodies well." He pulled the bow and the gown loosened. He did the same to the next bow, exposing more of the slope of her breasts.

She was breathing fast, her mind a rush of desire and worries of inexperience.

When the material was loose enough, he pushed it aside so her breasts were uncovered. Her pale-pink nipples were tight and pointed and her sternum shone slightly with perspiration. She studied his face—he appeared enraptured, mesmerized—and then he cupped the outer edges of her breasts and brought them together.

"Philip," she gasped, his touch on her tender flesh so new and exciting.

He tipped forward and took her left nipple into his mouth.

She caught her breath as wet heat sent a new shot of desire through her chest, her belly, and to her cunny. Her nipple hardened further, until it almost throbbed, and she ran her fingers into his silken hair and tugged at the roots.

After a moment, he switched to the other nipple and she closed her eyes, pushing her chest up for more. The sensation was heavenly and had set her entire body aflame with lust.

"I want to kiss you all over," he said, trailing his lips to her sternum and then up her neck to her mouth.

"Yes," she managed against her lips. "I want that. I want it all."

Her words seemed to increase his need and he tore at his tunic, throwing it aside, then sat and pushed at his boots.

Joanna's eyes widened as she watched the muscles in his shoulders and back bunch and flex. His skin was perfect, smooth and tan, and a sprinkle of dark hair sat at his sternum. She could look at him forever. He was more perfect than any Greek or Roman statue.

"We should take this off properly," he said, turning his attention to her gown.

She nodded and lifted her hips, pushing at it, fumbling with the sleeves, getting frustrated.

But then it was gone and she lay there, flat, legs together, arms at her sides and utterly naked before him.

He stilled, his lips damp, his eyes wide, and his breathing heavy. The look he gave the length of her, a heated caress with his eyes, had her skin prickling and a delicious shiver wending up her spine.

For so long, she'd wanted to know what it was like to lie with a man. To be desired. To want and be wanted.

Now she knew, in one look of adoration from the archduke, exactly what that felt like.

"In the good name of the Lord, all my prayers have been answered," he said quietly. "You are perfection."

"I am happy to please you."

"Oh, you do…you will." He lay on his side next to her and kissed her cheek as he cupped her breast. "And I will please you, too." He caught her damp nipple between his thumb and finger and tugged gently.

She moaned and closed her eyes. Her virginal body was his to do with as he pleased.

"Tell me," he whispered against her ear.

"What? Tell you what?"

He didn't reply. Instead, he slipped his fingertips downward. Over her belly, into her navel, then lower, to the small crop of hair that grew at the juncture of her thighs. "Tell me, have you ever touched yourself here?"

"Philip." She looked up at him. His face was so close. "That is a sin, as well you know."

"I didn't ask whether or not it was a sin," he said, stroking the short hairs this way and that. "I asked if you'd touched yourself here. In the dead of the night, when all alone. Have you touched yourself and wondered what I'd be like?"

She paused for a moment then nodded.

"Is that a yes?"

"Yes, it's a yes."

"Good, because I wondered what it would be like to lie with

you, to feel you around my fingers, under my tongue, gripping my cock."

"Oh...I...really...I..." Her mouth formed a perfect 'o' as he slid between her cunny lips and pressed on the small nub that gave her pleasure.

"Open up," he whispered onto her mouth. "Let me in."

She hesitated.

"What is it?" He frowned.

"I..."

"Tell me. Whatever it is. I need to know."

"I am untouched by a man, Philip, as you well know and..."

His frown softened. "And you are scared?"

"No." She shook her head. "I am not scared, I want it. I want you..."

"So what is it?"

She touched his cheek. "Please, I just ask this: Be gentle with me."

"My beautiful wife." His eyes shone with emotion. "You are my most treasured possession. I will treat you more gently than if you were made of Murano glass, or the finest porcelain. That is my promise to you."

Her chest ballooned with gratitude. She had no idea what was in store for her, but if Philip promised to be gentle, she believed him.

"Now part your thighs and let me know your sweet womanhood," he whispered.

She did as he'd asked, her belly trembling with anticipation.

Once again, he kissed her, and as he did, he ran his fingers through her cunny, stroking the plump flesh, finding her damp entrance and then stroking back up to her nub.

She shivered with longing and gripped his biceps, feeling them tense as he moved his arm, his hand, his fingers.

He was exploring her and spreading the moisture that had grown between her legs. She smelled her own arousal and groaned, pressing her head into the pillow. "More," she gasped.

She knew exactly where she needed to be touched, but would he know?

"You are demanding of me?" he asked, a note of humor in his voice.

"I want you to show me what you know."

"Oh, I know a lot."

She opened her eyes and looked up at him. "And who taught you?"

"Why do you need to know?"

"I just do."

He found her entrance with the tip of his finger and eased in an inch.

She gasped and tightened her grip on him.

"I have been taught by the girls at court," he said, "in preparation for this exact moment. I needed to be ready for when I had a wife, whose pleasure is my everything."

Joanna couldn't answer—the sensation of him there, inside her, was overwhelming. And now he was going deeper, sliding in through her moisture.

"Heaven help me," he murmured. "You are so tight."

"Philip," she gasped, running her hand down his arm to clutch his wrist. "Oh…it is…"

"It is going to feel so good for you…and me." He kissed her and connected the heel of his hand with her cunny, over her bud.

She moaned softly and curled her toes. Yes. That was where she needed it.

Her husband seemed to know this and rocked his hand, pushing his finger into her and rolling over her most sensitive spot.

She inhaled sharply and canted her hips. The connection increased and she drew up her knees, greedy for more.

He added another finger, tunneling deeper into her cunny.

"Oh, yes…yes…" she said, pulling him in for a kiss. "Philip."

He kissed her with enthusiasm and worked with skill and determination. Soon, the pleasure she'd known before, on her own, was building. A pressure that had started in her pelvis and was growing, swelling, demanding release.

She was panting now, her heart rate soaring and her pulse deafening in her ears. Her body was alive with need and it was something only Philip could satisfy.

"Don't stop." She gasped desperately. "Oh, please, don't stop. Don't stop."

He stopped and pulled out.

She wailed. "No, I... Oh... Why...?"

In one swift movement, he'd rid himself of his breeches. His cock sprung out, thick, long and hard. The dark end was bulbous, the root springing from a tangle of pale-brown hair.

"This is the right time," he said, moving over her. "Trust me. Trust me in this moment the way you have never trusted anyone before."

She nodded, parting her legs so he could settle between them. In an instant, his cock was probing at her entrance. So wide and hard, she didn't think it would ever fit.

"Your pleasure was just about to take you," he said, locking his arms and looking down at where they were about to join. "And it would have been good with my fingers, do not doubt that, but with my cock, you will feel like you have landed in paradise."

He curled his hips, claiming more of her, and let out a groan.

"My love." She reached for his chest, cupping his defined muscles.

"You feel so good," he said. "Your body is so warm and wet."

"And you are...so hard...and big." She battled to take him; he was going deep, stretching her, filling her. "Oh..."

Suddenly, he dropped down and caught her mouth in a kiss. Her breasts flattened to his chest and his body pressed up against her nub.

"Oh, my..." She arched her back and gripped his hips with her knees. He went deeper, so deep, his balls pressed up against her cunny.

"Find your pleasure," he whispered, rubbing up against her.

"You were just about to find it again."

She nodded, canting to meet him. The pleasure was there. A burst of bliss just waiting to grip her entire body.

"And when you do..." he said, moving over her, in her, and on her with purpose. "I will find mine and we will be as one."

"Please...don't stop this time."

"I won't, my love. But please, find your pleasure...soon." He closed his eyes and appeared in deep concentration.

Wrapping her arms around his shoulders, she concentrated on the pleasure growing between her legs. He was stimulating her with skill and the pressure was building. She trembled and shook and held her breath. It was there. Ready to release.

And then it did. She cried out, a pleasure-soaked wail, and dug her fingernails into his flesh as she was held hostage to ecstasy. Her cunny squeezed around him, holding his cock then releasing over and over. White-hot fingers of bliss stretched over her skin, shaking her limbs and creating pulses in her spine.

He half withdrew then pushed back in, then repeated the action, extending her bliss and finding his own.

His cock throbbed and he groaned long and gutturally. A full-body tremble attacked him and she held him tighter, holding him together, so it seemed.

"My love," he gasped, lifting his head from the crook of her neck. "You are... We are...perfect together." His brow was shiny and his face flushed.

"You are perfect," she said, pushing his hair back from his forehead. "I thank the Lord for you, for everything about you, but most of all, your gentleness and understanding."

"It is Him *and* our parents we should thank." He smiled. "It is not often my father has gotten it right for me, but you are most definitely right for me, Joanna of Castile."

Chapter Eight

Philip sat up on his pedestal in the Aula Magna and looked at the familiar faces all turned his way. His new wife was beside him on her seat, her back straight and her chin tipped regally. She really was incredibly beautiful, goddess-like with her long, pink-kissed hair; perfect skin; and seductive, dark eyes that sparkled with intelligence.

Once again, the sun was shining and a long streak of light poured through the window and landed over her. It didn't touch anyone else. It was almost as if God Himself had joined in their ceremony and wanted all of Brussels to see how beautiful she was.

"My love," he said, gesturing to his grandmother, who stood before them holding his sister's arm. "I would like you to meet my grandmother, Margaret of York."

"It is a pleasure to meet you," the dowager said, bowing her head but not taking her eyes from Joanna. "I hope you will be very happy here with us."

"Thank you." Joanna smiled, a warm and genuine smile that made Philip fall for her just a little bit more. He adored his grandmother and anyone who did the same had a place in his heart. "I am sure I will be, Dowager. Coudenberg is beautiful and so far, the archduke has made me feel very much at home." She turned to him, her smile still in place and her eyes flashing.

He shifted on his seat. Was she remembering their first night together? Was that why her cheeks held the faintest blush? It had been incredible. She was like no other girl he'd ever lain with. But then, she wasn't a *girl*. She was a princess, her blood was royal, and even more than that…she was his precious wife.

He reached for her hand. "That pleases me, that you feel at home." He clicked his fingers. "And I have a present for you."

"A present?"

"Yes, and it is why I wasn't here yesterday when you arrived. Sourcing it took longer than I had anticipated."

"Could you not have sent a courtier?"

"To choose a wedding gift for my bride?" He pressed his hand to his chest. "Oh, no, what kind of husband would that make me?"

"One who is where he is supposed to be when he is supposed to be there." She raised her eyebrows at him.

For a moment, he was shocked by her words, then he chuckled. She had wit—that was one thing he knew for sure about her.

A courtier stepped before them holding an armful of neatly folded material. Another stood at his side, then another. All holding sumptuous cloths.

"What is this?" Joanna asked, standing and then stepping down from the plinth.

"It is a trousseau, linen for your married life," he said, watching her run a fingertip over an exquisite piece of soft weave the color of a jay's wing. "We have excellent weavers and seamstresses here. I hope you will take advantage of them."

She turned to him, a frown marring her brow. "You do not like what I wear?"

"My love." He stood and cupped her cheek. "I love what you wear very much, but in Burgundian court, our style is different. I thought you would enjoy following the fashion, as you are a modern woman and there will be many feasts and music festivals for us to attend throughout the year."

"Mmm." She looked at the material again. "I do aspire to be progressive thinking and perhaps my gowns are a little...extravagant in comparison to those of the Flemish women."

"It is very beautiful material," Beatriz said.

"The best in all the world." The dowager nodded seriously.

"Yes, it is rather lovely." She turned back to Philip. "I thank you for your thoughtfulness. It is a wonderful gift and yes, I will have new gowns made and one for Beatriz too."

Beatriz smiled and curtsied.

"I am glad you approve." Philip turned to the room. "Now let us feast, enjoy good wine and music, and celebrate the joining of Burgundy and Asturias and the families Habsburg and Trastámara."

The doors burst open and there was a round of applause as servants carried in platters of roasted pheasant, woodcock, and venison. There were trays of fig-stuffed apples, cheese, bread, and pickles. Glass bowls of sugared almonds and candied spices were set about along with lettuce, poached quince, roasted carrots, and turnips soaked in honey.

Delicious scents filled the air and Philip breathed deeply as he looked around. For a moment, a stabbing pain caught in his chest. His father wasn't with him on his official wedding day. That hurt. His mother neither, but that wasn't her fault. Both absences were a darkness that sometimes weighed heavily on him like a wet, woolen cloak. But today wasn't a day to brood. It was a day to celebrate and then later, he'd lie naked with his sweet wife and have her panting his name all over again.

Music started, a flute, and he took his seat at the head of the feasting bench alongside Joanna. Her knights moved with her, never far away, always silent. He wasn't sure if he'd ever get used to them. Hopefully, he wouldn't have to. When she'd been his wife for a while, produced an heir, then surely, Belmonte would see that he was more than capable of protecting her.

"The food is delectable," she said. "Your cooks are very skilled."

"They are the best in the world."

She popped a wine-soaked cherry into her mouth. When

she'd swallowed, she leaned close. "You seem to think that everything you have here is the best in the world."

"It is."

"How can you know? Have you traveled the world?"

"I have been told by my grandmother, who hails from England."

"Ah, I see." She turned and stabbed at a piece of meat.

"What does that mean?" he asked. "'Ah, I see'?"

"You have been *told*. Do you not wish to travel the way Columbus has?"

"I will travel out of necessity. For war, to conquer, to discuss matters of politics and Habsburg business."

"Will you come to my homeland?"

"Perhaps, if the need to arises."

She nodded. "It is very hot, hotter than here, and the grasses dry out in the summer. They turn the color of your hair and blow in the scorching winds."

"'Scorching' winds?"

"Yes, the wind is hot. But the olive trees like it." She paused. "The horses and dogs, not so much. We rest in the afternoon. Take to our bedchambers and wait until the sun begins to slip from the sky and takes with it the heat of the day."

"And in the winter?"

"It is cold, it is true." She paused. "But I suspect I will be colder here, this winter."

He leaned close and kissed her cheek. "I will keep you warm, my love. Do not fear."

"I will hold you to that." She touched his arm, her small, slender fingers delicate on his dark tunic. "Every night."

He caught his grandmother watching him and smiled at her. He hoped she approved of his new bride as much as he did.

"Tell me about your family," he said, reaching for a thick slice of venison.

"My parents are pious monarchs with great ambitions to spread the word of God in their new lands."

"It is a noble cause."

"We were raised to be God fearing, to confess our sins."

"And I know you committed at least one." He popped in some food and studied her face as he chewed.

"Archduke," she said with a frown and glancing around. "I beg you not to talk of such things, of our private conversations."

"No one is listening. No one is interested in us." He grinned.

"*Everyone* is interested in us and everyone is always listening." She stared straight ahead. "That is what I was frequently told growing up in court. And it is why we took lessons in etiquette and good manners, amongst other things."

"What other things?"

"Mathematics, grammar, reading, law, history, languages." She paused. "The list goes on."

"So…go on." He was curious to know his wife's skills.

"Classical literature and poetry, Juvencu and Prudentius, Seneca and the Saints."

"That is a lot."

"Needle arts, drawing, dancing, clavichord and monochord, Latin—"

He laughed. "And French too. I cannot fault your accent."

"I thank you." She glanced at the window. Sunlight still poured in. "And outside pursuits were not forgotten, hawking and hunting, equestrian skills—"

"I do not wish you to ride."

She frowned at him and crossed her arms. "But I love to ride."

"It is my wish that my wife, the mother of Habsburg heirs, does not ride." His jaw tensed and he gripped his goblet of wine. A flash of a memory popped into his head. The memory of his mother's accident, which she'd never recovered from. "Do you hear me?"

"Ah, Archduke, may I please offer you and your honorable bride my sincere congratulations?" Thomas stood at his side.

"Thank you." Philip nodded.

Thomas leaned closer, his hand on Philip's shoulder. "A gift that I hope will serve you well." He set a heavy silver candlestick holder upon the table.

"How pretty," Joanna said, a smile returning to her face. "I thank you, Thomas—if I may call you that?"

"It is my name, Your Highness." He grinned. "So please, call me 'Thomas.'"

Joanna smiled then returned to picking at her meal.

"Thank you, my friend," Philip said. "Now I wish you to carry out an instruction." He made a *come closer* gesture with his fingers.

"Of course." Thomas leaned in.

"Ensure the stables do not allow my wife to ride on the Spanish horses Belmonte and his pesky knights rode in on. In fact, they must not let her ride at all."

Thomas glanced at the knights who stood tall and silent. "I will instruct the groomsmen this very day."

<hr />

THE FEASTING AND dancing went on until night had fallen. Philip's legs ached and his head spun with all the wine. So much so that when he fell upon his bed with Joanna, day was breaking and he was snoring within minutes.

When he opened his eyes she was gone. There went his chance to enjoy her sweet body once more.

He rang for hot water, honey, and bread then pulled on his clothes. Where was she? He looked out of the window at the flat landscape that stretched into the distance. There were more clouds in the sky today, but still, it shone bright. Above, a pair of buzzards circled, their graceful outlines in silhouette.

It was then he spotted movement in the distance. Horses. Three of them. They were advancing at pace toward the palace, cantering over the vivid, green lawns.

He placed his hands flat on the glass and peered out, eyes narrowed. It was a gray horse and two bays. Atop the bays were knights; their shining armor was unmistakable. And on the gray was a woman riding not sidesaddle, but legs astride.

"In the name of the good Lord." He sucked in a breath as a shot of anger burst into his veins. Heated and tormenting, it made his ears ring and his heart pound.

He turned from the window and stomped across the room, dragging on a pair of breeches as he went. He pulled open the bedchamber door then stormed along the passageway, thundered down the staircase, and marched for the main door.

Once outside, Belmonte rushed up to him. "Your Grace, you look...angered."

"*Angry* is too calm a word." He threw a withering look at Belmonte. "I am furious beyond all comprehension." He clenched his jaw so hard, his teeth hurt.

How dare she disobey him like this?

How dare she test his good nature?

"Thomas! Thomas! Where are you?" Philip didn't wait for a reply. He paced across the formal entrance area, down more steps, and made his way in the direction of the horses.

Belmonte rushed at his side. "What has made you furious? Can I help the situation?"

"It is the horses you brought that made the situation." He clenched his fists.

"I do not understand."

"I told my wife I did not want her to ride, yet there she is, as clear as day, making haste on horseback...and for what? Pleasure?"

"She has always ridden, Your Grace. And a very good rider she is too."

"I will not stand for it!"

"Because she is not using a sidesaddle?"

"It has not helped the situation."

The horses turned toward them and slowed.

Philip's fears were confirmed. It was Joanna atop the huge, gray steed—its neck as strong and thick as a carthorse and its withers standing at a man's chin level.

"Wife of mine." Philip shoved his hands on his waist and stood with his feet hip-width apart. He squinted up into the sunshine. "Dismount this instant."

She rode toward him and halted with an innocent smile upon her face. "Good morning, husband."

"Your Grace. Your Grace." Thomas rushed up, cheeks red and out of breath. "I'm sorry. I…"

"You what?"

"Fell asleep after the festivities. My plan was to visit the stable first thing this morning and tell—"

Philip held up his hand, silencing him. He should have done the job himself.

"What is it?" Joanna asked.

"Get down from the horse." He had to consciously unclench his teeth to speak. *"Now."*

"You are angry?" Her smile dropped.

"Get. Off. The. Horse."

She let out a sigh then did as he'd asked, slipping nimbly to the ground still holding the reins. Her gown was creased as it fell to her ankles covering her lower legs, which had been exposed.

The two knights, close behind her, also dismounted. One of their horses let out a neigh, as though sensing the tension.

"I don't know why you are so vexed," she said. "This is a beautiful Spanish horse who has served Belmonte well and is a safe ride. Honestly, Philip, I'm a good rider. My parents put me in the saddle the day after I took my first step."

Each word enraged him further. It was all fueled by fear. Fear for her. Fear for himself at the thought of losing her. Fear of her being broken by a fall. His stomach contracted. Sweat popped on his forehead and under his arms.

"I cannot stop riding, which is one of my favorite pursuits, just because—"

"Silence." His fists clenched. He was aware of Belmonte taking a step closer. He didn't care. His frustration at being disobeyed was all-consuming now. "I ordered you not to ride, just yesterday. Then this morning, I wake and you are not in our marital bed, you are outside, riding, doing the very thing—"

"I am not good at taking orders." She tilted her chin and glared at him. The horse shook its head and pawed the ground.

"Why. You..." He raised his hand and stepped forward, reaching for the reins. He had to get her away from the giant horse, away from Belmonte, so he could explain his fears in private.

But the moment his arm lifted higher than his head, his movements were stopped.

The slice of metal on metal as two swords were withdrawn screamed through his ears. Between one heartbeat and the next, the steely tips of the knight's weapons were tucked beneath his chin. If either one swiped an inch, he'd be dead.

He stilled instantly.

"How dare you?" Philip's nostrils flared and his mouth dried. Cool metal prodded dangerously near his life blood. "Belmonte. Tell them to back off," he managed, glaring at the knights.

Belmonte, hand on the grip of his dagger, looked between Joanna and Philip and then at the knights. "Your wife's protectors clearly consider you to be a threat to her wellbeing in this moment."

"I said...*tell them to back off.*" Philip didn't dare move. He was fond of the blood vessels in his neck.

Thomas, who had also drawn a dagger in preparation of protecting Philip, snapped at Belmonte, "You dare to threaten the archduke like this, on his own land?"

"Our loyalty is to Joanna of Castile," Belmonte said, his deep voice low and menacing. "Though I will agree, this situation is not ideal."

"Not ideal." Joanna turned and frowned at the knights. "Remove your swords from my husband's neck. Immediately."

Nothing.

"I command you." She stomped her foot. "Remove your weapons."

Still nothing.

"I believe a little reassurance from your husband in necessary, Your Highness," Belmonte said.

"He was not going to hit me or hurt me. My husband is a kind and gentle man, I know that already. He was reaching for the reins." She slipped the reins into Philip's still-raised hand. "See. Like this."

"I want her away from this horse so she does not get hurt by it," Philip managed as he curled his fingers around the leather. "Why would I hurt her when that is my biggest fear?"

No one spoke. Philip could hear his pulse in his ears. Sunlight glinted off the two blades and the narrow slits of the knight's helmets gave them an ethereal quality.

Then, as quickly as the weapons had appeared, they were gone. Slid back into their sheaths.

"My love." Joanna stepped quickly up to him and touched his neck. "Are you hurt?"

"No." He closed his eyes for a moment, composing himself. So many emotions charged through him—relief, anger, indignation, surprise—it took a few breaths to control them.

"I will not ride again," Joanna said. "Now I have seen how it disturbs you."

"For that, I would be grateful." He opened his eyes. The tremble in his limbs, the fight instinct, was reducing. "Now let us go back to the palace, where we can conduct ourselves with a little more civility." He threw a glare at Belmonte and then curled his arm around his wife's small waist and pulled her fragile body toward his. He kissed her temple. "And I wish us to be alone. It's like being in a battlefield being wed to you."

"You are dramatic." She giggled and pressed her hand to his bare chest as she leaned close. "Though as you said yourself, I am not just some girl of the court, I am Joanna of Castile, third in line to the kingdom of Asturias and of royal blood. I am everything you need and more."

He studied her sparkling eyes—they were full of confidence and ambition. She was indeed unique and he knew in that moment she'd keep him on his toes. She'd keep life at the palace interesting. Very interesting.

CHAPTER NINE

JOANNA WALKED INTO the cool bedchamber, relieved to have the stern knights stay on the other side of the door.

At the angle she'd been standing after dismounting, she'd known Philip had been reaching for the reins. Admittedly, he'd been about to snatch them from her, but it hadn't been an arm raised ready to strike.

And the look on his face—the anger and surprise in his eyes—that he'd been drawn against on his own land had made her heart flip. Seeing the deadly tips of swords at his neck had generated a rush of nausea in her. To see him harmed, to see his blood, would pain her likely more than it would pain him.

The door closed with a solid bang.

"I am sorry to have disobeyed you," she said, turning. "But you have to understand, riding, especially early in the morning, is one of my favorite pastimes."

"A dangerous pastime."

"I am a skilled rider."

He walked to the table and poured two goblets of wine. He passed one to her. "As was my mother."

"Your mother?"

He walked to the window and stared out.

She studied his broad shoulders and narrow hips. The way his hair curled slightly at the ends and his breeches hugged his long legs. Suddenly, she remembered something her own mother had told her. Mary of Burgundy had fallen from her horse and never recovered.

"Philip?" she said softly. "I—"

"My mother had an accident while out hunting. She fell from her horse, injuring her spine." He spoke quickly, as though keen to get the words out and over and done with. "My father's life, and mine and Margaret's, changed forever that day."

Joanna set down her wine and walked up to him, wrapped her arms around his waist, and pressed her cheek between his shoulder blades. "My love. I am so very sorry for your loss."

He hitched in a breath. "So you will understand," he said, his voice tight with emotion. "That I do not wish to lose you, my dear, beloved wife, to the same fate."

"I promise I will not ride again." She felt wretched for scaring him so and humbled that already he did not want to lose her.

He was silent.

"It's just after last night, in bed, with you, I..." She held him tighter. "I felt renewed and I wanted the wind on my face, to hear the sound of hooves on the ground, and...to rejoice in being alive."

He set his wine on the sill and turned, folding her into his arms. "I do not wish to speak of it again."

"I understand, my love." She pushed his hair back from his face and stared into his eyes. "I only want to make you happy."

"And I you." He dipped his head and kissed her.

A deep, passionate kiss that had her knees weakening. She moaned softly and clung to him. His body against hers lit a fire inside her, heat spreading and her blood pumping hotly.

He tipped his head, deepening the kiss, and pulled her to him so tight, her breasts squashed up against his chest. His breath quickened and he cupped her behind over her gown. Her headpiece fell to the floor.

"Philip," she gasped.

"If you think your knights want to keep you safe, their resolve is nothing to the lengths I would go to in order to protect your life," he murmured against her lips. "You are the perfect match for me. If I could, I would keep you in here, away from harm's way, tied to the bed so I can ensure your safety."

"Tied to the bed?"

"Yes." He glanced at the four-poster, but then his attention lingered on its shiny engraved posts and rich canopy. When he looked at her again, a mischievous grin danced on his damp lips. "In fact…I might just do that."

"Philip. What are you saying?"

Suddenly, he released her and she felt the void of space around her as he stepped away.

"I need…" He flipped open a chest at the end of the bed and began pulling out blankets and embroidered cushions, tossing them behind himself. "Ah…here they are." He withdrew two lengths of black silk, the kind that would have been used as swags. "Perfect."

A coil of excitement wound in her belly. Exactly what did her intriguing new husband have in mind? One thing was for sure: He was determined it would happen and he appeared pretty excited about it.

He stood and held either end of the silk in each hand. He pulled, making the material taut with a snapping sound. His gaze settled firmly on her. "My love, prepare to be bound and pleasured."

"Bound and pleasured?" She could hardly get the words out, her mouth was so dry. She could hardly hear them for the bellowing of her pulse in her ears.

"I know you're not going to disobey me when I tell you to remove your clothes."

She gulped. "Now? You want me to remove them *now*?"

"Of course now." He nodded at the door. "We will not be disturbed. Your knights will ensure that."

Joanna dragged in a deep breath and let her attention slip to his breeches. Behind the material, there was a long outline of flesh she now knew to be his big cock. He was erect again, the way he'd been before.

He wanted her. His body craved hers. That thought alone thrilled her in a way that made her cunny clench and her limbs tingle.

"Joanna." He raised his eyebrows and tipped his head. "Remove your gown...now."

She hesitated.

"If you don't, you can say goodbye to it, for it will be ripped from you without a care for its future."

With fumbling fingers, she tugged at the laces and buttons, freeing the bodice. When it had loosened around her ribs she pulled at the sleeves and withdrew her arms.

The material gaped at her chest, her small breasts shifted with each of her breaths, and her nipples were hard.

"My love," Philip murmured, watching her intently. "Do not be shy. The time for that is over."

She beat down a wave of nerves and pushed at her gown. It caught briefly on the swell of her hips then pooled at her feet.

"And the rest." He raised his eyebrows. "I wish to see all of you."

She'd worn a soft undergarment for riding. Now, she pushed it down her thighs, past her knees and shins, and kicked it aside.

"Phew, I am a lucky man." Philip blew out a breath as his gaze roamed her body with unashamed and unabashed desire. "You are the woman I dreamed about, but now you have a face."

Summoning bravery, she walked to him, hips rolling and the air cool on her nakedness. "And you are the man I dreamed of."

He smiled then nodded at the bed. "You should lie down and prepare yourself to be pleasured with skill and devotion."

"Skill. That is quite a claim."

He chuckled. "A claim I make with confidence." He nodded at the bed again. "Lie down so I can begin."

With nerves fluttering in her belly, she lay on the bed on her back. The bedding was colder than she'd expected when she stretched her limbs straight. A heaviness filled the air and a quiver set up in her belly.

"Arms out to the sides." Philip looked down at her with hungry eyes. He licked his lips. "Right out. You are at my mercy, so show it."

She did as instructed, feeling even more vulnerable in the new position.

He dropped one silk tie on the bed and then carefully looped the other around her right wrist several times.

She didn't speak but watched his movements intently as he fastened the silk to the bedpost, making it taut so her arm was outstretched and harnessed into position.

"Feel okay?" he asked.

She nodded.

He smiled and dipped his head, swiping his tongue over her peaked right nipple.

She gasped as the hot, wet heat of his mouth sent desire winging through her body.

"You are so responsive," he said softly and then he licked his way to her other breast. He took that nipple into his mouth and sucked gently.

"Philip," she murmured. In all of her dreams and fantasies, she'd never imagined her husband would make her feel this way—so wanted and revered, so utterly feminine.

"Do not fear," he said, straightening. "I will give you everything you need and more." He scraped his hand through the blond strands of his hair in a way she'd noticed he did often.

"Now for the other side." He picked up the second ribbon and walked around the bed. The bulge in his breeches was significant and sent another thrill through her. The size still shocked her, though, and she hoped he would be as gentle as he had been previously.

He tied up her other wrist, securing her, sacrificial almost, to the bed. Very gently, he touched her inner arm then ran his finger up past the crease of her elbow, her pale upper arm flesh and to her armpit. From there, he stroked to the button of her collarbone. "You are so soft," he said. "And beyond tempting."

"What are you tempted to do?" she asked, not sure if she'd be able to handle the answer.

"Why don't I show you?" He smiled and walked to the end of the bed. Once there, he bent and removed his boots then hooked his fingers into the waist of his breeches. "What I can tell you is I won't be needing these."

Joanna trembled and blinked rapidly as his light-brown body hair was revealed and then his cock came into view, dark and hard, the tip glossy.

He took hold of her ankles and pushed them apart.

She gasped. "Philip!"

He didn't stop and widened her legs until her thighs were separated and her cunny was on full display.

She squirmed with embarrassment, self-conscious of the damp folds and dark hair.

"You are beautiful," he said, moving between her legs. "Do not think anything otherwise."

She was breathing fast, her breasts shifting with each panting intake of breath.

"And I wish to worship at the altar of your body." He flashed a wicked grin then dropped down between her legs, his face nestled at her cunny.

A sudden, wet lick ran up through her lower lips, over her entrance, and to her nub. "Oh! I... What...are...you?"

"Relax," he said, looking up at her with hooded eyes. "And enjoy, because you will...a lot."

Relax. How in God's name could she relax with her husband's face between her legs, licking her most private place?

He did it again, his hands on her inner thighs and his nose burying into her pubic hair.

This time, she closed her eyes and willed herself to relax. But it was impossible. The sensation was so new, illicit, dark—and surely sinful.

"You taste better than any feast." He murmured, slipping a

finger to her entrance. "It may take some time for me to sate my appetite for you…if ever." He pushed his finger into her wet, tight cunny.

"Oh…Philip." She thrashed her head from side to side and pulled on her binds. "What you do to me…it's…"

"Perfect for you. Now take your pleasure when you want it, there is no rush. I am quite happy down here."

His words were shockingly delightful and she clenched her fists and strained against the ribbons. The bed creaked and this seemed to spur him on.

He stroked his tongue over her nub, fast, little circles that had her hips canting to meet his mouth. "Oh, yes…yes…"

The pressure was mounting, the pleasure increasing. And being tied into position, at his mercy, only added to her arousal.

He added another finger to her cunny, gently pumping in and out of her the way he had his cock.

Instantly, the pressure intensified, the need to race to release gripping her.

She arched her spine and curled her toes, the sounds of his fast breaths and kisses adding to her lust. She groaned and her belly tightened. Her burst of pleasure was almost there.

Her cunny squeezed his fingers and her nub was hot and swollen beneath his clever tongue. Never had she imagined such a carnal moment as this. It was incredible, her body held hostage by sensuality.

And then it was there—the huge wave of release was about to crest. She held her breath and her heart thumped. When it reached the point it could no longer be contained she let out a wail and clamped her legs to Philip's shoulders, keeping him there.

He stayed with her, working her cunny and her nub. Her skin prickled as heated bliss spread through her body, making her limbs tremble and bright lights flash behind her closed lids.

On and on he went, extending her pleasure. The silk was at full stretch and so tight around her wrists, her fingers tingled. She didn't care and kept bucking for more of the magic he was creating.

Eventually, she calmed and her cunny's spasms receded. "Philip...oh, that was surely...a sin...but it...felt so good."

"My love." He lifted his head and kissed her patch of pubic hair. His eyes were sparkling and his lips shiny with her arousal. "What a man and wife do to find pleasure is not a sin. You should remember that."

"I...I will try." Another full-body quiver took control and she shook from her toes to her fingers. "Oh...please."

"Please?" He grinned and rose to his hands and knees. "What are you asking for?"

"You, my love. I want you to find pleasure."

"Pleasuring you *is* pleasure for me." He came over her. "But we do have the small matter of producing an heir."

She went to hold him, but her arms were trapped.

He grinned. "And while you are pinned down and at my mercy, I will see to that."

"You like that I can't move?" She could see the dark desire in his eyes. It gave him away.

"What is not to like about you giving your body to me?"

"It is yours." She breathed in his rich scent. "Please...do it."

His cock was there, nudging at her pliant entrance. Then as his mouth caught hers in a kiss, he pushed in. A slow but determined ride to full depth.

She groaned and her cunny fluttered around him.

"Heaven help me." He gasped. "I cannot last... I am too..." He pulled out halfway then rammed back in.

She cried out at the intense bliss of his cock filling her so absolutely.

He groaned and released his seed in three fast thrusts. Slapping into her, every muscle in his body turning to stone.

Excitement winged through her. To see and feel him in this moment was exhilarating. His fierce self-control was slipping and all because of his lust for her. She clung to his hips with her legs and buried her face in the crook of his neck when he collapsed over her, only just holding his weight.

Their chests pressed together, and sweat slicked over their bodies.

"My love," he whispered against her ear. "You excite me like no other."

"I am glad." She looked up at the canopy. "Because you will never have another, not now we are wed."

"I will not want anyone but you," he whispered. "You are everything and more than I will ever need."

CHAPTER TEN

"How did you enjoy the service?" Philip asked Joanna as they walked back to their solar many months later. The corridor was quiet, apart from the sounds of their footsteps and the knights' clanking armor.

"It is always excellent and with such a large congregation, I enjoy the hymns."

"Good." He squeezed her hand. "And what should we do after lunch? I have no business to attend to today."

"I am glad. You have been in meetings all week."

"No meetings today. It is the day of rest."

"I wish you could rest on another day too." She couldn't help but pout. The last few weeks, her husband had been engrossed in the details of governing and raising money with the Estates General.

"You married a busy man with great responsibility, as you know, my love."

"I do know that, but I can't help wanting to spend time with you." She paused. "I have been educated in many things, including politics, you know."

"And for that, I am grateful, for I should have hated a stupid wife." He chuckled. "But I don't wish for you to worry about such matters."

"What if I promised not to worry, but instead to help find solutions to problems? I could be of assistance."

"I will bear that offer in mind."

"Do more than *bear it in mind*."

They turned the corner. Several female courtiers scurried ahead holding armfuls of material. A brunette girl looked over her shoulder, her pretty face flushed and her eyes wide.

"You are of course right. I will consider it most seriously," Philip said. "Are you hungry?"

"Er, yes, I suppose I am."

"Me too. I will organize us figs; bread and honey; and perhaps some goat's cheese too." He gestured to the door of her bedchamber, which he used too on most nights. "Wait for me, my love."

"But…?"

He held up his hand and called, "We are having luncheon in our private chambers."

The courtiers, realizing they were being given an order, stilled. The brunette was the only one to turn around; the others continued on their way. In her arms were two of Joanna's new French-style gowns that needed cleaning. Joanna hadn't seen her before.

"Please, I will join you shortly, Joanna," Philip said. "Please go and pour the wine."

"Who is that?" Joanna asked.

"A servant, Joanna." He frowned slightly. "Go… I insist."

For a moment, she hesitated then stepped into the bedchamber and closed the door. She removed the hennin she always wore to church and set it aside, then stood with her hands on her hips.

Philip's voice came from the corridor. A string of words. More than just ordering bread, honey, and cheese. Then a female's voice. A giggle. Philip talking again.

Heat spread on her chest and up her neck—a stinging rash of jealousy. Her jaw clenched and her toes curled in her shoes. She reached for the handle and stepped out, stomped past her knight standing to the right, and froze.

Philip was indeed talking to the pretty courtier. Standing close too, a smile on his face as she tucked a stray lock of hair behind her ear.

"Who are you?" Joanna asked, raising the hem of her gown and stomping up to the girl.

Shock washed over her face and she stepped back, quickly looking at the floor.

"I said, *who are you*? Who are you to my husband?" Joanna stabbed her finger in the direction of the girl.

"Joanna, what are you doing?" Philip curled his hand around the top of Joanna's arm.

She was vaguely aware of her knights filling the space in her peripheral vision.

"You tell me to go into our private chambers so you can talk and giggle with this...this...*wench*." She glared at the girl, hating her delicate features and perfect skin.

"She is not a wench. This is Natalie. She has worked here since she was very young. I have known her since *I* was very young."

"And that gives you permission to act as though you are not married?" Joanna tilted her chin. "Not married to *me*?"

"I am allowed to speak to other women." Philip frowned, his voice was low.

"You are not." She tipped her head and glared at him. "Unless it is a business matter or a family member."

"You are being ridiculous." He looked at Natalie and jerked his head to the right, dismissing her.

She took a hurried leave, quickly disappearing from sight.

"*I* am being ridiculous? How would you like it if I carried on with the stableboy I have known since childhood?"

"Stableboy?" Philip raised his eyebrows and his lips tightened. "What stableboy?"

She flicked her arm, dislodging his hold. "Exactly...what stableboy? You do not need to fear, for we are in *your* home. And I would bet silver coins she is one of the girls with whom you honed your bedchamber skills." Joanna's body stiffened at the thought of Philip tying another woman to his bed and pleasuring her. It made her feel physically sick and she pressed her hand over her mouth as an acrid taste spread on her tongue.

"My love, do not think of that." He rested his hands on her shoulders. "Why would you? It is in the past."

"It hurts me." She blinked as her eyes moistened. "To think of you with another."

"I am not with another. I am with you. My wife."

He pulled her into a hug and she did not resist. His strong body against hers was what she needed—reassurance that he loved her, adored her, and would never leave her for another.

But what if he did?

A sob escaped and she squeezed her eyes closed.

"Hush, my love. Do not upset yourself when there is nothing to be upset about."

"But why did you want to speak to her alone?"

"We were not alone." He pulled back and cupped her cheeks. "Your knights were right there. I was planning a special Sunday luncheon for us and ensuring all the flavors I know you adore were going to be on the platter."

"You were?"

"Yes." He kissed the tip of her nose. "Now let us go to the solar and have some alone time." He glanced at the knights, his eyes narrow. "And your silent guards can go back to their places."

She nodded and swiped at a tear rolling down her face. What had gotten into her? Her emotions were like a rushing storm cloud racing from east to west and getting heavier with rain.

She allowed Philip to lead her into the bedchamber, then dabbed her face with cool lavender water from the basin and brushed her hair.

Philip went into the solar, the room they used when they wished to be alone eating, reading, or talking.

Joanna walked to the bedroom window and stared out at the landscape she'd become used to despite its flatness. For a moment, Raul's face popped into her mind. She wondered if he'd found a wife. She hoped he had and that hope didn't bring with it any jealousy or twisting of her guts, not like the thought of Philip with another. That was like a dagger to her heart and stole her breath as though she were actually being strangled.

Her attention was drawn to a flowerbed full of roses. It was alive with bees and butterflies and a small songbird hopped on the gravel path that ran alongside it.

A sudden idea came to mind. A sinful idea, admittedly, but one that would get her what she wanted. She'd make a love potion. Yes. That was what she'd do. As soon as she had a spare moment, she'd gather rosebuds and crush them with honey. Then when Philip wasn't looking, she'd add some to his claret wine. He'd never notice, and as long as she was the woman who had made the potion and was with him when he drank it, it would be her with whom he fell totally and utterly in love.

And she needed him to, for she was so in love with him, it made her bones ache when she wasn't with him.

THE NEXT AFTERNOON, when Philip was with his noblemen and advisors, Joanna set her Bible aside, hooked a small basket over her forearm, and slipped from the room. As she walked down the stairs, her knights close behind, Beatriz appeared.

"Can I get you anything, Your Highness?"

"Yes…I mean no. This is something I must do myself." She hurried out of the main entrance and turned left, toward the rose garden.

"Whatever are you doing?" Beatriz rushed to keep up with her. "Surely, I can help."

"Not in this instance, no." The sun heated her cheeks, making her feel alive and positive. This would surely work.

"But please, I am here to serve."

Joanna came to a halt and turned. "I am lovesick, Beatriz. There is no one who can help me but me."

"Lovesick?"

"Yes." She shook her head slowly, as though it really were a very uncomfortable affliction—perhaps it was.

"Your husband?"

"Of course. For whom else would I be lovesick?"

"I am glad, of course, that you feel this way about him." Beatriz took Joanna's hand. "And does he feel the same?"

"What do you think?"

Beatriz said nothing. A buzzard called overhead. In the distance, the chime of a church bell carried on the breeze.

"See, you do not think he loves me." Joanna huffed and turned around. She carried on walking fast.

"Joanna, Princess, I did not say that." Beatriz rushed after her. "From what I see, there is great affection and he speaks very highly of you, lavishing you with time and gifts. I have no reason to suspect he doesn't love you."

"Lavishing me with time," Joanna threw over her shoulder. "Perhaps in the first moon of our marriage, but not now. Now he spends all of his days debating and poring over scrolls."

"It is his duty as archduke."

"It is his *duty* to be with me." Joanna stopped at the rose bed and surveyed the flowers before her. They were in various stages of blooming, but she only wanted the tightest buds, for they held the most power.

"What are you doing?" Beatriz stood alongside her.

"I am making a love potion."

"A love potion? But that is really quite a sin and—"

"I do not care, and you must not tell a soul about it."

"Of course your confidences are safe with me." Beatriz paused, as though thoughts were spinning through her mind. "And what will you do with the love potion?"

"I will put it into his wine, of course, this very evening."

"And you do not think he will notice?" Her eyes widened.

"Not if it is the third or fourth goblet of wine, no." Joanna chuckled, feeling pleased with her cunning plan. "Now here, hold the basket while I choose the buds."

Beatriz swallowed tightly then took the basket. "Yes, of course."

Joanna found three deep-red buds with petals still tightly wrapped around themselves. She plucked them carefully and dropped them into the basket.

"What else do you need?" Beatriz asked, glancing around.

"Honey, as freshly gathered as possible. And a pestle and mortar."

"Shall we go to the kitchen?" Beatriz nodded to her right.

"Yes. And you can get it for me. That way, no one will know but us. I don't want anyone getting suspicious that I am using spells."

"That would be very wise." Beatriz looked worried and then glanced left and right again. "To keep it a secret. It could cause problems if it were known."

"It will be unproblematic. I am Joanna of Castile, wife of the Habsburg Archduke, remember. I am clever as well as cunning and I have you to help me. Don't I?"

"Yes. Of course. Always." Beatriz bobbed her head. "Let us get this potion made before your husband concludes his meetings for the day."

That evening, after eating with Philip, the dowager, Beatriz, and Thomas, Joanna excused herself, complaining of feeling a little green.

Which was the truth; she'd felt that way all day. Perhaps it was the thought of Philip and the courtier girl. Perhaps she was nervous about casting her spell.

"I will join you soon." Philip held up a full goblet of wine and grinned. "Beautiful wife of mine."

She nodded and left the room, the knights close behind. Philip had drunk well during the meal and would no doubt have more back at their bedchamber. To help him sleep without worries, he always said.

And it was that last drink that she'd put the love potion into. Excitement filled her. Soon he'd feel as drunk on love as she did.

The knights didn't follow her beyond the threshold to her bedchamber and with the door safely closed, she found the small, brown bottle she'd filled with her potion and hidden beneath the bed.

A fresh jug of wine waited on the table beside the large tapestry—red-and-gold embroidery depicting a unicorn, a lion, and a pomegranate tree—and she quickly poured two goblets.

One she set aside, and the other she left on the tray then removed the cork of her potion bottle.

"With rose and honey, I cast this binding love spell over my dearest Philip," she whispered, carefully adding a few drops to the wine. "May honey sweeten your love for me, your devoted wife, and rose remind you of the thorny pain we would both feel should we be parted." She closed her eyes and tipped her head back, clutching the bottle to her chest. "For we are meant to be, as the moon is to the sky and the snake is to the desert. Our love is as vast as an ocean and can withstand storms, hellfire, and the devil himself." She paused, emotion almost overwhelming her. "May you know love the way I do, Philip. May it embrace you, consume you, fill your mind and your heart." She opened her eyes and stared at the wine, the surface still now of ripples. "I love you so, and you shall love me so."

Quickly, she stood and replaced the potion in its hiding place. The moment she had, the door opened and Philip walked in.

"My love," he said, pausing. "You still have your headdress on."

"I have?" She touched the small hair roll that had lace hanging down the back.

"Usually, you remove it immediately upon return to our private chambers. It annoys you."

"Ah, yes." Quickly, she removed it and set it on a chair. "I was thinking of other things."

"Oh?" He picked up the wine on the tray, the one with the potion in it.

She held her breath.

He raised his eyebrows. "What were you thinking of? These other things?"

"Oh, just home, what my parents are doing. I have not heard from them in a month."

He drank some wine the way he always did, several big mouthfuls.

Joanna held her breath, wondering if it would taste different. If he'd notice.

He shrugged and set his attention on her. "I am sure you will receive a letter soon. They are doting parents. The knights who follow you everywhere are proof of that."

She nearly sighed with relief that he hadn't noticed anything different about his wine. "Are the knights really so tiresome to you?"

"Yes." He drank more wine. "They are." He gestured to the door. "We have an adequate number of skilled warriors here at Coudenberg to ensure our safety. And quite honestly…" He reached for the jug of wine and poured more. "I find it offensive that they think I would hurt you."

She smiled. How could he hurt her in any way, now that he had drunk the love potion?

"I shall order them to be gone," she said, waving her hand in the air and walking to him. "I will speak to Belmonte at dawn. He will not have a problem."

"That would be most agreeable." Philip set the jug and his refilled goblet aside and cupped her cheeks. "My love. My wife. My beautiful Joanna."

Her heart skipped. The potion was working faster than she'd thought. "Philip."

"Have you noticed something different?"

"Different?"

"Yes." He stroked his thumbs over her cheeks.

"I don't know what you mean?" Her heart clattered. He must have guessed about the love potion. He'd be angry, she was sure. He'd demand that she stop any kind of witchery or spell-making. That she confess her sins.

"You are…" He frowned.

"I am what?"

"Pale and you have barely eaten this last week."

"It is true, I have been sick. And I know why…" She paused. "But I don't want to tell you why?"

"You don't?" He raised his eyebrows.

"No." She shook her head and downcast her eyes. It really was most embarrassing to be afflicted so.

"Please, tell me. I want to hear it from you."

"I fear you will not be happy with me."

"Oh, my love, do not think that. I will be. I will be the happiest man in all the land."

"You will?"

He nodded and his eyes sparkled.

"In that case…" She paused. "I am lovesick, I know I am. I love you so much, it has stolen my appetite and made me think I am quite crazy with desire for you."

"Lovesick?" Surprise crossed his face.

"You see?" Irritation suddenly clasped her in its grip. "You are not happy. I knew it."

"Of course I am happy that you love me." He pulled her closer and pressed his lips to hers. "I love you too."

"You do?"

"How could you doubt it?" He frowned.

"But you have not said it."

"I am saying it now. I love you. I love you. I love you."

He kissed her again. He tasted of wine and cloves and the figs he'd eaten at dinner and she melted into him.

When he pulled back his expression was serious. "But what I thought you were going to say is…"

"What? Please, tell me."

"That you are pregnant, Joanna. You have not had menses for some time. I thought you were going to tell me you are expecting our first child and that is why you felt sick."

"Menses. What do you know of...?"

"I know enough"—he slid one hand to her flat belly—"to know that we are to be parents, Joanna. You and I have made an heir, and I can't wait to meet him."

"I... I... You really think so?" She stared at a small, wooden cross on the wall. "We have been blessed, by God, with a child?"

"I believe so, my love."

He kissed her and Joanna felt such joy, she wondered that her heart wouldn't beat right out of her chest.

Chapter Eleven

Several months later, Philip paced outside the bedchamber door. Likely, he thought, doing the exact same thing his father, Maximilian, had done on the day he'd arrived into the world. Creaking the same floorboards.

He clasped his fingers together at the base of his spine and turned, retracing his steps toward the urn of flowers perched upon a table. He'd wear the green rug out very soon.

A sudden, bone-chilling scream belted out from the bedchamber. It curdled his blood and pained his heart.

He stilled and stared at Thomas, who was pale and tapping his fingers together. "How much longer will this go on for, Thomas?"

"As long as it takes." Thomas downturned his mouth. "Could be days."

"In the name of the Lord, I hope not. I do not envy women childbirth." Philip scraped his hand through his hair then gestured to a courtier. "Bring us food, and drink. We have been here for hours." He paused. "And some for my wife. She must also be hungry."

"Yes, Your Grace."

"I do not think she will eat," Thomas said.

"I have to offer her something. I feel completely useless." Philip resumed pacing with his hands clasped behind his back.

Another scream and then silence—a silence that weighed on

his shoulders as though his horse had toppled upon him. He held his breath and stared at the door.

What was happening?

His mind went through the worst scenarios. His wife was dead. His son was dead. Both were dead.

He gulped and pressed his palms on the door, wishing he could see through it.

And then a high-pitched wail—an infant's indignant scream—that filled his heart with joy.

Thomas jumped up and clasped Philip's shoulder. "It is over. You are a father."

"Thanks be to God." Philip crossed himself and spun to Thomas, who pulled him into a hug with much back slapping.

The wailing continued and several noblemen, including the bishop, rushed up to him. Each had smiles on their faces, each keen to rejoice at his son's arrival.

"It is great news," the bishop said.

"Congratulations." Belmonte shook his hand.

Wine was poured and a toast made.

Then Beatriz poked her head out of the door and set her gaze on Philip. "Your wife wishes to see you."

"In there?" Philip asked. "Now. Already?"

"Yes." Beatriz smiled. "Come."

"That is not usual," the bishop said. "This is women's time."

"She wants you," Beatriz said. "*Really* wants you."

"And likely will not settle until she sees her husband." Thomas directed at the bishop. "That is her way."

"Yes, that is true. I will go to her. I am archduke and she my wife. We can do as we please." Philip felt like he would burst with happiness as he strode in.

And the sight with which he was met caught his breath. Joanna sat up in bed, her hair cascading over her shoulders and at her breast a swaddled child suckling. At her side, a birthing woman from the village held a strip of wet muslin.

"My love." He rushed to Joanna. "You are well?"

"Yes." She smiled softly and nodded. "Just tired."

He stroked her hair from her warm brow and kissed her there. She had circles beneath her eyes. "You frightened me. It went on for so long and was so…loud."

"You have not heard a woman in labor before?"

"No."

"I heard my mother give birth to my sisters. I knew to expect great pain and I got it, in bucketfuls." She stroked the baby's round pink cheek. "But it was all worth it, and now she is here."

"'She?" Had he heard her right? A daughter? A sinking feeling caught in his stomach, but quickly, he beat it away, not wanting to acknowledge the treacherous emotion.

"Yes. You have a daughter, Philip." She looked up at him with clear, curious eyes.

"Oh." He straightened. "I was convinced we were having a son."

"You *hoped* we were having a son." Her lips flattened and her eyes narrowed.

"Naturally. I need an heir to rule when I am gone."

"Do not speak of being gone." She reached for his hand. "And do not keep love from your daughter because she doesn't have a penis."

He thought for a moment, realigning the plans he'd had for a son arriving on this day.

"Philip." She withdrew her hand. "It is God's will we have a daughter first. A son will come next, I am sure of it." Her tone was sure and firm.

Again, he pushed down the rise of disappointment. He wouldn't let it take hold and he certainly wouldn't let his wife see it. Not after what she'd just been through. "You are right. We will have a son in due course." He paused. "What shall we call her?"

"If it were a boy, I'd planned on John, after my brother." She closed her eyes and pulled in a breath the way she always did when she spoke of her departed older sibling. "But now…"

"Please, do not upset yourself about John on this happy day."

He kissed the top of her head. Her grief at John's passing had been hard to witness. The letter that had arrived from King Ferdinand and Queen Isabella heart-wrenching as they'd described his demise from weakened lungs.

"Eleanor," she said suddenly. "I like Eleanor. It was my great-grandmother's name."

He thought for a moment. "I see no reason why we shouldn't call her Eleanor. And I like it." He smiled down at the baby. "Hello, sweet Eleanor, and welcome to the world."

Joanna smiled and he relaxed. Her fractious state of late pregnancy had set him on edge. She'd been uncomfortable and demanding of his time. He hoped now that Eleanor was here, his wife would return to her usual fun and congenial state.

"We will write a letter to your parents," Philip said, watching the baby suckle at Joanna's breast. "And tell them of our news."

"They will be thrilled to be grandparents." She paused. "Happier news this time, after poor Margaret's ordeal."

Philip's heart squeezed for his dear, gentle sister. How awful she must have felt to go through labor but have a child without a breath at the end of it, and no husband to comfort her. He closed his eyes and hoped he would see her soon. Coming home would be good for her, he felt sure of it.

"Yes, with more children to come." Joanna went on. "I suspect my elder sister, Isabella, will be with child by now. Her marriage to Manuel of Portugal was some time ago."

Philip walked around the end of the bed then sat at her side and took her free hand. He kissed her knuckles.

Isabella had been in mourning for her first husband, Alfonso, and as a devotedly religious woman, she hadn't wanted to remarry. It had been on the insistence of her parents that she'd been sent back to Portugal to wed again and her plight played on Joanna's mind. "I am sure she is happy now, Joanna, as happy as we are."

"I wish I could believe you."

"You should. You should trust me."

She smiled and looked at the baby again.

"So I will go now and write a letter, have it sent by special envoy. Our child's arrival is stupendous news to be celebrated." He paused. "And while I write, I will also inform King Ferdinand that I am to hold the title of Prince of Asturias."

She looked up at him with wide eyes. "You will do what?"

"It is only right." He spoke measuredly, for it was something that had been playing on his mind. "Your brother, the prince, is dead, and as your husband, I am the only living male relative in the kingdom. The title should be mine."

"My father will never allow it."

"He will not have a choice. I claim the title."

"Just like that?" She frowned.

"Do you not believe it is mine?"

She was silent.

"Who else's should it be? We do not have a son." He nodded at baby Eleanor.

Joanna nibbled on her bottom lip. "Very well, write and ask him." She paused. "What does Maximilian say to this plan?"

"He agrees wholeheartedly." The truth was Philip hadn't spoken to his father about it, but he knew Maximilian well enough to know that staking a claim on any title with land would be approved of. Maximilian, like Philip, thrived on power and expansion of the Habsburgs.

"We should plan a Christening," Joanna said.

"Yes, a christening should be held at the earliest convenience. I will go and speak to the bishop now." He kissed Joanna's cheek and stroked the baby's downy hair. "And I thank God and Jesus and all the heavens for my wife and child coming through this day."

Two days later, the Aula Magna was swamped with guests, who had all come to meet the new princess and see her blessed into Christendom. A feast had been set out for afterward and the bishop stood on the plinth before the thrones with a Bible in his hand and a font at his side. He looked as though he might pop with his self-importance.

"For you." Thomas handed Philip a scroll. "It has just arrived by horse."

Philip took it and examined the seal. "It is from King Louis of France." Philip stepped aside from the crowd and turned to the wall to read it. "The new king is either declaring war or sending good wishes. Which is it to be?"

Thomas huffed. "I know what I'm hoping for."

Philip studied his friend. "You wish for war?"

"No." Thomas frowned. "I am a man of peace until pushed, as well you know. And why would he send soldiers here? His are all in Naples battling for control of Italian territory."

Philip didn't answer. It was no secret King Louis didn't like the Habsburgs, and since the new monarch's succession upon the death of King Charles, Philip hadn't been feeling as confident with France as a neighbor.

He broke the seal and unraveled the scroll.

Archduke Philip of Austria and Princess Joanna of Castile

It is with great pleasure that I congratulate you on your first child, a daughter. It is my wish that she grow to be a healthy and pious monarch who serves you well.

I would also like to extend a hand of friendship to you and your young family. Perhaps we could discuss this further if you came to stay at French court. It would be my request that your father, Maximilian, King of the Romans, also attend.

May God be with you.

King Louis XII of France

"That wasn't what I was expecting but not ungratefully received," Philip said, handing it to Thomas.

Thomas read it quickly, his lips twisting as he took in the words. "Only two days old and Eleanor is brokering diplomacy."

"It is the way of the modern world." Philip shrugged. "I heard he has reduced the pensions of his nobles and has plans to reduce corruption in the tax system with more judges and laws."

"I have faith that he will achieve that. He is proving to be a determined man." Thomas paused. "It will make for a rich country and an efficient system."

Philip nodded. "One with whom it would be good to be friends."

"I agree. Do you think your father will travel to France?"

"He may now it is no longer Charles in power. He had a deep dislike of Charles going back many years." Philip rubbed his freshly shaven chin. "A treaty that ensures peace and stability in our region can only be a good thing." He turned back to face the room. "I will write to my father this very day and explain the situation, and also to King Louis thanking him for his kind words."

"That would be prudent." Thomas paused. "If you do visit, would it be wise to take your wife?" He nodded at Joanna, who held the baby beside the bishop.

Eleanor's cream, lace gown was so long, it nearly reached the floor.

Philip thought about the question. "It is no secret that France and Spain do not see eye to eye, but Joanna isn't an heir. Her elder sister lives and may give birth to a son at any time."

"That is true."

Something in Thomas's tone had Philip facing him. "What are you not saying?"

"If you take the title Prince of Asturias as planned, then *you* are Spain visiting France."

Philip frowned.

"And taking your wife, from whom you have succeeded the title, will only remind King Louis of that."

"I will claim that title. It is my right."

"I am not disagreeing. What I am saying is it would be wise not to rub King Louis's nose in the fact the Habsburgs have made a powerful alliance with Spain and there is nothing he can do about it."

"The Habsburgs are making many alliances and will make many more." Philip suddenly grinned and clasped Thomas's shoulder. "Being seen to have much power is a good thing, right? I do not consider it a problem."

"Power is a responsibility I do not envy."

"Ah, but stick by my side, dear friend, and you will enjoy the fruits." He gestured to the grand Aula Magna with its gold gilding, tall, glass windows, and decorative fireplaces. "For this banqueting hall is all mine. It wasn't built by me, no—it was my mother's grandfather who commissioned it. But now it is mine to do with as I wish and one day it will be my son's."

"Or daughter's. Remember your mother inherited from her father and from what I hear—"

"Enough." Philip held up his hand. "I do not wish to speak of my mother on this day." He straightened his tunic and checked the brooch on his cape. "And I have things to do, a daughter to baptize."

"Yes, Your Grace." Thomas dipped his head. "I congratulate you on this happy day."

Chapter Twelve

Joanna watched her husband with his daughter. It was a lovely June morning and they'd taken a blanket to the lawn beside the rose garden, along with bread and cheese and mint tea.

"Look, Joanna, she can sit up on her own," Philip exclaimed.

"Almost."

Eleanor babbled and flapped her little arms as she wobbled in a seated position. Her head looked too big for her body and her cheeks were flushed red, like little apples. She really was a very becoming infant to behold.

"You're so clever," Philip cooed as he spread his hands, ready to catch her. "Such a clever girl."

"Just like her parents." Joanna tore at a piece of bread. "And as an intelligent person, I cannot understand how it took so long for me to be informed of my sister Isabella's death in childbirth. It is not as though we live on the moon." She gestured to the sky, where a half moon hung dappled and white in the blue expanse.

"My love." Philip frowned. "Please do not upset yourself about that again, and have you not thought that perhaps that was God's will, so that you could grieve for John and then for Isabella separately?"

"But I can't let it go." She swallowed the lump that had suddenly grown in her throat. Poor Isabella, she'd been pushed into wedlock twice, and then into a motherhood that had taken her life. "I feel so far from home."

"This *is* your home." Philip gestured at the grand palace. "It has been months since we found out the dreadful news." He plucked a buttercup and handed it to Eleanor. "Here, smell this."

She giggled and swiped for it.

"And poor Miguel," Joanna went on. "A babe in arms and his mother dead. It is said he is quite sickly. Don't let her eat that, Philip."

"He is?" Philip nipped the flower between his fingers and held it away from baby Eleanor's mouth. "Who said he is sickly?"

"Belmonte told me." Joanna knew this would interest her husband. His petition to her father to claim the Iberian title as his own had been turned down on account of Miguel's arrival."

"How would Belmonte know the state of the child?"

Joanna shrugged and studied her husband. If something happened to her nephew, then she would be first in line to the throne of Castile and Aragon, making her, one day, Queen of Asturias. Queen of the new Kingdom of Spain.

"I will pray for the child's good health," Philip said, handing Eleanor a small sliver of apple. "That God have mercy on his young soul."

Eleanor reached for the piece of fruit and babbled something in her own little language.

"I have also been thinking," Philip said, setting his attention on Joanna. "It is time we had another child. A son this time."

"We have been trying these last months." Joanna bristled slightly. It was bothering her that she still hadn't fallen.

"Perhaps not trying hard enough." He reached across the blanket and set his hand on her ankle. "And as it is Sunday, a day of no meetings or debates, I suggest we continue our quest." His touch sneaked beneath the material of her gown and he ran his warm palm up her leg to her knee. He leaned closer, his eyes sparkling and his body heat radiating onto her.

"Philip." She glanced around, but she didn't shift away from the caress. "What if the courtiers see you doing that?"

"Do I look like I care?" He twitched his eyebrows and bit on his bottom lip, as though holding in a wicked grin—a grin she adored. It was one that made her feel feminine and needed and as though she were the only woman he had eyes for. "This is my home," he went on, his voice low and gravely, "and you are my wife. All of this belongs to me, including you, and I will do as I wish…exactly as I wish, most especially with you."

"How you tease me so." Her heart thumped in her chest as she touched his cheek. "With your sinful promises."

"Promises you know I can fulfill." He ran his hand up to her thigh, her gown bunching at his wrist.

"Philip." She caught his forearm.

"Wife of mine. I suggest you call for Beatriz to take care of Eleanor. Otherwise, I will be mounting you here on the lawn, as though we are a stallion and mare."

She laughed. "You're outrageous to say such a thing." She swept her lips over his, all of her worries evaporating. Her husband was distracting her in the way he was so very good at. "But I agree, we should not like to get a reputation for behaving like animals. We should take to our bedchamber."

"At once." He suddenly jumped up and held out his hand to her. His erection was evident behind his breeches. "Beatriz, where are you?" he called.

Joanna allowed him to pull her to standing, and by the time she'd straightened her gown, Beatriz was bustling over the grass toward them. "What can I do to serve, Your Grace?" She batted at a wasp that was making a bid for the picnic.

"Please, take care of Eleanor," Philip said, wrapping his arm around Joanna's waist. "My wife and I have important business to attend that simply cannot wait."

Beatriz's eyes dipped to his groin. "Oh." A flush of pink rose on her cheeks and she averted her attention. "I see…yes, of course, Your Grace, leave Eleanor with me."

Joanna giggled and gripped Philip's arm. "We should go," she whispered, "before you shock any more of our staff."

Quickly, they traversed the lawn and up the stone steps to a side door in the palace. From there, they used a back staircase, a quicker route and one used mainly by staff, to the bedchamber.

Philip was breathing fast, marching with intent and pulling her along. She got the feeling he'd march into battle the same way. It thrilled her that he wanted her so badly, that his need was great, and she would be the one to satisfy him.

"You drive me *loco* with longing," he said as they reached the bedchamber door and he pushed it open. "My body aches for yours."

"As does mine for you." She stepped inside the brightly lit room and the moment she had, he slammed the door and dragged her close.

She clung to him, a groan of need escaping her lips. His tongue found hers and he slid his hands to her buttocks and gripped them through the gown, hauling her to the length of his body.

Excitement winged through her, his urgency sparking a new, thrilling desire in her.

"Lord help me." He stooped to kiss her neck as he walked them backward, until her behind hit a walnut desk. "But I will release in my pants if I do not get inside you soon."

"So hurry." She gasped, sitting up on the desk. She dragged at her gown, exposing her knees, thighs, and finally, her cunny. She spread her legs in invitation.

He scrabbled with his breeches and released his cock. And then he was there, probing her entrance and kissing her again.

She clung to him as he curled his hips and drove in deep. She cried out in bliss. The fast, determined filling was a wonderful edgy sensation somewhere between pleasure and pain.

"You like that?" He grunted.

"Yes, more. Give me all you've got."

This spurred him on and he set up a wild rhythm, slamming in and half withdrawing over and over again. The table knocked up against the wall. A tray of empty wine goblets crashed to the floor and rattled as they rolled toward the window. His somewhat unholy praises to the Lord filled her ears.

"Oh, Philip…don't stop." She coiled her legs around his hips and clung to his shoulders. He was rubbing up against her nub almost violently and it felt amazing. The encroaching orgasm was the only thing that mattered in her life at that moment.

"Find your pleasure." He gasped. "My love…"

"I will… I… Oh…" She closed her eyes and squeezed his cock with her cunny, driving her pelvis in time with his so he hit that hot spot inside her at the perfect angle. "Oh…oh, yes…yes…"

She didn't care about the noise they were creating. All that mattered was finding bliss together. "Philip… I… Oh…" Her climax claimed her and she flung back her head and wailed through the powerful, pulsating ecstasy that slammed through her body.

"Ah, yes…I am… with you…" He filled her with his seed, crying out with each thrust.

She reached for his face and stared into his passion-filled eyes. Never in her life had she been so close, so in tune with another person. She thanked God and all the angels in heaven that Philip was her husband.

"My sweet Joanna, that was…wonderful." He found her mouth in a kiss and pulled her closer still.

She kissed him back, and while she caught her breath, she said a silent prayer that God would bless them with a son this time—a son and heir to make her husband happy. For if he were happy, she would be happy.

Chapter Thirteen

1500
Coudenberg Castle

"The infant in Portugal has died." Philip looked up from the scroll he'd just received from King Ferdinand and Queen Isabella. Two deep frown lines plowed over his brow. "It saddens me to read such news to you, Joanna, it really does. I am so very sorry."

"Miguel, Prince of Portugal, my sister Isabella's baby son?" Joanna crossed her chest and her eyes moistened. She held her own sleeping son closer. The thought of losing baby Charles to sickness was too much to bear—losing him for any reason was terrifying and she didn't think she'd be able to breathe if his little body was drained of life.

"I am afraid so." Philip passed the scroll to his new chamberlain, Antoine de Lalaing. A small man with both a pointed nose and pointed beard and with an astoundingly sharp mind.

"God bless his soul." Margaret, Philip's sister, kissed the cross that sat at her neck. "Today and always."

"From whom does the news come?" Thomas asked, pouring five goblets of wine and then standing beside Antoine to read the scroll.

"The king and queen themselves," Philip said. "Joanna's parents. Apparently, the first messenger was killed by bandits, which is why it has taken so long for this news to arrive with us."

"Oh, what a shameful thing to happen." Joanna shook her head. "What else do they report? Are they well?"

"There is no mention of ill health in either your mother or father." Philip took the two wines Margaret offered him. "Which I know will gladden you, dear wife."

"Yes. It does." She sighed. "It has been so long since I have seen my beloved parents. Years now."

"In which case their instructions, written on this scroll, will please you." Philip passed Joanna a goblet and sat at her side on their favorite seat in their solar.

She set the drink on the table. Wine didn't suit her palate when she was pregnant and she still had a few months to go with her third child, with whom she'd fallen pregnant not too long after Charles had been born. "What instructions are they?"

"Don't you see?" Philip said. "You are, after all, an intelligent person."

"See what?"

"You are now the heir presumptive of the Crown of Castile." He paused. "Princess of Asturias. One day to be queen."

"A noble title and future, indeed," Antoine said, re-rolling the scroll.

She nodded slowly. Yes. She did know that. It just hadn't registered, as she'd grieved her tiny nephew whom she'd never met but had loved all the same. "Yes. I am aware of my new title and its weight."

"And..." Philip said. "How do you feel?"

"Sad that I had to lose a dear brother and beloved sister to be in this position, not to mention a stillborn niece and infant nephew." She reached for Margaret's hand and squeezed. "I would wish them well and happy and on this Earth more than having any title."

"I know you would, dearest sister," Margaret said, her eyes sparkling with emotion.

Philip knocked back his wine and strode to the window. He stared out with his back to the room.

"You said the instructions would please me," Joanna said. There was something about his stance that was prickly. What else was written on the scroll?

He turned. "We are to travel to the kingdom of Castile, where you will receive fealty. You as princess and I as your consort."

"Consort?" She nodded as realization set in. No wonder he was tetchy all of a sudden. "And this displeases you, Philip." She didn't mean it as a question. "Your title."

"I am already Prince of Castile." He jabbed his thumb onto his chest. "As you and everyone knows, except, it seems, your parents. That title came to me when your brother died and there was no one but me to take on the role."

Joanna nodded. This had been a sharp subject for many moons. One she'd avoided because seeing her husband vexed and irritated was one of her least favorite things to witness.

"And now they give me the title of 'consort'?" He huffed and his jaw tensed. "I will not have it. I will not."

"While my father is alive, you have no choice." She shrugged.

"How can you care so little about this snub I must endure?"

"I *do* care, my love." She sighed, tiredness coming over her. "We will sort this matter out when we arrive in Castile."

"Which will not be for some time." Thomas held up the scroll. "They have requested that you do not travel, Joanna, until you have given birth."

She passed the sleeping Charles to Margaret and sat back with her hand on her belly. "Can you give him to Beatriz for me?"

"Of course. Right away." Margaret held Charles tenderly and slipped from the room.

"I will be quite able to travel if we leave soon," Joanna said. "Before my belly gets too big."

"No." Philip shook his head. "This is one matter your parents and I do agree on. I do not wish you or our child to be rattled around for weeks on end. Goodness only knows what that could do to you both and I simply won't risk it."

A part of her thrilled at his desire to protect her. She adored it when her husband showed that side of himself.

"We will wait and when we do travel…" He bit on his bottom lip.

"Go on?" Joanna said, wondering why his eyes were alive with plotting and scheming.

"We will not travel by boat, as you hated that so much, my love." Once again, he sat and took her hand. "You've talked of it often, the awful Bay of Biscay. How sick it made you. How terrible the storms were. How you wanted to die rather than endure the sickness of the sea."

"I can vouch for that!" Margaret said firmly. "Awful way to travel."

"But it is the only way," Joanna said, "France is too dangerous for us to pass through."

"Ah, but it is not." Philip grinned. "King Louis himself has invited us to spend time with him at court."

"At court? At French court?" Her eyes widened, hardly believing what she was hearing. "That would be asking for death. He cannot be trusted. He is a snake in the grass waiting to bite."

"He has been nothing but trustworthy thus far. No snake-like qualities."

"How can you say that?" She shook her head. "He is waging war in Italy and—"

"And we are not Italian." Philip shrugged.

"You are the *son* of the King of the Romans." She tapped her temple. "Or did you forget that?"

"Of course not." Philip stood and paced to the fireplace, tossing another log on, even though it was not cold.

"The king and queen will not be happy if you put their heir and daughter into such a precarious position," Antoine said.

"I agree," Thomas added.

"It is I who will decide what is safe for my wife." Philip turned and set his hands on his hips. "She is mine, not theirs."

"Yes, my love, that is true." Joanna stood and went to Philip, slipping her arms around his waist. "I am yours. So do not upset yourself."

He hugged her back. "I am not upset, just determined, for this will be good for us, to have King Louis's favor. Very good. We must have strong friends and neighbors."

"But what if he does not give his favor? What if he hurts us? Kills me to spite my parents… his enemies?"

"He won't."

"How can you be so sure?" She looked up at him. The thought of entering the lion's den didn't appeal to her in the slightest. And what of her children? What if he took out his wrath on them? A sudden thought popped into her head. "Are you making deals with France? Behind my back? Behind the backs of the king and queen and your father?"

Philip looked as though he'd been slapped, such was his shock. "No, of course not."

"I don't believe you." She tilted her chin and stepped backward, still studying his face. "You are a nominal vassal, after all."

"Do you think I would do such a thing? Do you think I am crazy?" His eyes were wide.

"I would never accuse you of being *loco*, Philip. It is a cruel thing to do to an intelligent person."

"I agree."

"And do you also agree that the throne of Castile is at stake just by my being in France?"

"I do."

"So how can you know I will be safe? How can you possibly guarantee that unless you have made deals?"

"Because, my love, as you pointed out, my father is the King of the Romans." He took her hands in his and squeezed them gently. "Do you really think Louis will risk upsetting Maximilian? Which would be the case if you were harmed. And to anger the King of the Romans would bring hellfire upon him, of that I know and I am sure he knows it too."

She thought about it and her mood mellowed. "Your father

and King Louis signed a peace treaty, didn't they?"

"Indeed. So I think we will be quite safe. In fact, I *know* you will be quite safe. You might even enjoy a taste of French court."

She huffed. "I am sure it will be garish. With nothing to eat for the children. Eleanor is quite fussy these days."

"We will not travel with the children."

"What? How can you even—?"

"My love." He cupped her cheeks tightly. "It would be cruel to put them through such an ordeal. They will not understand the nature of travel and the arduousness of it."

"But…"

"They will be well cared for by Margaret until we can send for them. When the babe is weaned."

Much as the thought of not being with her children hurt Joanna, she did see the sense in it. And it would only be for a short time, surely.

Belmonte would travel with her, of course. "And Belmonte," she said. "My parents will insist that he and his men escort me through enemy territory."

"I have no doubts we will receive word of such as soon as they hear of our plans." He rolled his eyes and released her cheeks. "They do have opinions on everything, after all."

"Philip." She frowned. "When we meet my parents you will have to be utterly charming."

"Am I ever anything else?"

"At times, yes, when you do not get your way." She paused, testing the waters. "You angered them when you claimed John's title for your own. That is why you are to be named 'consort' and not 'prince.'"

His jaw tightened and he stepped away, picking up a small brooch and examining it closely, even though it was one he'd seen many times.

Joanna waited for him to speak.

Eventually, he set his attention on her again. "As Thomas here bears witness, I will get you safely to Castile, my love, so that you can become the official heir and I your consort." He tipped his chin. "That is my promise to you."

<hr />

SEVERAL WEEKS LATER, another scroll arrived from Ferdinand and Isabella. This time, it was Joanna who broke the royal seal and read it first. As soon as she'd finished, she passed it to Philip, who snatched it from her.

"As I suspected," he said, looking at her with a frown. "Your parents are not happy about you traveling through France."

"That is to be expected."

"And what is more, Belmonte is to write to them regularly with news of our journey."

"Again, that is to be expected." Joanna rubbed her growing baby bump and then stood. She spread dill butter on bread and took a bite. It was her favorite snack of late.

"I wish they would trust me to care for you." He put the scroll down and took her hand. "I am as capable a husband as I am a ruler, am I not?"

"Yes. You are a perfect husband and I love you very much."

"And I you." He kissed her tenderly.

"There is news of my sister Catherine too," Joanna said, helping herself to more bread and butter. "Did you read that bit?"

"Indeed, it seems she has found herself preparing to depart for England already."

"She is fifteen and has been betrothed to Arthur, Prince of Wales, for some time. I am sure he will find her most agreeable."

"And we should hope that he will be a true and loving husband."

"That is what she so deserves. Little Catherine is a delight. Curious and talented at many things, and also a dear and gentle soul."

"Though if anything like her elder sister, gentle but intelligent and strong of will." Philip poured wine and took a sip.

"You flatter me." She laughed. "But it is a truth."

She studied his relaxed posture and took a deep breath. "So when this child is born, if I am so intelligent, you will allow me to attend council and meet with the Estates General about political matters here?"

He turned to the window, his fingers curling around the base of his goblet. "We will be traveling, my love, or had you forgotten?"

"I had not forgotten, but I know that we will return to court at some point. And if I am to be ruler in Asturias, then surely, I should be ruler here too."

"*I* am ruler here." He spun to her. "Do not forget that I have inherited everything around you from *my* ancestors."

"I could not forget that, and I am doing my duty by giving you heirs to pass all of this on to." She tipped her chin.

His eyes dipped to her belly. "For that, I am grateful, and every day I thank God for His benevolent gifts to us."

"I just wish," she said, walking to him, "that you would see me more of an equal in state matters. I had a good education and knowledge that could benefit you if you'd let me share it."

"My dearest Joanna." He smiled and shook his head. "Do not think that I do not know of your wisdom. It shines from your eyes. But your duty"—he stroked her belly—"right now is to give birth to a healthy child and emerge from labor healthy yourself. It is an arduous task and it fears me each time you go through it. Your pain is my pain. Your screams scar my soul."

She hated seeing the concern on his handsome features. "I am up to the task. It is hard work, exhausting and painful beyond all imagination, but I have proved that I am fertile and able to produce fine sons, have I not?"

"And that is all I want you to concentrate on for now. You do not need the added anxiety of matters of the state. It would not be good for you or the baby."

Joanna sighed, though she tried to suppress it. Being a mother was all well and good, and she was relieved that she fell pregnant easily and without much sickness at the beginning. But having babies didn't mean she couldn't think. Couldn't be a positive contributor around the political table. And now that she was heir presumptive to Spain, it was a task that would indeed fall to her one day.

If only her husband could see that too.

Chapter Fourteen

Joanna looked down at the three lockets on her lap and studied her children's faces. She missed them terribly, even though they'd only been traveling for two days.

Eleanor and Charles had cried when she'd left—Eleanor having to be pried by Margaret from around Joanna's neck, her small face going beetroot red and tears dripping from her chin.

It had broken Joanna's heart.

Little Isabella had barely noticed. At the breast of a wet nurse—a nobleman's wife from a nearby village and an upstanding Christian woman—she'd continued to feed greedily during the commotion.

And now, with each pace of the horses, she and Philip were getting farther and farther away from their beloved children and closer to France and King Louis.

"We will return home soon," Philip said, glancing at the lockets and then up at Joanna. "After the ceremony in Toledo, we will journey back through the Pyrenees. A shorter route."

"That cannot come soon enough," she said, holding in a sob. "I wish they had traveled with us, the children. I'm sure they would have been perfectly fine."

"It would have been foolhardy of us, not least because it would have put Charles, our son and heir, also in Louis's court."

"If Louis had harmed a hair on his head, Maximilian would have dropped the weight of his army upon him. My father would have done the same. Louis wouldn't dare."

"That might be the case, but do we really want to risk our only son?" Philip took her hand. "It is enough risk that you are going to be there."

Joanna thought for a moment. "I will not curtsey to him."

"I beg your pardon?" Philip's eyebrows shot up.

"I will not curtsey to Louis in court."

"You must, Joanna. He is a king."

Her jaw tightened and she turned and looked out of the carriage window. Her new status was weighing heavily upon her, but with it, also came a sense of power. Power she'd never thought she'd have as she was the third child, a second daughter. Yet here she was. Heir presumptive and her destiny changed. She was going to grab hold of it, tightly, for she had an educated brain and the heart and soul of the bravest king and queen in the world. She would make everyone proud and rule with surety and wisdom.

THE JOURNEY TO Loire was long and hot and much as Joanna had trepidations about arriving at the home of her parents' French enemy, she was relieved to finally arrive at Château de Blois and have the rattling carriage come to a halt.

Beyond the carriage door, Belmonte gave instructions to her knights. They were to stay no more than five paces from her.

Philip scowled at the back of the carriage, in the direction of the knights. They'd always irritated him and she knew it wounded his pride that her parents didn't think that he, her husband, could protect her.

She touched his cheek. "You are a patient man," she said gently, "and for that, I thank God, but do not think of anything else now other than getting us through this visit with Louis and then continuing our journey."

He ran his hand through his hair, his brow furrowed.

She flattened down a tuft that had stayed upright. He was so handsome, so regal, she'd have to stay close and make sure no ladies of the French court set their desires upon him.

They were not greeted by the king, but by smartly suited courtiers, who directed them across the courtyard.

The red brick and gray stone chateau was three stories tall and then taller still with gothic spires and ornate pillars. The steep roof was dark and the black windows somewhat menacing, as though eyes could peer out, yet it was impossible to see inside.

They were escorted through a series of lobed archways, footfalls echoing around the stonework, and then through to a lobby holding a small, glass chandelier.

"How very modern," Philip commented.

Joanna looked around. The interior was lavishly decorated with flowers and gilded walls. To her right, huge, wooden doors were thrown open to a vast room with a tiled floor and an elaborately decorated ceiling featuring dark-blue squares decorated with small, golden crosses.

"That is the *Salle des États Généraux*," a courtier said, pausing at her side. "Quite beautiful, don't you agree?"

"Yes, indeed." She nodded and took in the canopied golden throne set upon a red, rugged plinth.

"I am sure you will get to admire it further, during your visit," the courtier went on, his accent heavy. "This way, please."

Joanna followed, Philip at her side, the knights and Belmonte close behind. Then came their entourage, carrying luggage and gifts of material and wine for the king and his wife.

After climbing a set of stone steps, the courtier opened a door and gestured to Philip. "Your chambers, Your Grace."

"Thank you." Philip looked at Joanna.

"There is an adjoining door to the ladies' guest room."

"I'm sure the princess will be quite comfortable." Philip stepped inside.

Joanna was escorted a few more paces and then shown into a

westerly-facing room that was bright with sunlight.

Belmonte stood in the doorway and looked around. "That is the door to the archduke's room?" He pointed to the left.

"Yes." The courtier tipped his chin at Belmonte. "And who are you?"

"I am the personal protector of the Princess of Asturias under the orders of her parents, King Ferdinand and Queen Isabella."

The courtier looked him up and down, seeming to downturn his mouth very slightly as his attention settled on Belmonte's ever-growing black-and-gray beard.

Belmonte didn't seem to care. "And the princess's knights will be on guard outside this room and by her side at all other times. You should ensure the king is aware of that." He paused. "Though I should mention it is non-negotiable."

The courtier huffed, then stepped out of the way as Beatriz bustled in carrying a trunk. "This way," she called over her shoulder.

Five more trunks arrived and were set beside a wooden-paneled wall and a highly polished walnut table.

"Dinner will be served at dusk," the courtier said, straightening his cravat. "Promptly. The king does not like to be kept waiting."

"I trust there is hot water," Beatriz said.

"Naturally." He turned and stepped out.

Belmonte followed, closing the door behind. He spoke to the knights guarding her door, his voice muffled by the heavy wood.

"Your Highness, you must be exhausted. I will prepare you a lavender bath."

"Thank you, but not lavender—that will make me sleepier still. I'll have sage or peppermint."

"You are very wise with herbs." Beatriz dipped her head. "I will call for some immediately."

Joanna went to the window and looked out. She was higher than she'd expected and her view was over trees and then a wide river, complete with a stone arched bridge. Small houses peppered the landscape, interconnected with tracks and hedgerows, and a flock of sheep grazed on softly rounded hills in the distance.

The sun glowed rich orange, jewel like, as it sank into the water, stretching dazzling fingers of light over the river's surface. A small boat meandered toward the shore, leaving a jagged wake.

She poured wine and sipped, then discarded her shoes. It was strange to feel tired after sitting in a carriage all day. She'd forgotten how wearisome traveling was. Philip was right; the children would not have enjoyed such a journey. She was thankful for his wisdom.

Soon, Beatriz had a barrel of hot, steaming water scented with herbs ready for her to sink into. It felt heavenly to have the heat surround her bones and she dabbed her face, glad to wash away the dust and dirt of the road.

"Which dress shall I lay out for you?" Beatriz asked, fussing with the trunks.

"The red one."

"This one?" Beatriz pulled out a new, scarlet dress decorated with images of golden pomegranates and artichokes.

"No, no not that one." Joanna pointed, dripping water onto the rug. "That one."

"This?" Beatriz pulled it from the trunk and held it at arm's length. "But…"

"It is a traditional Spanish dress, yes, and I think that would be appropriate for me to wear to meet the King of France."

Beatriz studied Joanna and then the boned skirt on the dress.

It was made of sumptuous, red velvet encircled with five dark hoops and it was shaped like a bell. A black velvet stomacher in the shape of a 'v' gave way to padded shoulders and long, red sleeves that gaped over the wrists. The neckline was low, but not as low as some of her dresses from Ghent and Flanders.

Beatriz laid it on the bed. "I'm really not sure—"

"And the black headdress." Joanna gestured to the trunk to her left. "And the necklace my mother gave me, the one with the emerald set in gold."

Beatriz found the headdress and placed it on the bed beside the gown. She added the necklace next to it.

"And I should also like the cloak."

Beatriz's eyes widened. "It is very warm, Your Highness."

"I wish to look the part."

Beatriz studied her for a moment then set the spectacular and heavily decorated cloak on the bed. It depicted the coats of arms of Castile, Aragon, and Trastámara and would drape from her shoulders and pool at her feet. In this outfit, no one would mistake her for anything other than Spanish royalty.

She smiled, then dunked under the water, wetting her hair.

When she surfaced Beatriz was there, ready with a jug of rosemary water to rinse through the strands. "Are you sure you know what you are doing?"

"Perfectly sure." Now that she had a plan, in all honesty, she was quite looking forward to meeting the King of France.

"MY LOVE, ARE you ready?" Philip's voice came through the door.

"Almost," Joanna called. "But please. Wait there. I will come to you."

"But..."

"One moment," she called, shrugging to adjust the weight of the heavy cloak. Already, she felt hot in it. And the dress was tight at her waist, the voluminous sleeves hanging halfway down her legs, adding to her discomfort. But what was a little discomfort when she had a point to make?

Philip banged on the door again. "We must hurry. The king hates to be kept waiting."

"Calm now, husband. I am ready."

Beatriz dusted Joanna's nose with powder then fussed over a loose strand of hair poking from her headdress.

"How do I look?"

"Spanish."

"Spanish royalty?" Joanna raised her eyebrows.

"Indeed, Your Highness. That is exactly how you look and I believe exactly what you intended."

Joanna smiled. "Coming, my love."

The door opened and she swept toward it with her head held high and holding the dress slightly off the floor so as not to trip.

Philip stood dressed handsomely in dark breeches and a pale tunic. A dazzling Habsburg pendent sat around his neck and his hair was still damp from bathing.

His mouth formed a perfect 'o' when he saw her outfit.

"Come, come," she said, gliding past him and her tall knights. "We will be later still if you do not."

"Joanna!" He gasped and stood as though pinned to the spot. "What in God's name are you doing?"

She turned to him. "Going for dinner with the King of France, which was your idea, if I remember correctly."

"But...But what are you wearing?" His tone was sharp as he gestured at her outfit. "What is *this*?"

The knights tensed, a subtle but definite low, metallic clank.

"It is my Spanish dress, as you can see." She placed her hands on her waist, her elbows sticking the cloak out wing-like.

"But you look so..."

"Beautiful? Adorable? Regal?" She raised her eyebrows at him, enjoying seeing him struggling for words for once.

"So...Spanish." He took a step closer. "You look so utterly Spanish."

The knights followed him, hands on their sword hilts.

"I *am* Spanish, or had you forgotten?" She raised her chin higher still and set her gaze on his.

"Of course not, but I had no intention of rubbing the king's nose in your...Spanishness."

She let out a brittle laugh. "Then why did you bring me here? Tell me that. Why on Earth did we not board a boat?"

"You hate sailing and France is on our way to Toledo."

She twisted her mouth into a smile. "Yes, of course. You are right, my love. I hate sailing."

He frowned. "You will anger King Louis with this formal attire. That is not wise."

"Do you really think it will vex him?"

"Yes." He folded his arms. "Now go and change."

She mimicked his action, the cloak hanging heavily once more. "I do not have time to change."

"I will wait."

"That might be the case." She laughed and turned. "But the king won't, so come on, let's make haste."

She paced across the landing to the stairwell with her outfit flowing. Thickly framed landscape paintings adorned the walls. She was aware of Philip and her knights close behind and her heart beat faster now at the thought of meeting this king her husband revered so.

In the Estates General room Joanna had admired earlier, a lavish banquet had been set on a long table strewn with candelabras. Her mouth watered at the sight of the boar's head with an apple between its jaws, the side of beef already sliced, the pies and figs, the herbed butter and steaming bread. How hungry traveling made her.

Around the sides of the room, French noblemen stood dressed in finery and sipping from pewter goblets. Beside them were French women in long gowns with square-cut necklines and cuffs made of sable, hair pinned and half-hidden by dark headwear.

Upon her arrival, they stopped talking and turned to study her. A few of the women whispered behind cupped palms, their eyes sparkling as though they'd just been told the most wonderful gossip.

Joanna let her gaze rest on each person in turn.

Philip drew up beside her, a shoulder taller, his chin also tilted as he assessed the room.

"Your Highness," Belmonte said, appearing with a goblet of wine for her. "You look…like your mother."

"Thank you, Belmonte. I will take that as a compliment." She smiled at him but gestured the wine away.

"As you should. She is a beautiful woman." He dipped his head then took his place behind her, with the knights, the way he always did.

The high-pitched trump of a brass instrument made her startle, but she disguised it, or so she thought, for Philip pressed his hand into the small of her back, as though telling her he was there for her, no matter what happened next.

She was glad of the turn in his mood.

The king's arrival was announced by a courtier wearing feathers in his hat. "Lords and ladies, please welcome the esteemed and adored King of France, King Louis XII."

All eyes turned to the head of the room.

Joanna consciously slowed her breathing. She had no intention of looking perplexed or nervous or intimidated by King Louis. If she gave him one inkling that she was, he'd play her like a puppet.

She heard his heavy, echoing footfalls before she saw him. And then when he did appear, his emerald-green cloak caught her attention first. Floor-length and made of sumptuous fur, it accentuated his broad shoulders and tall stature.

He wore a heavy, golden chain over it, and upon his head a black cap, from which flowed silken hair the color of a chestnut. His skin was pale, his nose was large, and his chin wasn't strong and angular like Philip's; it was shallow and his neck long. This didn't make him an ugly man, just not one to her taste.

Behind him his wife, Anne, Queen of France. She wore a golden silk damask gown with the fashionable square neckline, though her gown also had an ample skirt and train. Her gown cuffs were trimmed in fur and her kirtle sleeves red and embroidered in gold. A glittering, heavy, pearl-and-diamond-encrusted gold necklace sat around her neck.

The king's dark eyes surveyed the room then came to rest on Philip and then finally on Joanna. He paused, as though taking in her dress, surprised by it, then stepped forward.

"Ah, our guests are here," he said, flinging up his arms and displaying the capes slits and his red, velvet sleeves beneath. "Finally."

He strode alongside the banqueting table, the attention of everyone in the room upon him.

"Philip of Habsburg." He chuckled. "Why, you are a most handsome prince, indeed. It is a truth I have heard but now see with my own eyes. In fact, if it were up to me, I would declare you 'Philip the Handsome' and be done with it."

"You are too kind, Your Highness." Philip inclined his head. "And thank you for inviting us to be your guests. It is always a pleasure to visit France, and of course, on this occasion to meet you."

Louis huffed slightly. "And you have married since your last meeting with my predecessor, Charles." He turned to Joanna. "An interesting choice of bride." He paused. "Your father's, I should imagine. He is a conniving and cunning character."

Joanna held the king's curious gaze. Her fists clenched so tightly, her nails dug into her palms. A rash of heat spread up her spine.

"Please, allow me to introduce my wife formally, Your Majesty. This is Princess Joanna of Castile, Archduchess of Burgundy, the Low Countries, and Luxemburg." Philip's voice was tense.

Silence hung heavily then stretched uncomfortably when Joanna didn't bob her head, or bow, or curtsey. She simply stood tall and proud and unaffected by the king's stare.

Eventually, Joanna did break the silence. "It is a great pleasure to meet you."

Louis raised his eyebrows, his lips a thin, tight line. He glanced at Philip and then back at Joanna.

Behind her, Belmonte and the knights' wariness practically crackled from them. They were ready for trouble.

Louis cleared his throat and rubbed the point of his small chin. "You do not bow to the king?"

"You are not my king," she said firmly.

Philip stared at her, his brow furrowed and a rise of color growing on his cheeks. "Joanna. Apologize at once."

She ignored her husband. "You are not my king," she repeated to Louis. "For I am heir to the throne of Aragon and Castile, Princess of Asturias. One day, I will be Queen of all Spain and we will be equals." She tried to read his expression—it was impossible—but she pushed on regardless. "Equals do not bow to one another."

"Your Majesty, I—" Philip started.

Louis held up his hand to silence him. "And this is why you wear such a gown, Princess, to remind me and all in this esteemed room exactly who you are?"

"I am proud of my heritage and will be prouder still as Spain gains power and new territories."

"Power." Louis stepped closer to her. He breathed deeply as he stared into her eyes. "For people such as us is the elixir of life, is it not?"

"And comes with great responsibility to do good," she said, trying to ignore the bristling anger coming from Philip. This was clearly not how he'd imagined introducing her to his mighty new friend. "To do good for the people who serve us. To do good for the people who rely upon us."

A flash of amusement crossed Louis's eyes then he tipped his head back and a great, roaring laugh emerged. It echoed around the room as his noblemen looked at each other.

He then stepped to the right and clasped Philip's shoulder. "Oh, my, Philip of Habsburg, Philip the Handsome, you have found a willful wife, indeed. One with a great mind and, I would imagine, great stubbornness. I will give you one word of advice for managing such a woman, something I have learned from experience." He paused and his mirth subsided. "When the wind blows it is best to be a pliant willow bough that bends with it rather than breaks. For if you are too rigid, like an old oak branch, you will be snapped—in this case, by her."

"Wise advice, indeed," Philip said, though there was a note of annoyance in his voice.

"Do not seek to control her," Louis went on. "Instead, go with her, for a future queen is a feisty creature and when she is queen she will be more complex still."

"Perhaps you confuse 'feisty' with 'intelligent' and 'determined,'" Joanna said.

"My dear, you are right." Louis stood before her again and set his big hands on her shoulders as he stared into her eyes. "And I should do well to remember that, as one day, we may meet on the battlefield."

Chapter Fifteen

PHILIP SIPPED WINE and then some more. He wished the drink were cooler. He was so hot sitting in the grand room surrounded by stiff conversation and polite formalities.

Louis was seated at the head of the long table, Joanna sat to his right and Philip to his left so they were facing each other.

Behind her stood her knights, though Belmonte was seated at the far end of the table, eating and enjoying the company of the queen and a pretty young nobleman's wife.

"I have grand plans for extending Château de Blois," Louis said.

"You do?" Joanna replied politely.

"Yes, a chapel to the right of this room and perhaps something decadent."

"Like what?" Joanna ate a single berry.

"A staircase that spirals like the side of a snail's shell. It is a vision I have."

"A very interesting vision." Joanna smiled. "But, if I may ask, what is your vision for Naples?"

The king studied Joanna, then sat back, elbows on the table and fingers steepled. "Your parents have asked this question coming from your mouth?"

"I have not seen my parents for many years, not since my marriage." She gestured to Philip. "But I am sure my husband would like the answer to that question. My father by law also."

Philip sat up straighter, it was true, he did want to understand Louis's plans in Italy, but it was a conversation he'd planned on having later, when more wine had been imbibed, tongues were looser, and menfolk alone.

"Isn't it obvious, *ma chère?*" Louis directed at Philip, despite the endearment to Joanna. "I wish to control the Kingdom of Naples. I wish to control and own it fully. It is my right."

Louis paused, staring Philip down.

Philip held his gaze as he spoke. "You believe it is your right because your predecessor, Charles, declared it to belong to France?"

"Indeed, it does belong to France. The House of Anjou has served there for many years as monarchs."

Philip nodded slowly. "You would not have pressed as far into Italy as you have if it weren't for Milan's help."

"They have been…a benefit." Louis shoved a chunk of meat into his mouth and chewed.

Philip did the same, then took a gulp of wine, the smooth muscles in his neck flexing. "My grandfather wished for peace and my father does also," he said. "So do I."

"There is something to be said for peace," Louis said. "Indeed, my ink has stained many a treaty."

"Which is what I'd like to talk to you about." Philip leaned forward. "It would please the King of the Romans very much if a treaty could be signed securing borders."

Louis looked from Philip to Joanna. "What do you think? Which borders should be protected?"

"France and Burgundy, to begin with," she said quickly.

Philip knew his wife was thinking not just of her children and home, but also the people of Burgundy and the Low Countries. Loyalty was a good quality of hers.

Louis appeared to ponder the suggestion. "And then?" He turned to Philip.

Philip hadn't expected the question to be turned on him, but he thought quickly. While his father held northern territories with an army, he, Philip, as consort and one day King of Spain, had to think bigger. "Spain," he said. "A treaty with King Ferdinand of Aragon would be of great benefit and very progressive of everyone involved."

"Disregarding current territorial disputes," Joanna said with a firm nod. "That is essential."

"Naturally." Louis inclined his head.

"Because…" She paused. "There is no winning in war for our people. Instead, let us think of peace for them because that, and low taxes, is winning."

Louis was quiet.

"I understand that my view is different," Joanna went on, "and although I was brought up by pious parents, I am capable of seeing the world for what it is. Indeed, I have read the diaries of Columbus himself. My views of the world are far-reaching."

Louis raised his eyebrows.

So did Philip's. Columbus, this was news to him.

"The world is a complex place, but not when it comes to a roof over your head, food on the table, and the safety of family," Joanna said. "That is something everyone wants, no matter their wealth, creed, or birthplace. It is human nature the world over."

"You see, Archduke"—Louis pointed at Philip—"you have yourself a wise woman, indeed." He chuckled. "I will consider these treaties carefully. We all have enemies in common, except for the pope, naturally. So plans must be made, alliances sought where possible." He tore a chunk of bread. "Now come on, eat up, and then we will dance and drink and be merry together this night."

PHILIP DRANK HEARTILY throughout the rest of the meal and watched his wife charm Louis in between making small talk with the wife of a councilor sitting to her other side.

What Philip really wanted to do, now that the subject of a treaty had been broached, was obtain a promise of marriage between his infant son, Charles, and Louis's daughter. It would secure his position and his son's going forward, and on top of that, Maximilian would jump for joy.

He'd never imagined to witness Louis so captivated as he spoke to Joanna. It made Philip feel both proud and irritated and he didn't enjoy the warring of his emotions. His wife was utterly beautiful, yes, and her words were clearly the sweetest honey to Louis despite them being pitted against each other outside of this room.

It still irked Philip considerably that her parents hadn't given him the title of Prince of Asturias—that would have provided him with more sway than merely consort. If he were a prince, it would be *him* charming the King of France and suggesting treaties and discussing global issues.

But unless he could change Ferdinand's and Isabella's minds on arrival in Toledo in a very short space of time, he'd just have to be patient and seize his moment and princehood in the future—and patient he would be, not least because he wanted his son, Charles, to have the title of King of Spain and grow the Habsburg dynasty deep into the Iberian Peninsular.

Soon the banquet table had been emptied and pushed to the side of the room. The windows had darkened and fires and the chandelier lit. Between two tall candelabras, a harpsichord player struck a chord and a chanson rang out. The lilting verses seeming to draw people into a circle the way a siren might call to sailors.

Philip spoke to a nobleman's wife about the weather and they admired the gilded walls. She was pretty and smiling and keen to point out the details of a tapestry depicting the Garden of Eden.

"My love," Joanna said, suddenly appearing at his side and clasping his arm. "You have been otherwise engaged for quite some time." She switched her eye contact to the woman at his side.

"I'll bid you goodnight, Your Grace," the woman said quickly.

"I must seek out my husband for a dance."

He nodded at her politely. "Indeed. It was a pleasure to make your acquaintance."

"Philip." Joanna scowled up at him as she walked away. "Who is that woman to you?"

"No one. And I am sorry." He smiled at her and was relieved when the crease on her brow softened. "Small talk is all. Being polite."

She kind of huffed and looked about to say more, but he jumped in first. "Come. We should also dance."

She shrugged and allowed him to steer her toward the outer edge of the jollity, where they joined in.

But the dance was stiff and somber and all the time he could feel the pent-up energy in Joanna's body. He'd seen her dance with a frantic tempo in the soles of her feet and her hair spinning and coiling around her face. Had him speaking politely to the wife of another guest upset her so much? He wouldn't put it past her. Jealousy hovered around his wife like a threatening storm.

"That dress is so unbecoming." A voice to his right.

"I know. What was she thinking? She looks like a Spanish vagrant." A mocking giggle.

"Old-fashioned, likely full of moths too."

"The sun has scorched away any good fashion sense."

Philip turned, his hackles rising with each word he'd heard spoken.

Two French courtiers, powdered faces and tightly pinned hair, took a step back. "Your Grace," one of them said, bowing her head and stiffening.

"Do. Not." He pointed at them and fought the heat that rose up his chest. "Do not speak of..."

"We were not speaking of your wife," the other one said hurriedly as she glanced at her accomplice. "Were we, Emmanu-elle?"

"No, we were not. Of course not."

"So of whom were you speaking?" A rush of anger was

mounting rapidly in him, itching its way up his back and tightening his chest. How dare they be so bold, so disrespectful?

"We were…just…"

"Philip?" Joanna squeezed his arm.

"Tell me," he demanded of the two women. "Confess."

They both looked at Joanna. It was clear they were not going to own up.

"Do not," he said again, "speak of the princess that way." He gritted his teeth. "Do not speak of my *wife* that way."

"Philip." Joanna touched his cheek and turned his face to hers. "My love, I thank you."

"For what?"

"For keeping the snakes at bay." She turned and glared at the women. "Though eventually, I have no doubt they will become bitter and twisted and killed by their own venom. A fitting end."

The two women shrank backward, into the crowd, quickly retreating to the other end of the long room.

"I should demand they leave court," Philip said, "for disrespecting a guest of the king."

"I did not expect to make friends here." She paused. "And I didn't think you wanted me to wear this gown, yet you defend it."

"I didn't want you to wear it because I knew it would be another thing for which I would have to defend you."

"I can defend myself."

"That might be the case, but you are mine. You have not just my heart, but also my protection." He held up his finger. "And do not say you have your knights, for if they are your swords, I am your shield." He grabbed her hand. "Let's dance again."

"This dance is dull."

"It is French."

"Exactly."

"Shh," he said. "We are guests of the king, remember."

"Of course I remember."

The next dance started, legs crossing to the right and then

left, followed by a slow turn. A flute joined the harpsichord, picking up the pace a little.

To Philip's horror, Joanna broke away from him and raised her hands with her fingers bent and pressed against her palms.

"This tune reminds me of *jota Aragonesa!*" She smiled broadly, her mood suddenly shifting. "My favorite dance." She twirled around, her gown expanding like a bell around her legs and her veil flowing.

"Joanna!" he said, glancing at Louis, who was staring at Joanna with wide eyes. His wife, the queen, did the same at his side.

"Joanna, stop that." He reached for her, but she slipped from his grasp.

"Come on, dance with me." She tipped back her head and laughed then stomped her feet to an even faster tempo and clicked her hands as though she held castanets.

"Joanna." Heat rose on his chest, up his neck, and to his back. He looked around at the aghast faces.

She was whirling and twirling, clapping too, her feet slapping the floor.

"Joanna." He managed to get close to her and curled his arm around her waist. "Stop this."

She stilled. "But I want to dance how I always dance."

"This is not the place for such displays." He steered her away from the center of the circle that had formed around her. "You rub the noses of these people into your Spanishness too much."

"Rub their noses." She laughed. "If they had any sense in the brains behind those noses, they'd dance with fun and freedom in their bodies."

He glanced at Louis. "Please excuse us, and thank you for your hospitality."

Louis inclined his head, his attention locked on Joanna. Thankfully, he appeared more amused than angry.

The crowd parted as he pulled his wife toward the exit of the grand room, her knights close behind. When they stepped outside the music resumed and the hum of conversation picked up.

Conversation about them, no doubt.

"What in heaven's name are you thinking?" he snapped as he strode along, urging her with him.

"What was I thinking?" She bristled. "I was thinking that I had no intention of dancing a stupid French dance when I am not French."

"We are guests of the King of France, or had you forgotten?"

"And you are married, or had you forgotten that?" She tried to pull away from him. "You are married to the heir to the throne of Spain." She paused. "Yet you dare to... You dare..."

He kept her close. "What are you talking about?"

"You. Speaking to that woman. That... that stiff, snub-nosed tart who was at your side before the dancing started. She was spilling words of desire into your ears. I know that because I saw how she looked at you."

"What?" He stared at her, horrified. "The nobleman's wife? I do not even remember her name and she did no such thing."

"I saw you, and I saw her. Lust practically dripped from her eyes."

"She, like me, is married. There was no lust on either side." Philip could hardly believe what he was being accused of.

"You think I am blind?" She shoved at him. "You think I cannot see how you look at other women? Simpering courtiers are just the start."

"How dare you accuse me of such a thing?" He clasped her hand and turned her to face him. "It is wholly untrue and quite unfair."

"So you deny that you flirt with other women?" She laughed, as if he couldn't deny the statement.

"Yes. I do. Wholeheartedly. I only have eyes for you, my wife." He marched her up the stairs.

Her jaw tightened as they headed for their bedchamber, the music fading.

"You do not believe me?" he asked.

"I am in two minds."

He stilled with his palm flat on the door. "I beg your pardon?"

"I have two minds." She shrugged. "For I have not had enough of your attention of late."

His jaw tensed and through the dim light, he studied the flash of daring in her eyes. She was goading him, and she knew exactly what to expect when she did that.

He turned to the knights. "We are to be undisturbed. Ensure that is the case."

The knights said nothing but took up their usual places on either side of the door, hands on the hilts of their swords, eyes staring straight ahead from the dark slashes of their helmets.

"You want attention, wife," he said, shoving at the door so hard, it bounced off the wall. "Step in and you'll get it."

She bit on her bottom lip. Her cheeks had reddened and her breasts were rising and falling with her rapid breaths.

"Joanna," he said. "You ridicule me, rile me up, then accuse me of philandering. You must have known I'd react. I am not a passive man."

Her nostrils flared then with a swish of her dress, she stepped into their bedchamber, the veil on her headdress flowing behind her.

Quickly, he followed, back-kicking the door closed with a deafening slam. Oh, he'd show her attention. He'd make her realize that he had no interest in pretty courtiers or other men's wives. He'd prove it in the most basic, primitive way he knew how.

She tugged off her headdress and dropped it to the bed, turning to him with her hands on her hips. Her expression was defiant and challenging.

He was in front of her in an instant. He curled his fingers into the bodice of her dress and yanked, hard.

She gasped and staggered. The material gaped, her pale breasts, round and soft, spilling forward.

He cupped the right one. Her flesh was warm. He then lowered his face to hers, catching her nipple between two fingers. "I want you now as much I as did the first moment I saw you. And it is only you I want, Joanna."

Her pupils were wide and her lips damp from where she'd just licked them. "I want you *more* than when I first saw you."

"Can I say nothing right?" He growled.

"It is a fact."

He tweaked her nipple, tugging it until she whimpered. His cock was hardening rapidly and a wild, passionate need gripped him. "You are a frustrating woman."

She reached for his groin and grasped his cock over his breeches. "So satisfy yourself. It is clear from what I feel here, your frustration is great."

The smugness of her smile and the tease in her voice ignited a manic craving in him. It was wild, feral, and it consumed him. "Woman, you have asked for it now." He spun her light frame to face the bed, tipped her forward, then dragged down her hooped skirt so that it sat around her ankles.

"Philip," she panted, twisting and the material of her long sleeves pooling on the bed.

"Stay still." He palmed her pale, round buttocks and squeezed. "You are my wife. You are mine to do with as I wish when I wish, and right now, this is what I wish."

She whimpered and locked her elbows. Several strands of hair came free and bounced around her face.

He fumbled with his breeches, muttering when it took a second too long to free his throbbing cock. He was so hard, it hurt, his erection solid and needy.

"Philip, please…"

"Get ready." He grasped her hips and aimed the tip of his cock at her entrance. Anticipation of her warm, gripping cunny had his heart rate rocketing and he held her firmer so that she couldn't buck away when he entered her. Which he was about to do, hard and fast and as deep as he could go on the first plunge. "Get ready, Joanna, to be thoroughly adored by your archduke."

Chapter Sixteen

Joanna screwed up her eyes and fisted the bedding. She'd never seen her husband this way. Yes, he could brim with passion and urgency, but this was different. She'd pushed his patience, made a spectacle of herself and of him, and now she was facing the consequences.

He clasped her hips tighter, his fingers pincers that would likely leave rows of bruises.

She held her breath, her cunny quivering and getting wetter by the second. Her breasts ached and her belly was tight.

And then she felt the domed head of his cock, pushing at her entrance, finding purchase.

"Mine. You're mine." He forged deep, plunging the entire length of his cock into her cunny.

She cried out as he stretched her deliciously, determinedly, and almost violently. A thrill went through her at the basic instincts she'd unleashed in him and she arched her back, pushing onto him and taking him even deeper.

He released a strangled roaring sound then pulled partway out, only to plunder back in, his flesh slapping up against hers.

Air was shoved from her lungs and she clenched around him. "Oh! Oh! Yes…" she managed. "More."

"Don't worry, there's more…I've only just started."

He set up a frantic, pounding rhythm. Driving into her body with single-minded determination and fervor.

A hunger sparked in her and she reached down and pressed her nub with the tips of her fingers, giving it what she needed.

"Yes," he managed. "Touch yourself. Release your pleasure when I release mine."

It didn't sound or feel like he was far off from releasing his seed. His voice was tight and his cock as hard as it ever got.

But on and on, he ravaged her. The bed creaked, tallow candles flickered, and she worked her nub until she was panting and sweat beaded on her forehead.

"You. Are. Mine," he said hoarsely and punctuating each word with a pound of his cock. "And I only want you. Can you feel that? Can you feel how much my body desires yours?"

"Yes. Yes….oh, please…don't stop…Philip." Her arm ached, she was fretting herself so hard and fast. Each time Philip slammed into her, his cock rubbed a place deep inside her cunny that was greedy for more.

He grunted and gasped, sped up, and dragged her onto his cock with each forward thrust of his hips.

This tipped her over the edge and she clung to the moment of pure bliss before ecstasy swept through her. Her spine stiffened and she held her breath, caught in honeyed anticipation.

"Yes!" He cried out. "Yes! Now!"

Pleasure ripped through her, bursting from her cunny and spreading delicious, hot fingers of satisfaction over her body. Her cunny spasmed around his cock as he forged deeper and stayed there emptying his seed.

Her pulse thudded in her ears and she flung back her head, taking him so deep, she felt utterly owned by him.

He grabbed her hair, pulling her spine even tauter.

"Ah, yes, like that," she said. "Take me. Oh…my love."

Her hair roots tugged, sharply intensifying the bliss ripping through her. She trembled from head to foot and her toes curled. "Oh…Philip!" His possession of her was so complete, so uninhibited. She wanted the moment to go on forever. He might have been proving his ownership of her, but right now, she also owned his mind and body utterly.

He groaned, a low, guttural noise that thrilled her, then doubled over, his chest covering her back and his cock still lodged deep. "You drive me *loco*," he said, "and much as that drives me to distraction, it also makes me want you more, more than I ever thought I would want any woman."

"Good," she managed, staring at the fleur-de-lis pattern on the bed's curtains. "I want you to want me more than you've ever wanted anything or anyone."

He released her hair then pulled out.

She flopped to the bed with her head twisted to the side and her rump still in the air. Cool air washed over her hot flesh.

Breathing hard, he collapsed next to her and stared upward.

"Imagine," she said, studying him. "If we have created a child, a son, right here in French court."

He turned to her.

"A son who will be a brave warrior and a fine politician and will bring down all of France, including King Louis."

"Hush, my love. That is dangerous when spoken of here."

"But I only speak it to you."

"I would not like you to be overheard, or forget yourself after wine." He took her hand and kissed her knuckles. "The French are known for separating heads from necks with one slice of the sword."

"They would have to get past my knights first."

"And me." He frowned. "Remember."

"Yes, my love, and you." She paused. "But do not fear. I would not dream of uttering one perilous word outside of this bedchamber."

He huffed.

"You do not believe me?"

"Oh, I believe you not to speak ill of the king, but when you refuse to curtsey to him and flaunt your heritage in his face with your gowns and dancing, I have learned just how far I can trust you."

"Which is?"

"Let's just say I know to keep you within arm's reach at all times."

She smiled. "That pleases me, for I hate it when we are apart, even in separate rooms. It hurts me here." She pressed her hand to her chest. "You are my one and only love. My heart speaks your name with each beat."

He smiled and moved a strand of hair from her cheek. "We should get some sleep. It is late and we have had a long day with more long days to come as we journey to Toledo."

※

HER HUSBAND HAD been right. There were many long and arduous days to come, not least because they'd lingered overlong in French court enjoying fine dining and late-night conversations over wine.

During the journey through the Pyrenees, Joanna spent her days in a carriage, lamenting how it rattled her bones but enjoying gossiping with Beatriz.

Philip preferred to ride with Antoine, Thomas, and Belmonte conversing about matters of Burgundy and the Low Countries.

The scenery was beautifully rugged after the flatness she'd become used to, with towering, snow-capped mountains and dense, green forests, as well as babbling streams and wide rivers. The entourage stopped to make camp most nights, but on a few occasions, they stayed in small towns or villages, making the most of inns or local hospitality.

And with every mile, Joanna's heart filled with the knowledge that she would soon be in her beloved Spain again. She longed to see her parents, to show them the lockets engraved with their grandchildren's faces. To show Philip how grand a place it was with beauty in nature and grandeur in its cathedrals and castles.

She only hoped that he would charm them. For he could be

as stubborn as her father and the issue of his rightful title was not one he would drop.

"We are nearly at the border," Belmonte said through the window of the carriage as he rode next to it on his large, black horse.

"Oh, at long last." Joanna straightened. "Beatriz, how do I look?"

"Quite well."

"Am I not too pale?" She nipped each of her cheeks to give them some color.

"A little, but that is to be expected in your delicate state."

She rubbed her belly. "How quickly I have fallen with child again." She giggled. "My husband is quite the stallion."

Beatriz glanced away.

"Oh, my friend, do not blush. It is a truth. One only has to look at his fine jawline and pert buttocks to know that his seed is potent."

"Oh, dear Lord." Beatriz crossed herself. "What a thing to say."

Joanna laughed harder. "I am sure my parents will be at the border eagerly awaiting our arrival. I wish to look my very best so they know my husband keeps me in the manner to which I was previously accustomed." She touched her hairline, checking for stray strands peeking from her headdress. "Will this gown suffice?"

"It is a gown made of fine material."

"That is your only comment?" Joanna raised her eyebrows.

Beatriz was quiet.

"Beatriz?"

"It is, for my taste, plain, but then, I am used to a Spanish palate of vibrant reds and greens, orange, and yellow."

"This is traditional Burgundian. The embroidered roses are quite the fashion." Joanna stroked a silk petal sewn into the gown.

"Yes. It is very beautiful." She paused. "The truth is I long for the orange Spanish sun, and the deep green of ripe olives, the flash of blue when a kingfisher swoops over the rivers and..."

Joanna chuckled. "Yes, I know what you mean. The Low Countries are low in color as well as hills."

Beatriz covered her mouth and giggled. "Do not let your husband hear you say that about his land. He will be quite offended."

"He knows that my words run away with me, but as long as I do not upset his dearest new friend, Louis, I am safe."

Beatriz giggled harder and shook her head. "I do not know how you got away with that night. Your gown, your dancing...and heavens above, the fact that you wouldn't curtsey to the king and queen. God must have been protecting you. I certainly feared for you."

"I didn't get away with it entirely." Joanna grinned at the bedchamber memory and then rubbed her belly again. "I was taken in hand in the most basic of ways and now a new king grows inside of me, one whom I will train to bring down France, the very place he was conceived. Do you not think that is revenge enough against Louis for his greed in Italy?"

"Your Highness." Beatriz leaned forward and took Joanna's hands in hers. "You really should be mindful of your words. I fear for you if you become any more reckless."

"Do not fear, because soon, I am home, and a home I will rule over one day." She took her hand from Beatriz's and waved it in the air. "I hope my robes are finished for the ceremony in Toledo. I have no desire to wait around for seamstresses to work from scratch."

"The letter went ahead, with your instructions. Though it is just as well you do not yet have a swollen belly."

"It will come soon enough. Quite honestly, this has been such a long journey, I am surprised the child has not been born and is walking and talking." She laughed. "Don't you agree?"

"The border, Your Highness."

The carriage came to a halt and the door was opened.

Her knights sat on huge horses, sunlight glinting from their armor. Beside them, Philip was on his favorite steed.

Joanna stepped down, aided by a courtier. She looked at the river dappled in shade and the carriage marks that ran through the stones toward the narrow passing place.

Opposite, all was quiet. Sunshine glinted through the canopy, a light breeze rippled through a reed bed, and in the distance, a woodpecker hammered on a trunk.

"Where are my parents?" She frowned.

"It seems they are not here." Philip's horse turned in a circle as though impatient to continue his journey.

"But they must have known we were getting close?" She worried at her bottom lip.

"Perhaps they have miscalculated," Thomas said.

"And are on their way," Antoine added.

She blew out a breath, wishing the black sag of disappointment would go with it. Her parents had abandoned her. Forgotten her. They hated her.

"My love." Philip slipped from his horse and handed the reins to a courtier. "Please, don't upset yourself."

His kind words made her eyes sting with tears. "I am not upset."

He cupped her face and tipped it to his. He smelled of leather, and fresh sweat, and the outdoors. He hadn't shaved for several days, which was most unlike him, and he had a roguish appearance, one that reminded her of the sailors aboard the *Julia*.

"I can see that you are disappointed, if not upset, but Thomas and Antoine are right. Maybe they just got the day wrong."

"Do you believe that?"

He didn't speak.

"Philip?"

"I'll confess I fear it is me they do not wish to greet."

"Why would you say that?"

He shrugged. "I have it in my head they do not respect me. They have given me the lowly title of consort, after all."

She sighed. "Perhaps we should journey back to Flanders,

forget all about the king and queen, my parents, and go and be with our children, whom we both miss terribly."

"After all we have traveled?"

"If that is what will make us happy."

"No." He shook his head. "I should be a prince at your side, for all to see, and although my people see me as such, your people do not. That is why we must push on. We must acquire our rightful titles."

"I will speak to them about this matter. I told you I would."

"And, my love, that is why they are not here. They do not wish to meet their Burgundian prince." He kissed the tip of her nose. "Much as they approved of our marriage to begin with, now they regret it."

"Why would you say that?"

"I have taken you to French court, despite the fact I had every right to as monarch of a vassal state. And on top of that, I have laid stake to a claim of your brother's title and—"

"Oh, poor John. They must miss him terribly. He was always Mother's favorite." She closed her eyes and an image of her brother's youthful face danced in her mind. "I miss him. He was one of my best friends growing up."

"I am so sorry for your loss." He pulled her into a hug. "Now come, let us make haste. Soon we will reach Toledo and we can talk frankly and straighten everything out. And then, when you have given birth, we can return to our beautiful children."

"But John will not be there to greet me." Tears escaped and rolled down her cheeks. Throughout the journey, she'd foolishly pictured her family together again and waiting for her. Gentle John, beautiful Isabella and Maria, and sweet, little Catherine, who was now in England with her new husband, Prince Arthur. "None of them will be there, Philip. None of them, my brother and sisters and their little children and..."

"Hush now. Do not upset yourself." He rubbed her back soothingly. "It will do neither you nor the royal baby any good."

She melted against him, gaining strength from his solid body.

He was a balm slicking over her pain, a lullaby to her restless mind. He was her everything. Without Philip, who would she be?

"Your Highness," Beatriz said. "Please, alight the carriage once more. You must eat something—it has been hours."

Philip peeled back from her. "Yes, you are right, Beatriz, my wife must keep up her strength." He urged Joanna toward the carriage. "Please, I beg you, take care of yourself and your precious cargo and I will lead the way to Toledo and there, we can rest together."

"Do you promise? You will come to my bedchamber?"

"Of course, my love." He smiled gently at her. "It is where I always want to be."

CHAPTER SEVENTEEN

JOANNA STOOD BEFORE her parents, her heart pounding and her skin tingling with anticipation. Her gown felt strangely heavy and she'd just beaten down a rise of nausea she'd thought had passed with this pregnancy.

The king and queen sat sternly on their thrones, around them noblemen. Clergy and courtiers looked on with their lips set in flat tight lines.

"Mother. Father," Joanna said, then she cleared her throat. "It is good to see you after so long."

Isabella stood and smoothed her hands over her slim waist as though checking for creases in the perfect embroidery of her bodice. She stepped down from the plinth, her footsteps silent on the soft, red rug.

When she reached Joanna she took her hands and squeezed. Her eyes misted. "My darling daughter, you have been missed greatly. We thank God for your safe return."

Something in Joanna melted and she hugged her mother, pressing into her and having to hold in a sob. She could feel love in the urgent tightness of her mother's embrace, the cling of her arms, the hitch of her breath.

Eventually, she pulled back. "Mother, I would like to introduce my husband, Philip of Austria, Archduke of Burgundy and the Low Countries, grandson of the late Holy Roman Emperor and son of the Holy Roman King." She gestured to Philip, who stood tall and proud at her side dressed in traditional Burgundian court tunic and breeches paired with shiny, black boots.

She had never witnessed such a handsome man. He grew more so with age.

"Philip." Isabella reached for his hand and clasped it between her palms. "Finally, we meet the father of our grandchildren. We welcome you to Spain and thank you for getting our daughter here safely."

"Despite having journeyed through the land of our foe." Ferdinand's deep voice rang out as he stood. His crown glinted in a ray of sunlight as he stepped down from the platform and came to stand at his wife's side. He studied Philip.

Philip held his gaze.

"It is said that the Habsburgs are men of strong bones." Ferdinand rubbed his chin. "Is this also true of my grandson, Charles?"

"He is a fine, strong boy," Philip said. "He will make a great ruler and fine warrior and in turn make us all proud."

Ferdinand nodded. "And where is Belmonte?"

"Here, Your Majesty." Belmonte stepped from the shadows. For once, there were no knights at his side. Here, they were not needed. Joanna had an entire army outside the castle walls who would protect her and her family.

"Ah good. Tell me, how was the journey?"

"Long and arduous."

"And King Louis?" King Ferdinand turned his attention to Joanna.

"He was…" She paused and sought the right word. "Pliant."

"'Pliant'?" Ferdinand's eyebrows raised.

So did Philip's.

"Whatever do you mean?" Queen Isabella asked.

"I believe he can be made to see reason, persuaded, molded."

"You do?" Philip said.

"Yes, for didn't I skillfully show him that I was a royal Spanish subject and his equal? It only took a few moments for him to accept all that I was."

"Is this true?" Ferdinand asked Belmonte.

"It is, Your Majesty." Belmonte bobbed his head.

"Well, my dear." Ferdinand reached for Joanna's face, cupping it in his hands. "I congratulate your political skills and your patriotism." He kissed her brow. "We are glad to have you home, our beautiful daughter."

"Thank you, Father." Joanna breathed in his familiar scent and when she looked into his dark eyes flashing with love and pride, she really did feel like she'd come home.

"And with child." Isabella nodded at Joanna's stomach. "I have had enough of my own to recognize the gentle swell of a few months gone."

"You are right." Philip set his hand on the small of Joanna's back. "This will be our fourth, and another son, I am sure of it."

"We will pray for that, and for our daughter's safe passage through childbirth." Isabella kissed her cross and sent her eyes heavenward. "That must always be prayed for." Her eyes moistened again.

"Oh, Mother." Joanna took her hands. "I am so sorry for your loss, for all of our losses."

"Thank you. I take comfort from God, but..." She sniffed. "I so miss Isabella, oh, and poor John, my angel. I miss them so much. And John, he still had so much to do as Prince of Asturias and then one day King of all of Spain." She gestured to a courtier, who rushed over with a brass tray holding a scroll.

She took it and unrolled it. "I have been given a poem, a wonderful poem that brings me comfort. Let me read it." She unfurled the scroll. "'Sad, joyless Spain, everyone should weep for you. Barren, devoid of happiness that shall never return. Storms, sorrows, pains came and took residence in you. God sowed pleasures in you so pains would grow.'"

"Mother." Joanna gently took the scroll. "It is beautiful, a wonderful piece of work. But should we also think of happy times? Philip and I are here now."

"Yes." Isabella swallowed. "I will try to brighten for the festivities." She smiled, though it was stiff. "For you must receive fealty from the Cortes of Castile as Princess of Asturias, heiress to the Castilian throne, as soon as possible or the gown will not fit."

"And Philip, my wonderful, devoted, educated husband." Joanna turned to her husband with a smile and pressed her hand over her heart. "My love, my reason for breathing, he will also receive fealty as Prince of Asturias?"

The king cleared his throat and folded his arms.

"Father?" Joanna said.

Ferdinand set his attention on Philip. "You will be Consort Don Philip."

Philip's brow creased and his eyes narrowed slightly. Likely only Joanna would notice it, but she could see his mood shift to darkness. He'd felt sure, and she'd reassured him, that on arrival in Spanish court, his title would be amended.

"Father, don't you see?" she said, her stomach sinking. "I need a prince at my side, it is only right and proper."

"We do not know Philip yet," Isabella said. "Allow us time. He has just walked onto our land."

"But, Mother, he is my husband, the father of future Spanish kings. Please, I beg you." She clutched her hands beneath her chin. She wanted this so desperately for her husband. "I beg you to reconsider before the ceremony."

"That will not happen," Ferdinand directed at Philip. "And I should tell you I have heard from your father, His Majesty Maximilian, this last week."

"You have?" Philip seemed surprised.

"Yes. I wrote to him suggesting that your sister, Margaret, be wed to the Duke of Savoy. It seems he also thinks it would be a good match."

"But...why?" Philip shook his head. His right fist clenched. "She is taking care of our children and—"

"The union makes good sense. It strengthens the borders against France." Ferdinand paused. "Your father and I think alike—we see the benefit in such marriages and treaties. Until you, my new son, can prove that you also think this way, I have to title you 'consort.' Surely, you understand."

Philip said nothing, though later, when they were alone, Joanna was sure he'd have plenty to say.

"Let's presume you to be an apprentice," Ferdinand said with a smile that didn't reach his eyes. "Undertaking an apprenticeship for becoming a prince."

"France is pushing ever closer to Naples," Philip said, folding his arms and rocking back on his heels as though readying for a long conversation. "I spoke at length with King Louis about his intentions."

"Oh?" Ferdinand said.

"Indeed, he believes French monarchs have ruled this region for many years, which is why he wishes to claim it. And the help he is receiving from Milan is substantial." Philip paused, seeming to wait for Ferdinand to comment. He didn't. "I believe it would be pertinent for us to discuss war strategy, man to man, monarch to monarch," Philip went on. "We do, after all, have the same enemies, and the same goals."

"Do we?" Ferdinand raised his eyebrows.

A tendon in Philip's jaw flickered, the way it always did when he was growing frustrated or angry. "I do not understand why you doubt me, and if that is the case, why did you marry off your daughter to a Habsburg?"

"It was an astute choice when she wasn't heir presumptive. Now..."

"Now what, Father?" Joanna squeezed in close to Philip and took his hand. "Has it really changed things so much? I thought you'd be happy that we are in love, that we have provided heirs, that our people think highly of us, and our lands prosper despite our loathsome neighbor."

"Yes, it has changed everything," Isabella said. "And much as we are delighted to see you both so in love, and congratulate ourselves on the match, we must be wary of a man with no

Spanish blood laying claim to our throne."

"We married before God, a union that does give me Spanish blood now that Joanna is my wife," Philip said.

"I appreciate your pious view," Isabella said. "But we have a reputation to protect and would not like to be thought of as reckless with titles and crowns."

"Indeed," Ferdinand said. "Already, there are rumblings that a consort from a vassal French state is a traitorous move."

"I will swear my allegiance." Philip set his hands in prayer. "That is my God's honest truth."

"And you will in time," Isabella said. "But for now, it is Joanna who takes the title of princess and you will be consort."

Philip's teeth gritted and he puffed up his chest. "Very well. Now if you will excuse me." He turned and stomped from the room, his footsteps echoing and his arms swinging.

"Mother. Father. This is not quite the welcome I'd hoped for." Joanna pleaded. "I beg you to reconsider."

"It is the best we can do." The king returned to his throne and clicked his fingers for wine. "When your husband deviated through France, then lingered there at court, we would be fools to not suspect some kind of deal has been made with King Louis, our mortal enemy."

"'Deal'?" She was aghast. "The only deal that was made"—she rubbed her belly—"was between Philip and me when we conceived this child on French soil. We swore that this new son will be the downfall of France, that God, who works in mysterious ways, will ensure that is the case."

"I hope and pray you are right," Isabella said. "Now come. We must get you fitted for the gown. You have a larger waistline than anticipated."

"You look beautiful," Isabella said one week later as she

adjusted Joanna's headdress and veil. "A perfect princess for our people."

"Thank you, Mother." Joanna looked around for Philip. She'd yet to see him that day. He'd woken early and gone out riding, even though she'd asked him not to.

He was fractious here in Toledo. He couldn't settle. She blamed her parents for refusing to give him his due title. It had unnerved him, belittled him, and pushed him from her.

"I do wish you would re-think Philip's title," she said, adjusting her silk gloves. "If I am to be heir presumptive to the crowns of Castile and Aragon, then—"

"The royal chefs have excelled themselves," Isabella said, as though Joanna had not spoken. "And a harpist has come from Cordoba, flamenco dancers from Seville. There will be plenty for you to enjoy after the ceremony."

Joanna didn't reply. It felt like half a celebration knowing her husband had been shunned, for that was how he saw it. She hated to see him unhappy; it pulled at her heartstrings. How could she truly rejoice when he wasn't?

"It is time." Belmonte opened the door. "Your people await, Princess."

"Yes, it is time." Isabella kissed the cross at her neck. "And I thank God this day has come." She kissed both of Joanna's cheeks.

Forty minutes later, Joanna was riding sidesaddle through the streets of Toledo with Philip at her side on a large, black steed. She was glad to be back on her favorite horse, Gianna, but not glad to see her husband's tense posture and narrowed eyes. Now he wasn't just cross about the title, but also about her being on a horse, something her parents had insisted upon.

"Philip, do not listen to them," she said as she waved to a group of women smiling at her and throwing petals into Gianna's path.

He didn't answer because it was impossible not to listen to the local men who stood beside a tannery shouting their way.

"We don't want a traitor on the throne!"

"Be gone, French supporter."

"Out with him."

"They twitter is all. They don't understand," Joanna said, her heart rate picking up. "Ignore them."

"If I were to be prince this would not be happening. They would respect me for who I am and the power I have."

"I promise I will make you prince as soon as I can, and then after that, you will be king of all this land and its people. That is my word."

"I appreciate your word, of course I do," he said stiffly, "but it may be sometime until you have the power to address this issue."

She stared straight ahead, her emotions tearing in two. How could she wish her mother or father dead so that she could make her husband prince and then king? If only they had just agreed, life would have been much simpler.

The way to the cathedral was lined with people, though her guards kept them at bay. Eventually, the tall-spired cathedral came into view. The sun had bleached the stones white and a brass bell sparkled from the tower. It was ringing loudly, booming around the cobbled streets.

Once down from her horse, Joanna rested her hand over Philip's aloft one and they glided up the steps and through the door. A clavichord played a familiar hymn as they walked down the aisle. So many faces turned to them, curious, smiling, suspicious. A few she recognized, but many she did not.

At the head of the altar stood her parents' favored clergyman holding a Bible. Candles on huge, golden sconces were lit around him and incense burned, spreading its smoky spiced scent.

Her parents were seated to the right, crowned and splendid, their expressions serious.

Philip held himself with dignity as the ceremony started with a long prayer, one of her mother's favorites. A hymn was sung and the bishop spoke at length about the duties of a monarch to the people. Not once did her husband fidget or even clear his throat—he was as dignified as a man could be, despite his displeasure.

Joanna was proud of him.

Eventually, they were each given a ring, which they kissed before the bishop placed them on their fingers and they swore their allegiance to Castile and Aragon, the lands and the people in the name of the Father, the Son and the Holy Spirit.

Then they turned to the crowd, who in a sudden rush of apparent relief that the long ceremony had come to an end, stood and clapped.

Joanna beamed, unable to stop her joy from overwhelming her. She was a true princess and these were her people and she loved them.

Philip kissed the back of her hand and she felt the tenderness in his touch. She could enjoy this moment, and knowing it would one day give her the power to grant her true love his wish made her all the happier.

Chapter Eighteen

Philip stood on the steps of the cathedral and studied the crowd. Congratulatory cheers for his wife rang out with the cathedral bells. The smiles, the petals fluttering in the air, the clapping, it wasn't for him... He was only consort. It was all for his wife.

Joanna clutched his hand and waved, her chin tipped regally and her eyes aglow with emotion.

He copied her and waved, though with less enthusiasm. He needed to fix this situation, and the sooner, the better. He was a Habsburg. He didn't lose. He didn't bow down to a Spanish king who was being stingy about bestowing on him what was rightfully his.

"Come, come." The queen gestured to the carriage. "Our feast awaits, as do our guests."

Noblemen and their wives, generals, priests, and scholars had all been invited back to the castle so the festivities could get underway. Queen Isabella was keen to show off her hosting skills.

Already, Philip's cheeks ached with the fake smiling. How would he get through the rest of the day?

Joanna glided down the steps, pink, yellow, and purple flowers landing in her path—it was as though she were walking in a spring meadow.

"My people," she called. "I thank you and promise to always serve you well."

More cheers went up as she climbed into a waiting carriage. He climbed in next to her.

"My goodness." She gasped. "I hadn't ever imagined such a large crowd."

"You are their princess and they have not seen you for many years."

"To be truthful, they didn't see much of me before I left to marry you. My parents weren't fond of parading us in public."

He closed his eyes and let out a sigh.

"What is it?" She clasped his hand, then rocked back slightly when the carriage began to move.

"Nothing."

"It is not nothing. I can tell by the set of your jaw."

"I am trying to hide my feelings."

"Not quite as well as you think—to me, at least. I know you well, remember."

He sighed. "In which case you know what it is?"

"You are not prince." She paused. "But you will be soon. Can't you just try to be happy with what we have? On this one day? For our hearts beat as one, our minds think as one, and we can rule as one."

"I wish it were that simple."

"Oh, Philip." She leaned across and kissed his cheek. "You are so serious all the time."

"Not our prince! Not our prince!" A shout came from outside. Philip tensed.

"Traitor from hell!"

"Get out of our country."

"Do not pay those men any heed," Joanna said quickly.

Philip's heart squeezed in anger and his skin prickled. He had to force himself not to burst from the carriage and push his fist into the men's mouths to shut them up.

"Please, hurry!" Joanna called forward. "Do not linger here, driver."

"They would stab a dagger into me, given the chance." Philip scowled. "They have no respect for me and won't until I have my rightful position. How can I be expected to rule this country?"

"It will be yours to rule soon enough."

The carriage gained speed.

"And until then, do not think of it," Joanna went on. "Twelve boars have been roasted in our honor. The banqueting table will be heavy with all of your favorite food and wine. Music will play and we will sing and dance and look forward to the birth of our second son."

He pressed his hand to her belly. "We *need* a second son. If something happens to Charles, we will only have daughters."

"I will give you a son, my love, I promise." She kissed his cheek. "Think of that and how proud you will be to report the news to your father."

>>><<<

THE FEASTING WENT on late into the night, as Joanna had predicted. And when the milky light of dawn spread over the terrace, Philip found himself sipping wine with the king.

This was his chance. He had to take the reins and he knew exactly how to do it. People wouldn't be pleased, would likely buck and rear in complaint. But that was tough. He had a family name to protect.

"I hear," Philip said, his voice soft amongst the first bird song, "that Granada is under threat."

Ferdinand sat back and crossed his legs, taking a sip from a golden goblet. His posture was relaxed. He'd likely have fallen asleep had Philip not been there.

"You defeated the Moors," Philip said, "a great and skilled victory."

"I thank you for the compliment." Ferdinand nodded slowly.

"Proof of the growing superiority of your kingdom."

Ferdinand said nothing, though his eyes sparkled, as though

curious as to what Philip was going to say next.

"Tell me, what do you propose to do about Granada?"

"Tell you? Why would I tell *you*?"

Philip was shocked by Ferdinand's snappish response. "I am your son by marriage, Don Philip of Girona. One day, I will be king beside Joanna."

Ferdinand said nothing and looked out at the horizon. His features were set, as though they'd been chiseled from marble. The sleepiness had lifted.

"Surely, we should discuss our military plans to defeat France," Philip said, leaning forward and holding out his hand. "Together. As one. I could be of assistance."

"As one?" Ferdinand frowned. "Are you not *as one* with King Louis?"

"As one with King Louis?" Philip pressed his hand to his chest. "I… No… I am not. I am most definitely not as one with King Louis."

"But it is true he is your friend."

Philip hesitated, then said, "I cannot deny we have an acquaintance."

"Exactly, so why in heaven's glorious name would I discuss anything with you that might be passed on to him and put us…Spain…at a disadvantage?"

Philip sat up straight, the words like a slap to his face. Did his new father really distrust him so? It seemed he did. But perhaps he could still work out a way around this. Use his friendship with Louis to his advantage.

"France is gaining in Naples and has ideas about Granada, I know this much," Philip said.

Ferdinand grunted.

"You are a wise and experienced man," Philip went on.

"You flatter me." Ferdinand raised his eyebrows.

"I speak the truth because I know that you will want to send me, as your negotiator, to France. Louis will listen to me. I can come to an arrangement to end the war in Italy and make him retreat plans for Granada."

"Huh, I doubt that."

"You should have faith. I might be young, but I have Habsburg blood and a cunning mind. This has allowed me to run my own state for many years now. The people of the Low Countries and Flanders and Burgundy thrive. Their taxes are low and their country is not at war because it is protected by solid treaties and strong borders."

"It is protected by your father."

"Who has not stepped foot over the borders for many years." Philip shook his head. "No, it thrives because of my decisions. It thrives because I keep enemies close so I can predict their next move." He spun his finger at his temple. "So I can know how they think, what they want, what they fear."

"Mmm." Ferdinand watched five swans fly overhead in a perfect 'V.'

Philip got the sense he was thinking about his proposal.

"Trust me, I'll give you my word on the Holy Bible I have Spain's interest at heart. Let me prove that to you." He stood and reached for the decanter of wine, filling up both of their goblets. "I love this country as if it were my own because it is my wife's country. My new family's country."

"You have the gift of talking sweetly," Ferdinand said, studying him. "It is true—and a beguiling face to go with it."

"So let me talk with sugarcoated words on your behalf. Let me go and negotiate with Louis, act as mediator. I swear I won't let you down. I understand him and his ways."

The king was quiet for several long, drawn-out seconds, then, "When will you leave?"

Philip had to stop himself from punching the air with triumph. "As soon as possible."

"Joanna will not be pleased."

"She must busy herself with delivering the next heir to Spain while I busy myself with matters of governing. For that is man's work."

Ferdinand nodded slowly.

"It is a very wise and considered move of yours," Philip said, snatching at the gesture of agreement. "And I thank you for the opportunity." He held up his goblet then clinked it against Ferdinand's. "Do not fear. I will deliver the best for you and for the future generations." He spoke with conviction and earnest because that was his promise. He would make deals and sign contracts and ensure his sons, and Ferdinand's grandsons, would get the maximum benefit out of any negotiations with France.

"WHAT?" JOANNA SCREAMED. "No, you cannot leave me! Not now. Not like this."

"My love." Philip glanced at the closed bedchamber door. "Please, do not fret so. It is not good for you or the baby. You must stay calm and restful."

"How can I be calm and restful without you? How can I? I need you with me."

"My love…"

She slammed her hands onto his chest, her small fists delivering quite the blow. "I forbid it. I refuse to grant you permission to leave me."

"You cannot do that." He grasped her wrists to stop the pounding. "Your father, the king, has set me the task of mediating."

"My father." She glared at the door. "I will go and speak with him, make him retract his instruction. Has he no sense?" She made a strange, low growling sound.

"He has plenty of sense, Joanna." Philip had never seen her so incensed. He knew she'd be agitated—angry, even—about him leaving for France, but this reaction was extreme. He could only blame her delicate condition and presume it had addled her mind. "I am to go and negotiate with Louis. I am honored your father has seen fit for me to carry out this important mission. I hope to prove to him that I am worthy of the title of prince."

"Of course you're worthy." She tipped her head back and stared up at him. "I will make you prince."

"You can't, not yet." He released her wrists and cupped her pretty, though flushed, face. "You know that."

"What I know is that I can't be parted from you, Philip, my love. You are the reason I breathe each morning, the reason my heart beats, the reason I put food in my mouth."

"And you are my reason also…for those things." He kissed her brow. "Please, calm yourself."

"I will come with you." She pulled back with her jaw set determinedly. "Yes. That is the answer. I will journey with you to France. I have been before. Nothing has changed."

"*Everything* has changed. You are an heir now, an heir with child. And I am sure a son sits in your belly. It is too dangerous."

"Do not tell me what is too dangerous for me and my son."

"I am the only person who can tell you." He caught her around the waist and pulled her near. "For it is my flesh and blood that grows in you. You must wait here. I will not stand for anything else. You must wait here until the baby is born."

"*You* will not stand for it." The volume of her voice climbed a few notches. "*You* will not stand for it, yet I have to stand for you leaving. Leaving me here… I cannot bear to be alone."

"Joanna." He pulled her into a tighter embrace and tucked her head beneath his chin. "This is the cross we must bear as monarchs. We must go onward, bearing our hardships, which in this case is to be apart."

"Do not throw piety at me now. It is that last thing I can cope with, what with my mother…"

"Your mother?"

"She is still sending out word to her new territories, to interrogate everyone and seek out non-Catholics, burn them, torture them, kill them… It is too much, this ongoing brutal inquisition of those poor people." She covered her face.

He stared at her. He'd heard rumors, rumblings, but was this really what Isabella was doing? He shook his head. He had his own problems at hand. "I have to go, and I will leave within the hour."

"No!"

"The sooner I go, the sooner I will return." He turned and walked to the door.

When he reached it he felt her behind him, her small frame pressing into his. "I beg you, don't go. I need you here, with me. I will die without you. Our baby will die without you."

"Joanna." He turned, his heart aching. "I have to go. I *have* to."

"You do not."

"I do. So wait, wait here in safety with our new son."

"I wish I were not pregnant." She pouted up at him. "Then I could come with you."

"Please, my love, do not say that. It is God's blessing that we have another child on our horizon."

"You will not be able to stand it without me," she said, holding his face between her palms and squeezing his cheeks. "You will grieve as though I am dead if I am not at your side."

"It is true, I will miss you."

"You will miss my face, my voice, my body." She slid her hands downward, over his tunic, past his chest, his abdomen, and settled her fingers on the waistband of his breeches.

"Joanna?"

"You will miss how I do this?" A flash of darkness crossed her eyes. It was mixed with lust and excitement and tinged with a hint of madness.

He frowned and shook his head. "I must go."

"No, I will make you want to stay with me…now." She folded to her knees before him, her gown puffing outward. "This is where you need to be. With me."

"What are you…?"

She peeled his breeches down and slipped her hand through

the material to find his cock.

He wasn't hard, but the moment her sweet and clever, little fingers surrounded his length, blood rushed to his groin and his erection swelled. She'd always had that effect on him. She was like the apple grown in Eden; her honeyed skin and flowery taste had become addictive. His body always responded to hers in an instant.

"My love," he said, looking down at her and locking his knees. "You... I need to go and... I need to..."

"You need to let me show you how much I love you, every inch of you." She pulled his erection free, then slowly, so slowly, poked out the point of her tongue and licked the tip.

"In the name of the Holy..." He swallowed tightly. The sight of her kneeling submissively before him, her dainty hand around his thickness and her pink tongue stroking his glans had his balls tightening in anticipation.

"Philip," she murmured. "You're not going anywhere, are you?"

"No... No, I'm not..." he managed as she opened her mouth and took his cock between her lips. "Not at the moment." He groaned at the hot warmth that surrounded him, and when she made her lips taut and sank down his length, taking him onto the softness of her tongue, he dropped his head back to the door and groaned long and indulgently.

Had anything ever felt so good?

She cupped his balls and rolled them gently, then sucked back up his cock. The coolness of air on his saliva-coated length sent a tremble through his belly. "My love, you have never...done this to me before and..."

She didn't answer. Instead, she sank back onto him.

The sensation was a potent mixture of darkness and bliss and he speared his fingers into her hair to hold her firm. "Oh, yes..." he managed in a low growl. "Like that."

She sucked up, taking her time, as if savoring him. Then she repeated the action, dipping low again.

Clenching his buttocks, he curled his toes in his boots. He closed his eyes and allowed her to hold him hostage in the sweetest, most sinful restraint he could imagine.

More blood rushed to his cock. He groaned. He was so hard, and each time she drew him deep, he could feel the back of her throat on his tip. Soft and hot, it made the release that was threatening nudge a little closer.

"Don't stop..." He gasped, filling his fingers up with her hair, tugging on the roots but unable to stop himself.

This seemed to spur her on and she picked up the speed, tightening her lips around him. She used her hand too, stroking his wet cock when she pulled back.

His balls were so tight, they ached, yet still, she fondled them. It was that which tipped him over the edge and he reached the point of no return.

"Joanna!" he cried. "I'm going to..."

In the name of the Lord, he was going to fill her mouth with his seed. He was going to release down her throat if she didn't heed his warning. Surely, she could feel and hear how close he was.

"Oh...in all the...ah..." Pleasure burst from him, throbbing through his cock in short, sharp pulses that gave him the most delicious satisfaction he could imagine.

And with each pulse, she swallowed, taking him into her body in a new way.

That thought added to his excitement and he swung his hips forward, claiming her mouth and grasping her hair. He tipped back his head and let an uninhibited groan rip from his chest. With it seemed to go all of his frustrations and worries. His wife was incredible.

Suddenly, he realized how firmly he was gripping her and how deep his cock was in her throat.

"My love." He pulled out and dropped to his knees before her. He held her face.

She was breathing fast. Her cheeks were red and her rosebud

lips puffy.

She stared at him with glazed eyes. "I told you…you'd want to stay."

"Of course I want to stay." He slanted his mouth over hers and kissed her deeply, tasting the salty tang of himself.

She melted against him, clinging to him as if her life depended upon it. Her need for him to be at her side at all times was a heavy weight. One he didn't mind burdening—oh, no—but right now, he had to go and secure their children's future. This was his one chance.

"Come, my love," he said. "Let us lie on the bed. I fear you have exerted myself."

"I am perfectly fine." She allowed him to steer her to the bed. "And how can it be considered exerting myself when I am just serving my husband."

"Serving me?" He chuckled and pulled her onto the bed with him. He wrapped her in his arms. "Is *that* what you call what you just did to me?"

"I am sure one of your young courtier tutors—"

"No, never." He kissed the top of her head. "And I'm glad you were the first to."

"And last."

"And last, but not for the last time, I hope."

"No, not the last time." She looked up at him, her eyelashes fluttering. "If you stay, I can do that every day for you, twice a day if you wish."

He smiled. "That is indeed a tempting offer."

He felt her relaxing, the tension slipping from her slender shoulders. "Sleep now," he said. "My beautiful wife, sleep now."

CHAPTER NINETEEN

JOANNA STRETCHED OUT her legs on the cool sheets then turned, reaching for Philip's solid body to snuggle against.
But the bed was empty, not even a warm patch.
She flicked her eyes open, instantly awake, and stared at the dent in the pillow his head had made. "Philip?"
There was no answer. Her heart skipped a beat and a familiar rush of nausea filled her gullet. "Philip? Where are you?" She flicked back the covers and stood, having to pause and close her eyes again for a moment when light-headedness gripped her.
"Philip. Please, where are you?" She staggered to the window and threw back a curtain. The courtyard was empty, apart from Raul sweeping out a stable.
She flung open a window. "Philip! Philip!"
Raul stopped sweeping and started up at her, squinting in the morning sunshine.
"Philip. Where are you? Show yourself." She leaned out farther, ignoring Raul entirely.
Isabella blustered in, Beatriz at her side.
"Joanna," Isabella cried out, rushing to her. "What are you doing?"
"Where is my husband?" Joanna asked, spinning to her mother and pointing her finger. "Who has allowed him to leave?"
"He can leave of his own accord," Isabella said with a frown. "He is not our prisoner."

"I forbade him to go without me," Joanna said. "I told him not to leave my side." Her eyes stung; tears were forming.

"Do not upset yourself so, Your Highness," Beatriz said. "It will not do the babe any good."

"It is impossible not to be upset." Joanna's voice rose with each word. "The love of my life is gone. How can I breathe without him? How can I *be* without him?" Through the fog of now-falling tears, Joanna saw the two women share a look. "You don't understand," she shouted. "You have never experienced the love that Philip and I share. It is transcending, it is consuming and it is—"

"Unhealthy," Isabella said, taking hold of Joanna's arm. "Your love for Philip is unhealthy and too much."

"Too much? Unhealthy?" Joanna stared at her mother. "How can love be too much? And didn't you want me to love the man you chose for me?"

"Yes, of course I did, but this is…this is not right. You have to be parted on occasion from him. That is the way of the world. Of your world."

"But I do not wish to be," Joanna snapped, pulling away. "I wish to be with him every minute of every day."

"That is not possible. You know that," Isabella said.

"Just because you and Father have a loveless marriage, that doesn't mean I have to."

"That is not true." Isabella's eyes widened so much, the whites were visible around her irises. "Why would you say that?"

"Because you allow him to bed other women." Joanna tapped the side of her head. "I remember you telling me that. I remember you saying that was the way of your marriage. Well, it's not the way of mine. Philip would not bed another. Oh, no… He only wants me." She spun away from her mother's shocked face. She looked as though she'd been slapped.

"Princess Joanna." Beatriz rushed up to her. "Please, do not say such things and—"

"Leave me." Joanna shrugged Beatriz off and stared once

more at the courtyard. "I am inconsolable." She dashed at her tears. Her chest was tight and her heart thudding. She stared into the distance, at the hills and the small track meandering over them.

In the dead of the night her husband had stolen away from her. Each trotting step of his horse taking him farther from their bedchamber.

Her throat constricted with the force of the scream she was holding in. How could he do this to her? He knew how much she loved him. How she couldn't stand to be without him.

Suddenly, the pain bloomed so hard and fast, it was unbearable. What if he did bed other women when he was at the French court? What if he did allow another's hands to roam his body, tease him, thrill him, pleasure him?

She screwed up her eyes and shook her head to try to rid herself of the image. It was sickening and it clawed a hole in her soul.

The room weighed down on her, the walls closing in. She had to get out of there. Get on Gianna and ride to France, to Philip. Nothing and no one could stop her.

She let out a wail, grabbed her nightgown upward, and tore from the room.

"Joanna," her mother called. "Wait."

She took no notice. All she could think of was Philip as she rushed along the corridor and down the stairs. She'd get on her horse and ride like the wind.

With her bed-mussed hair flying behind her, she ran across the courtyard toward the stable she knew her horse was kept in. It would only take a moment for Raul to tack up and help her aboard, then she'd be on her way.

"Stop! Please. Joanna," Beatriz called.

Joanna sensed her close behind, her mother too.

"I am leaving," she shouted over her shoulder. "I am going to my husband." It was all she could think of and the only thing that could happen.

"Madness has taken hold," Isabella shouted. "Raul, lock the gate immediately."

Raul stood still, his eyes wide.

"Raul!" Isabella said.

He moved quickly to do her bidding, shaken from his surprise at the scene.

"I do not have madness," Joanna said, turning but still making her way to the stable. "Unless you think I am mad with love, in which case I will neither deny nor apologize."

"This is not right. You must stay here," Beatriz implored, holding out her hands.

"Staying here alone, with you, is not right." She pointed at her mother. "I have to leave. I have to console my husband, who is distraught that you and Father have not given him his rightful title and treated him so harshly."

"We can discuss this," Isabella said.

"It is too late. He is gone." Once again, Joanna turned. She raced to the stable and unbolted the door. Rushed inside.

It was empty. The dusty floor swept and the trough dry.

"Where is Gianna?" Isabella demanded of Raul, who stood in the sunlight twisting a rag in his hand.

"She is in the meadow, Princess."

"Why? Why is she not here when I want her?"

"She is also with child." He nodded at her belly. "And the spring grass is good for her."

Joanna stamped her foot. "What ridiculously bad timing." She stormed forward and pushed past him. "I will have to walk to France."

"Your Highness," he said, "Please, I implore you in your condition—"

"What do *you* understand of my condition?" She huffed. "Have you ever carried a child in your belly?"

"No, but my wife has. Three times now."

She stopped and stared at his dark eyes. They were so different to Philip's, yet once upon a time, they had been her idea of perfection. They'd looked at her with adoration and longing back then. But now...now she saw pity and apprehension as he looked at her.

"I do not wish to discuss this with you, Raul." She tossed her hand into the air in a flippant wave. "Open the gate." She stomped over the cobbles, aware now of other courtiers and stablehands watching her. "I have a long journey."

"Princess." Beatriz was at her side. "Please. Come back to the bedchamber. You are making a spectacle of yourself."

"A spectacle? A *spectacle*? Because I wish to go to the man *she* made me marry, I am making a spectacle." Joanna gestured to her mother, who stood with her chin raised and her arms folded.

"Yes, I beg you." Beatriz clasped Joanna's hand, but Joanna snatched it away.

She took off at a run, but the gates had indeed been closed. Not only that, but a huge, iron lock and chain encircled them. "Open the gates." She ran up to them and gripped the cool metal. "I demand these gates be open!" She rattled the bars.

Her throat was tight and a gritty, acrid taste filled her mouth. How could this be happening? She was being held prisoner in her own home, in her own kingdom. "I demand you open these gates." She swung her attention to the nearest courtier, who took a step back, eyes lowered.

"You!" She directed at another. "Open the gates."

He too stepped away, head bowed.

"They will not," Isabella said firmly. "For they follow their queen's instructions."

Joanna's jaw tensed and fury burned through her veins. "Raul! I order you, as your princess, that you find the key and open the gate."

"I can't do that," he said, stepping closer to her with his hands outstretched. "How about you—"

"Stay away." She swiped at the tears falling afresh down her cheeks. These people were her enemies. They were keeping her from Philip. "Stay away from me. All of you."

"Your Highness, the baby has made you *loca*." Beatriz held out her hands. "I beg you, come with me. You need to rest."

"I know what I need and that is to be with Philip." She swung to the gate and stared at the track leading into the distance. "Let me out. Let me out."

Several passing villagers stared in, their eyes filled with curiosity and their baskets heavy.

A new strength came to her and she shook the gates with all her might, willing them to come off their hinges and release her from the burden of being separated from her husband.

But they did not and as her cries of frustration faded, so did her energy. She slumped to the hard ground, crying desolately, her chest aching and a hollow pit of despair opening up in her stomach. "My love. My love…" She sobbed. "You have been ripped from me."

"Joanna." Beatriz was at her side. "I beg you to come indoors."

"Get off me!" Joanna looked up at her with a snarl. "Unless you can open the gates, then leave me alone. I have no need of you." Her anger was reaching new heights. "Leave. Me. Alone."

Beatriz backed away but didn't leave.

Isabella did. She hoisted up the hem of her gown and flicked her head around, the veil from her hennin catching in the breeze. She walked back to the castle entrance as though satisfied with a job well done.

"I hate you," Joanna shouted after her. "You have ruined my marriage, ruined everything."

Isabella paused, said nothing, then carried on walking.

Joanna slumped into a renewed chasm of despair. How would she survive here alone? Her head filled with thoughts of Philip in another woman's bed, and her belly full of a baby that prevented her from going to him. The hopelessness of her situation filled her with gloom and misery and she dropped her head to her hands and sobbed until she was exhausted.

The day bled into night and with it, came cooler air.

She was aware of Beatriz nearby. Pacing, occasionally sending a murmured prayer heavenward, occasionally quietly asking Joanna if she was ready to retire.

Joanna ignored her. She'd show them all how strong her love for Philip was. That she was prepared to sacrifice herself and her baby to go to him. Then what would they be able to do? Nothing.

An owl hooted in the distance. The scent of burning wood filtered toward her along with the smell of herbs and meat cooking.

She shivered. Her stomach rumbled. Still, she stayed curled up in a ball, one hand gripping the gate. She would not be moved.

"Oh, but think of the baby," Beatriz said. "Your baby son. You must come in and rest."

"I am staying here. I am staying here until the babe is born."

"But why?"

"Because here I am nearer to my love, to France." She stared up at Beatriz. "Leave me. You are making my plight worse. Leave me."

Beatriz frowned and shook her head. "But, my dearest friend, I care for you. I care for you and your baby. I care for all of your children, whom right now, it seems you would see motherless."

"Which is probably what they believe because I have been gone so long." She swallowed. Her throat was dry and dusty. "Do you not wish me to be with them?"

"Of course." She paused. "When the time is right."

Joanna said nothing.

"And it will be," Beatriz went on. "When you have had this baby. When you are strong again. The time will be right."

"I am strong now." Though even as she said it, Joanna knew it wasn't true. She was exhausted, and cold, and hungry. Her heart felt like it was breaking in two and jealousy twisted her sinews and tendons so that it felt like she was a coil of bitter agony.

"Please, come with me," Beatriz implored. "You are making yourself sick lying on the dirt this way."

"No." Joanna thumped the ground, creating a cloud of dust. "Leave me be."

Beatriz clasped her hands together and stepped away, muttering another prayer.

Joanna went back to staring into the distance, ignoring the inquisitive villagers who were now gathered to see her spectacle. A shiver went up her spine and her stomach grumbled. Or was it the child kicking? She wasn't sure.

An hour passed. Then another. A thick cloud crossed the moon, casting a dark gloom over the courtyard.

Her body weakened, the shivering stopped, and her sore eyes closed. Maybe she should just die and end the misery she was enduring.

It was sometime after that she felt a blanket resting over her shoulders. She looked up.

Raul.

"You are cold, Princess," he said softly, the way he used to speak to her. "You are going to make yourself and the baby sick."

"Do you love your wife?" she managed, her voice croaking.

"Yes." He frowned. "Very much."

"More than you loved me?"

He hesitated, then, "I will always love you."

"So you understand love, and missing someone and not being able to breathe unless you are with them? That kind of love. Painful love."

"Yes, Princess. I do." His tone was calm and patient. "When you left I couldn't breathe or eat or sleep."

She frowned at him. "Yet you married."

"Life goes on."

"Not mine. I need to be with Philip."

"As he needs to be with you." Raul rested his hand on her shoulder. It was big and warm and not unpleasant. "But how can he be if you harm yourself by lying here all night? And cause the baby harm too."

"I don't want to hurt my baby. Philip's baby. He loves all of his children."

"I know you don't want to hurt anyone." He rubbed small circles on her back. "And Philip doesn't want that, either. Have you thought about how much the news of his baby being born still and lifeless will pain him?"

She looked up at him. "You think that will happen?"

"You are a princess. Your place is not on the dirt floor of the courtyard, gripping a metal gate." He nodded at her pale, cold hand still wrapped around the bar. "Your place is indoors, resting comfortably in your confinement, away from the watchful, gossiping gaze of your people."

She glanced at the small crowd holding candles and looking in at her. Her jaw clenched and a spark of pride lit her insides. Raul was right. This was no place for her.

Gingerly, she let go of the gate and pushed herself to a sitting position with her hair hanging forward. The effort was exhausting.

"Let me help you," Raul said.

She didn't answer. Instead, she straightened some more. Determination took hold. She was a princess. Only days before, these people had seen her in all of her finery and she'd promised to serve them with loyalty and dignity. What was she doing sprawled in the dirt like a mangy dog?

"That's it," Raul said, wrapping his arm gently around her upper arm. "Let's get you up."

Any other stablehand who'd dared to touch her she'd have admonished severely. But not Raul. Raul understood her. He understood love because he'd loved her the way she loved Philip.

Her spine was stiff and painful and her hips ached. Hunger gnawed at her belly and her temples pounded.

"That's it," he whispered, wrapping an arm around her waist. "Easy now."

"Oh!" Her knees buckled and she collapsed downward. But not far, because the next thing she knew, Raul had swung her up and into his strong arms.

In an instant, he was striding toward the entrance of the castle carrying her as though she were as light as a kitten.

Joanna closed her eyes, tucked her head against his shoulder, and whimpered. She felt wretched and drained, defeated and hopeless.

The sooner her child was born and she could escape her parents' home, the better. She needed to be with Philip the way she needed air.

CHAPTER TWENTY

"BEATRIZ," JOANNA SAID the next morning as she sat up in bed. "You need to help me."

"Anything, Your Highness. I will do anything for you."

Joanna gripped her hand. "You must go to Philip. Get a horse and ride to French court."

"I beg your pardon?"

"You must go and report to me what my husband is doing."

"But...they will never allow me into French court."

"They will. You are part of the prince consort's entourage. You have been there before."

"As *your* lady, not his."

Joanna waved her free hand in the air. "What does that matter? I insist you leave today, immediately. Raul will sort out a horse and carriage while you pack a trunk."

"But...I really—"

"There is no discussion to be had. You must leave and write to me daily, reporting on his actions." She leaned forward, desperate for Beatriz to understand the urgency of the situation. "If you don't, I feel I will lose my mind."

Beatriz tenderly tucked a strand of hair behind Joanna's ear. "I cannot, my friend. My place is here with you. When the babe is born, you will need me."

"I have given birth lots of times. I can do it alone." She raised her chin.

"That is not wise. I beg you."

"What is not wise is for you not to follow my instructions." She nodded at the door. "Go and ready yourself. And be sure to pack scrolls and ink for the reports."

Beatriz frowned.

"Now."

"No, Your Highness. I will not. The queen will not allow it, either. I am sure of that."

"What my mother wants is none of my concern." Joanna fisted the sheets. Why didn't Beatriz understand the gravity of the situation? "This is an arrangement between you and I. I need you. I need you to do this."

"I can't." Beatriz shook her head, her eyes downcast.

"You can."

"I am sorry." She backed away toward the door. "Truly, I am."

"You have failed me." Joanna picked up a brush and slung it at her. "You are supposed to be on my side."

Beatriz gasped and slipped from view. The brush clattered against the wall.

Joanna flung herself down onto the bed, burying her face in a pillow. She sobbed so hard, her chest hurt, her ribs heaving with each miserable wail of grief. For that was what it felt like without her husband. She grieved him. She wanted to be with him.

On and on, the tears came. She was lost to her own misery, twisted by an unhappiness that seemed to be never-ending.

Eventually, she fell into a deep, dark sleep. Drained and tired, her body gave up and relaxed. But her mind didn't. All too soon, she was being tortured by vivid nightmares.

Philip was in bed with a blonde French beauty, her hair running over his abdomen as she took his cock into her mouth. His face twisted with pleasure, his hands reaching for her soft, round breasts.

"No. No." Joanna was shouting in her dream. "Stop. Leave him alone!"

But the dream continued, the blonde on her back now, legs spread and beckoning Philip to enter her. He did. His long, strong body went rigid with desire as he pumped into her, driving them both to pleasure. He was lost to the woman, the wench, his memories of Joanna gone in an instant.

She screamed, the agony too much to bear, and tried to rip their bodies apart, but they were absorbed in their act and her demands fell on deaf ears—her scratching, yanking hands had no effect. Frustration mounted, jealousy twisting inside of her. Suddenly, a pair of scissors appeared in her hand and she raised them above the blonde's face, ready to bring them down, obliterate her beauty, slash away the pleasure in her eyes.

"Joanna, wake up. Joanna…please."

Her mother's voice, distant and weak, as though underwater.

"Joanna. You are dreaming. Wake up." The voice was louder this time.

She flicked her eyes open to the harsh light of day. She was breathing hard, her limbs twitching and her head spinning.

"It's just a dream," Isabella said, her brow creased with worry. "Just a dream. Pregnancy can do that at times."

"Mother." Joanna gasped, crying again, even though she'd been sure her tears had all but dried up. "Oh…it was so awful."

"My baby girl." Isabella scooped her close. "I hate to see you suffer this way."

"Then let me go to Philip." Joanna clung to her mother's gown. "Let me go to him this very day."

"We can't let you do that. You know why."

"But I can't be without him," she wailed.

Isabella pulled back and held Joanna by the shoulders. "You have to snap out of this. It's not right, this insane love you have for him."

"It is not insane. It is how a woman *should* love her husband."

"And does he love you this way?"

"Yes, of course he does. He tells me all the time he could not live without me."

"And I am pleased for you, that you share a great love with Philip. But don't you see, he is away performing his royal duties. He is mediating for Spain and as such, accepts his pain at parting from you. That is what you must do also."

"Yes, yes, it does pain him to be apart from me. From me and our children. It hurts him here." She banged her fist onto her chest.

"But he is strong and—"

"Are you saying I am not strong?"

"You are strong, Joanna, very strong, and now you must show it and speak no more of leaving for the French court or of missing Philip."

Joanna pulled away. "You do not understand my pain. You have no idea what I am going through."

Isabella was quiet.

"But I will show you I am strong. I will have this baby alone. I will stay in this room as my belly swells and I will labor alone. No one, not you or Beatriz, will tend me, then you will all know how strong I am, and then you will understand the burden of my love for Philip, the agony of being parted from him."

"Do not add to your burden." Isabella shook her head. "No woman should birth alone. It is a dangerous time."

"Please leave." Joanna pointed at the door. "If I am to be alone, I wish to be truly alone, with just my thoughts from this moment until my body expels this child."

"It will not be good for you. Pregnancy is a time for women to lean on women. God will be with you, but growing a child in your body is—"

"Leave, I beg you. And I don't care if God is with me or not." She turned and moved to the opposite side of the bed, then stood and walked to the window. Her head felt light and her knees weak, so she gripped the sill and stared out at Raul sweeping the yard.

A few moments later, the door clicked.

Her mother had indeed left her alone.

Philip surveyed King Louis XII of France's vast armory. The walls were adorned with swords, bayonets, and pikes. A wooden horse took pride of place beside the fireplace—large enough to stable the creature—wearing full military regalia. Every inch of the material covering the horse was emblazoned with Louis's crest. On its head, red plumes of feathers signified bravery and its tail was plaited with scarlet ribbon.

"What do you think, my handsome friend?" Louis asked, slapping his hand onto Philip's shoulder and clasping it.

"An impressive collection." Philip gestured to a set of shields. "Though they do not appear to have ever seen a battlefield. Not one dent amongst them."

Louis laughed. "These are just for show, to impress my esteemed friends. Such as you."

Philip nodded and took a goblet of wine from a nearby courtier. "I am happy to be here, as your friend and as King of Spain."

Louis's eyebrows raised. "King of Spain? I had not heard of King Ferdinand's death."

Philip smiled and dipped his head. "It is true, my father by marital law is alive and well…or at least last I heard. But he is an elderly king, one who is tiring with politics and weary with governing. I think you'll find that I am king before the year is out." Philip didn't think this would be the case, but it didn't hurt for Louis to believe it.

Louis was quiet. "For a tired king, he throws the weight of his army around."

"I have been advising him, as you can imagine." Philip paused. "But always with France in mind, and Burgundy, Flanders, and the Low Countries too of course." He took a sip of drink. "My marriage is quite advantageous, don't you think? For both of us."

"And how is your lovely wife? She is quite…charming."

Philip laughed and his heart swelled when he thought of Joanna. He hated being apart from her and knew his sneaking out at the crack of dawn would have enraged her, but what choice had he had? She simply wouldn't have let him leave and would have pulled all of her wily womanly tricks to get him to stay. "She is with child again. Another son, I am sure."

"Sons are a blessing, indeed."

"And I am glad you found her quirky ways charming." Philip remembered her wild dancing and flamboyant outfit swirling as she'd taken center stage at French court. "Her energy is to be admired, I hope."

"She is to be a powerful woman," Louis said, "and as she is energetic and headstrong, that is a lot to contend with for a husband. Are you sure you're up to the job?"

Philip frowned. He was a man. A Habsburg. Of course he could control Joanna. "I have handled my wife perfectly well over the years and that will not change because she gains a title."

Louis pressed his lips together as though holding in words.

"It will not." Philip sensed his rising temper. His scalp itched and his collar felt too tight. Who was Louis to cast such judgment?

"That is good," Louis said. "Because she may land you in hot water if not kept on…*a leash* is the wrong word, but you get my meaning."

"Speaking of hot water," Philip said, keen to move the conversation away from Joanna. "We need to discuss Naples, Sicily and Milan too, for that matter."

"Indeed." Louis gestured to two large, wooden chairs that were situated so they looked down the room. "Let's sit."

Philip did as instructed, the seat firm on his behind. "King Ferdinand is keen to get a resolution," he said. "As am I and my father, soon to be Holy Roman Emperor, for whom I can speak freely."

"And you are able to negotiate on King Ferdinand's behalf also?"

"Naturally." Philip scowled. "Why else would I be here?"

"This is good news."

Philip set down his drink. "As I said before, consider that you are in fact speaking to the King of Spain, right now, as we sit here."

"Very well. In that case, I want Naples. It is rightfully mine, and I also want compensation for the war I have had to wage reclaiming it."

Philip had to stop his mouth from hanging open. "You want compensation for a war *you* started?"

"Yes, it's been very expensive, this long dispute. I wish for money, from you...from Spain."

"I cannot agree to that."

"Is that you speaking or Ferdinand?"

"Me. Both. That is not going to happen. Compensation... It won't happen." His head spun. That was not what he'd been expecting Louis to ask for. He willed himself to keep calm and think through his next words. There was no way he wanted Louis to know he'd thrown him. "However, I have an idea..."

"Go on." Louis studied him, his beady eyes searching.

Philip smiled. "I do know how both you and I, France and Spain, can cement an alliance, and in turn secure Naples in the future."

"Go on."

"We will sign a treaty, a secret treaty to overturn Frederick of Naples and draw an end to this war in more ways than one."

"I don't understand."

"Ah." Philip tapped his nose. "The first part is easy. Claiming Naples from Frederick, we have good armies already in position, but the second part of my plan is a long game. We must be patient." He paused for dramatic effect. "Can *you* be patient, Your Majesty?"

"Right now, you hold me in suspense and my patience is thin ice."

Philip smiled. "We must wed my eldest son, Charles, to your

eldest daughter, Claude, so that eventually, Naples and Sicily and all of the north will be in their hands entirely. Ultimate power in this vast Italian region. Don't you see? It is a simple solution and we both win."

"I want Naples now." Louis frowned.

"You can have it, kind of." Philip nodded for more wine. "Because in the meantime, as will be stated in our pending treaty, France can rule Naples and the north of Italy and Spain the south. It will only be a generation and the entire country will be as one and under our rule. When I say 'ours,' I mean yours, France."

Philip smiled, knowing what a prize it would be for his son, Charles. He'd have territorial stakes in France, Spain, and Italy, as well as the Low Countries and Burgundy and beyond. It was a grand inheritance for his son, the greatest ever sought, and all because of a well-matched marriage. Philip felt flush with power and ambition. It was all going to plan.

Wasn't it?

"Ferdinand will never agree to this." Louis paused while his goblet was refilled with claret. "He hates me."

"It is true his fondness for you is lacking," Philip said. "That is why I am here. So we can speak truthfully, intelligently, and civilly."

Louis waited.

"And don't forget, my son, Charles, is Ferdinand's grandson. Ferdinand wants the best for Charles and this marriage is the best for him, for Charles."

"Mmm." Louis scratched his chin. "I had not accounted for that…"

Philip waited, his heart thudding. He wanted nothing more than for Louis to agree to this marriage. It would solve a host of problems along with the treaty.

"I will agree." Louis nodded slowly. "I can see this way Claude, my daughter, will eventually win not just Naples, but many more territories with this marriage. It pleases me."

"You are very wise and patient and think in a progressive

manner." Philip retrieved a scroll from his pocket. "And in preparation I have drawn up the agreements necessary." He stood and unrolled the scroll.

Outside, he heard voices. His advisors, Louis's too. They wouldn't be happy that Philip had gone along with his plan. They'd claimed Ferdinand would be furious, that he had no interest in treaties with France. That the king wanted Naples and Sicily for himself without compromise.

But what did they know? He, Philip of the House of Habsburg, had accomplished in a single conversation what Ferdinand and his advisors hadn't managed in years of battle.

What was more, he'd secured a French crown for his son. How excited he was to tell young Charles this.

And it would be soon.

He would go to Flanders shortly. Check on his children and his Estates Generals. He'd been gone too long and a powerful man like him had to keep hold of the reins in all of his territories.

In all of his growing empire.

Chapter Twenty-One

Joanna doubled over, catching her breath. The familiar waves of agony clutched her womb with mean, gripping hands. But she didn't cry out, she didn't shout for help. And she didn't ask God to have mercy. Instead, she bit on a rag and screwed her eyes up tight, turning inward, owned by the pain.

It was all that existed.

True to her word, she'd spent her pregnancy alone in her bedchamber with the door closed, save for food being passed in, which she'd picked at miserably.

And now her confinement was almost over. The onset of labor was a blessing. The sooner the child was born, the sooner they could travel to Coudenberg.

The pain subsided and she dragged in a breath and stared at a painting of a castle on a hill. The frame, made of thick, dark wood, had a layer of dust along the top. It was a picture she'd studied many times. It reminded her of Coudenberg Palace the way it sat tall and proud and with pine trees to the left.

How she longed to be back there. Philip had written to say that was where he'd gone after his meetings in France. At first, she'd been furious with him, written straight back, and demanded he come to her. But the children missed their parents, he'd said, and at least one of them should be there with them.

Another searing rush of pain clutched her belly and she groaned long and low as the tightening reached a crescendo. Each one was more punishing than the last. But what was this pain after the pain of being parted from Philip? If she could bear that, she could bear anything.

The wave of torture waned and she staggered to the bed. Cramps tightened her inner thighs and beads of sweat peppered her brow. It took effort to climb onto the mattress she'd spent so many hours, days, weeks, and months lying on in her miserable slumber, yet she gained strength knowing her prison sentence was coming to an end. As soon as the baby was born, she'd order a carriage and they'd leave.

"Oh, Lord, have mercy." She gritted her teeth as yet another contraction gripped her. Her belly turned to stone and the first urge to push came with it, along with a gush of fluid. For a moment, she wanted to yell for her mother, for Beatriz, but she didn't... She would do this alone. She would bear her cross in solitude.

"Please...enter this world smoothly," she gasped as the contraction ebbed away.

She flopped onto her back, legs spread, knees drawn up. Experienced now at giving birth, she knew what was coming next. There was nothing for her to do other than what her body needed to...eject this child.

Like a malevolent storm rushing in from the north, the next contraction left her dizzy and breathless. The urge to push was growing.

Again, she bit on the rag, closed her eyes, and fisted the blanket beneath her. Would she survive this pain? Was this the birth that would kill her? Certainly, she felt on the edge of death. If she reached out, she could touch it. Perhaps it would be a blessing to end the suffering.

But then it was there. The urge to push was overwhelming and she grunted long and low and went with it. The energy within her was bright and urgent and even though she was exhausted, she pushed with all of her might—her body stretching, opening, expelling.

The baby was half in and half out. She stared at the ceiling, knowing the pain was coming again. It did. This time, the slippery body slid from her onto the bed and the relief was instant.

Frantically, she reached for the bloodied newborn and turned it over.

"Oh, my love, we have a son." She gasped, scooping him up. "Another son. Ferdinand. Our beautiful son. Welcome."

She clasped him to her breast as he let out his first wail.

Soon her mother, Beatriz, and other courtiers would come running. They'd see that she was a strong wife who delivered sons, future kings, future rulers. How could they doubt her now? How could they deny her?

Almost immediately, the bedchamber door opened. Her mother and Beatriz rushed in. It was almost as if they'd been hovering outside, listening, anticipating.

"Princess." Beatriz rushed forward holding a damp towel. "You have given birth."

"To a son, Ferdinand." Joanna looked directly at her mother. "And he is healthy, as am I."

Isabella's jaw tightened. "This is good news, indeed. I will send thanks to God."

"You will also send for a carriage. We will be leaving shortly."

"That is out of the question."

"You deny me again? After I have done as instructed and waited all these months alone?"

Her mother said nothing.

"Philip has written saying he wants me with him, that he needs me at his side, as do my other children. He misses me desperately. I must go. Now." She swiped at the sweat on her forehead.

"You are not strong enough."

"I am. Can you not see how strong I am? I gave birth alone, with barely a noise. I am strong and capable and—"

"Joanna. You are not strong. You have been confined to your

bedchamber, eating barely enough to sustain yourself, let alone a child. It is only by God's will that the child is alive."

"How dare you? I would never hurt my son." Did they really believe that? She would never hurt her child. Never.

"Your Highness…the afterbirth." Beatriz had her hand on Joanna's knee as she examined her.

"Yes. Yes," Joanna said. "I know." She trembled, her limbs tensing and relaxing as the afterbirth slipped from her and she watched Beatriz cut the cord that connected it to the baby.

"It is also thanks to God that you had the strength to push him from your womb," Isabella said.

"Why does everyone doubt my character? Have I not proven myself enough times?"

"If you mean wailing at the castle gate, then once was enough."

Joanna frowned. "That was months ago."

"And the villagers still talk of it."

"All the more reason for me to leave." She sat forward, but the moment she did, small, black dots danced in her vision. She slumped back closing her eyes.

"Joanna." Her mother was at her side, clutching her hand. "Please, let us not fight. Get your strength back then we can talk."

"Talk about what?" Joanna asked with her eyes still closed.

"About Ferdinand staying here when you journey to Flanders. I do not wish to stop you from going to your husband and children, I know how much you miss them, but you cannot take a possible heir to Spain with you. He must stay here when Charles is so very far away."

Joanna opened her eyes and blinked in the suddenly harsh light. "Not take Ferdinand? But Philip will want to see his son. I have to take him to Flanders with me."

"Philip will have to come here and meet baby Ferdinand…" She tipped her chin and sniffed. "If he dares."

"Dares? What are you talking about? My husband is a brave and courageous man."

"After his bold treaty-making and rash promises of Charles's marriage to Louis's daughter, it is clear he does not have the courage to show his face before the king. That is why he returned to Flanders. What is more, he holds the infant Charles there."

"But…I…" Joanna's head was spinning. Was that really what had happened?

"You did not know." Isabella raised her eyebrows. "About all of the agreements made during that meeting?"

"Of course I did." She'd known of the planned marriage, as Philip had told her this in his letter. But not of the treaty. "And I support him fully. He is a wise man and a great governor. I'm sure his father is also in agreement."

Her mother huffed. "We shall see."

"Mother." Joanna leaned forward. "I can't leave my baby here. I have to go to Philip, with Ferdinand."

"I agree. You must go to Philip."

"Good. Yes." Joanna nodded.

"But not for three months at least. You must get your strength back after childbirth."

"Three months?" They could not be serious.

"Yes." Isabella folded her arms.

"One month."

"Two."

Joanna sighed. "I will agree to that." She did feel exhausted, but if she felt well sooner, she'd simply go.

"And Belmonte will accompany you. Along with Beatriz."

Beatriz reached for Ferdinand. "Shall I clean him?"

"Yes. Thank you." She studied Beatriz. Their last words had been spoken in anger. But that had been months ago. Perhaps Beatriz had forgotten. She certainly was acting like she had.

"Beatriz and Belmonte," Joanna said. "Naturally. But not the knights. Philip detests them."

"Not the knights, and not Ferdinand," Isabella said, nodding at the baby, who had stopped wailing and was looking up at Beatriz with big, blue eyes. "He stays here, in his rightful home."

"His rightful home is with his parents and siblings."

"We cannot allow it. Had your husband been more considerate of Spain in his discussion with King Louis, then maybe we could have entrusted him with our grandson, but now—"

"But he is Philip's son! You can't keep him."

"We aren't claiming him as our son, only our heir should we be kept from Charles."

"'Kept from Charles'?" Whatever did her mother mean?

"Yes, kept from him by Philip, as we have been to date. It would be within our right to obtain papal permission to bypass him as heir should the need arise."

"No…I…"

"You could stay, Joanna. Stay and care for little Ferdinand yourself."

"But what of my other three children? They need me. They miss me. Philip tells me so in his letters."

"You must do what you must do." Isabella stood. "But remember, I am not just your mother, I am also queen and I will be obeyed." She paused and set down her shoulders. "Ferdinand stays. What you do is up to you."

EIGHT WEEKS LATER, Joanna rattled along the track toward Coudenberg Palace. The journey over the Pyrenees and through France had been long and her arms had ached for her baby boy. How she missed the scent of his wispy hair, the grasping little fingers that curled around hers, the feel of his warm body when she held him close.

But the sorrow of parting was laced with anticipation and excitement and that had kept her going on the trip through the mountains and across the seemingly endless forest paths. How her heart sung with the thought of seeing her other three children. They'd been separated for so long. She wanted their chatter in her ears, their laughter filling a room.

And Philip. Each step of the horse's hooves drew her closer to her lover. She yearned for his arms around her in a way she'd never known. It was a need greater than breathing, even. She had to be with him. God had given her this powerful love and now it was her burden. It was heavy and desperate and without him, she was sure she really would go mad.

Finally, the grand house came into view. Lit like the picture in her bedchamber she'd stared at so often by a blue sky and a white orb of sunshine.

Leaning forward, she pushed aside the curtain and took in the flat, green fields and the stream running through it. The air was clearer here. She was sure the dark cloud that had been hanging over her would be swept away by the pure breeze. Or at least she'd hoped it would. The cloud had been dank and cold and it had stolen any good thoughts she'd had. Almost as if it were a sinkhole for happiness. Even her dreams had been shadowed by it. The ones where Philip was with the blonde courtier had become so frequent that she'd feared going to sleep these last weeks.

What she needed was to sleep with him at her side so in the dead of the night when terror gripped her she could reach for him, hold him close, know that he was with her and no one else.

"Your Highness, we will soon be there."

"I know, Beatriz—it is exciting. Are you pleased to be back?"

"Yes, it is a beautiful place." She paused. "But my duty is to be wherever you are, to serve you, to see that you are quite well."

"I am sure I will be from now on." She reached for Beatriz's hand. "And I thank you for being at my side when the storms come. You are a good friend—no, a *great* friend, and I thank the Lord for you."

Beatriz smiled and her shoulders seemed to relax. "And I thank the Lord for having you in my life." She paused. "How will you be without Ferdinand? He is so tiny—to leave with no idea when you will see him again? Do you not fear he will grow up not knowing his mother?"

"I will be with my husband, so my burden will be halved. He has the ability to make things feel right even when they are not." She stared into the distance again. Somewhere beneath that vast roof was the only man she would ever love. "Ferdinand is safe and secure with his doting grandparents. I have to think of my other children…for now, at least." But she would go to Philip first. The moment she arrived. She ached with longing to be with him, to feel whole again.

The carriage drew to a halt.

Before a courtier could even open the door, Joanna was out. She straightened her stiff spine and brushed down the front of her dark-blue gown. "How is my headdress?" she asked Beatriz.

"Perfect." Beatriz adjusted it.

"And my pallor?"

"A little pale, but that is to be expected after such an arduous journey."

Joanna hadn't found the journey arduous, just tedious. Impatience had clawed at her every step of the way—and was still clawing at her. She rushed up the wide, stone steps, eager to get to Philip.

She swept through the huge, arched doorway, barely noticing the courtiers bobbing at her sudden appearance. "Where is he?"

"In his bedchamber?" A young man holding a candlelighter said. "Your Highness."

"Thank you." She hoisted up the front hem of her gown and rushed up the stairs, seeming to float, such was her joy at finally being home, her true home, her home with her husband and children.

"Philip!" she called as she practically ran past an old, oak dresser and several portraits. "My love."

She flung the door to his bedchamber open, her smile as wide as any ocean.

Then froze.

Her smile slipped.

Her heart stuttered.

Sitting on the bed was Philip, and in a chair at his side, holding a rosary, was a pretty woman with long, blonde hair pulled back into a plait and secured with a black, velvet ribbon.

Fury gripped her as they both turned her way.

The woman lowered her rosary, the color draining from her face.

"Joanna, my love." Philip stood, his eyes widening. "You have arrived. Earlier than expected, which pleases me."

"Who is this?" Joanna demanded, stabbing her finger in the direction of the pretty woman. "Who is this?"

"I beg your pardon?" Philip frowned.

"Don't play dumb." Joanna glared at the woman, hate filling her veins and pain twisting her heart and lungs. "Who is this woman in your bedchamber? In *my husband*'s bedchamber? Who are you? Who are you, woman?"

Her mother's words from all those years ago came back to her. How she'd said a wife must accept adulterous behavior. Well, not Joanna. She wouldn't stand for it. Philip belonged to her and her alone.

"This is Carolyne, a courtier," Philip said. "We were childhood friends growing up here and—"

"Ha, one of the courtiers who taught you everything you need to know, right?" She clenched her fists. "Educated you on how to perform sexually on your wedding night."

"No...I... Please, Your Highness, I—"

"Don't speak to me." Joanna took in the room. An embroidery set lay on the desk complete with yarn and scissors. It looked as though she'd been there for a while, making herself comfortable. Making herself at home.

"Please, Your Highness. I mean no harm, I was simply—"

"I have no interest in your excuses. You are a harlot, a slut, and you had plans to steal my husband from me while I was not here to see your conniving, wily ways."

"That is not true..." The woman clutched her rosary beneath

her chin and blinked rapidly. "We are simply friends."

"Joanna, you have got this all wrong," Philip said in a sharp tone. "As I said, Carolyne and I are old friends. She grew up here and…"

"All the more reason for me to distrust her." Joanna lunged for the scissors and swiped them up. Red-hot fury blasted through her. She was shaking, panting. Her skin tingled and her limbs trembled. The glow of anger reddened her thoughts, misting them, stealing her sanity.

She grasped the woman's shiny, long plait of hair and yanked it taut. Then, quick as a flash of lightning, she angled the scissors at the densest clump and hacked at it. Once. Twice. Three times.

The woman squealed and tried to break away but could go nowhere.

The plait came off in Joanna's hand. "Here!" She threw it into the woman's lap, where it landed looking like a beheaded snake. "Take this and get out of here or I will see to it that it is your *head* chopped off next."

Chapter Twenty-Two

"Joanna!" Philip said, his eyes wide. "What have you—?"

"Done? I'll tell you what I've done. I've shown what happens when people step into my territory. When people dare to betray me. That's what I've done. It is a lesson everyone at court should learn."

Carolyne stood, her long plait hanging limply from her hand. Tears emerged and rolled down her cheeks as she sobbed pitifully.

"Get out." Joanna gestured wildly to the door. "Get out and make sure I never see you again."

The woman glanced briefly at Philip then scampered to the doorway and slipped out, closing the door behind herself.

Philip paced toward Joanna. His cheeks were flushed and his jaw set tight. "You have behaved appallingly."

"You are not pleased to see me?" She placed the scissors down then set her hands on her hips. "Your wife, your love, the mother of your children."

"I am pleased that you have had a safe journey, but *pleased to see you*...when this is what you do upon arrival?" He gestured to the scissors. Their shiny blades still held evidence of several long, blonde hairs.

"How dare you?" She tipped her chin and did her best to look down her nose at him, but it was hard, given how tall he was. "How dare you question my behavior when it was *you* who was in your bedchamber with another woman?"

"A friend," he said, his eyes narrowing. "A friend from my childhood who has just lost her mother, a cook here. We were talking about shared memories." He pressed his hand over his heart. "I was fond of her mother too. She was part of my childhood."

"A likely story." Joanna huffed.

"A true story."

"You could have spoken to her outside, in the broad light of day. Why did you have to be in here?" She didn't believe a word he was saying.

"Some conversations are delicate and private." His lips tightened as he studied her, turning his handsome face even more angular. "Like this one."

"Exactly, like this one. Now let us become reacquainted as husband and wife. Perhaps I will give you more sons." Her cunny ached for him and her breasts were heavy with desire. She didn't care that he was angry; he'd soon forget that when they were naked and in bed. That always charged his passions for her.

"Reacquainted...yes..." he said slowly and somewhat menacingly. "I will reacquaint you with who is in charge, my sweet Joanna. Remind you who runs this house, these lands, and this marriage, for I fear you have forgotten."

He reached for her and she went into his embrace, eyes closed waiting for his kiss. Longing had reached a crescendo inside of her.

But the kiss didn't come. Instead, she found herself locked in his arms and being dragged to the bed. "Oh...Philip."

His need for her was clearly very intense.

"My love." She gasped as he sat, feet on the floor, and dragged her onto his knee. "Show me how much you love me," she pleaded. "How much you have missed me."

"I do love you and I have missed you." He cupped her face. "But I see now that my absence from your life has led to you being misguided—deluded, even—and that needs to be rectified."

His eyes flashed dangerously as he stared into hers.

"I don't understand." She frowned.

"Behave like a child, wife of mine, and you will be punished like one."

The next thing she knew, she was face down over his knee. Her world had upended. Her headdress slipped to the floor and her hair hung by her cheeks. "Philip," she gasped, kicking up her heels and trying to right herself.

"Stop that." He held her firmer. The highest part of her body was her rump and her toes were only just skimming the floor. "Keep still, woman."

"What are you doing? Lord have mercy. Philip. What are you doing?"

"The Lord will not save you from this spanking." He yanked at her gown, pulling it up past her knees, her thighs, and then over her buttocks. "A spanking you know full well you deserve."

She yelped and tried to cover herself, twisting and turning, but he batted her hands away and held her firmer against his hard body. How could this be happening? The image she'd had of their passionate reunion did not include her bare bottom being exposed for his hand.

Slap.

A hard, sharp smack suddenly landed over both of her cheeks.

She jerked forward, crying out at the shock of the hot sting of his palm colliding with her delicate flesh.

Slap. Slap. Slap.

He'd spanked her again, hard, precise swipes that had heat flooding to her rear and between her legs. She yelped and squirmed but to no avail. Her husband held her exactly where he wanted her.

"Be quiet," he said. "I don't want those knights of yours rushing in and I'm sure you don't, either. You look quite the sight, Princess Joanna of Spain, with your blushing bottom on show like this for all to see."

Before she could deliver a scathing reply, he delivered another set of spanks.

Slap. Slap. Slap.

She felt so humiliated, so chastised and utterly helpless.

On and on the spanking continued, the pain and heat layering up and her breaths huffing from her with each resounding smack. The sound of her pulse pounded in her ears competing with the thwack of flesh on flesh.

"You must stop these jealous fits," he said, pausing and smoothing his hand over her smarting rump. "I will not stand for it."

Tears ran from her eyes, dampening her temples. "And I cannot stand you being with other women."

"I have not been with another woman since we wed. You have to believe that. I'll *make* you believe that."

He took out his frustration on her poor behind, smacking her soundly again.

"Oh, please…stop…" she begged.

He ignored her, spanking her until the heat was at its boiling point.

"Philip. I beg you," she wailed.

He stopped. He was breathing fast. So was she.

"No more." She sobbed. "No more. I promise to behave. I promise in the name of the good Lord."

"Are you sure?"

"I am sure. Please."

He said nothing. Instead, he traced the line between her thighs and buttocks, first the left and then the right. Then he slipped his finger down the crack of her buttocks.

She was hot and breathless, but she stilled and held her breath when he went lower, through the hot flesh of her cunny to find her entrance. She was wet for him, she knew she was, and when he slipped the tip of his finger into her body she let out a long, low groan of longing.

"You are so ready for me," he said quietly. "I hadn't expected that…"

"I want you," she said. "It is all I have craved, to be with you, as one." The words were stuttering and jagged but spoken with conviction. "Please…my love. Take me as your wife."

He added another finger, as though to tease her, and then pumped in and out of her cunny. She closed her eyes and moaned. Her toes curled in her shoes and she arched her back, pressing for more.

"Bad, little princess," he murmured. "Wanting this when you've been so naughty."

For some reason, his words, muttered so darkly, had her craving him more than she'd ever thought possible. "Philip."

"You need to understand your body is mine, as mine is yours," he went on. "Tell me you understand that."

"Yes. Yes. I understand." At this moment, she'd say anything to get him to give her everything she needed. "I am yours and you are mine."

"And you will apologize to my friend for chopping off her hair."

"What?" She twisted.

"You heard."

"I am the heir to the throne of Spain. No, I will not apologize."

He withdrew and set a resounding spank on her buttocks.

"Oh!" She lurched forward. "Yes. I will…oh… Please, no more…and but…more…"

He chuckled, his mood seeming to shift. "Luckily, I want you as badly as you want me."

Suddenly, she was being hoisted upright. He moved her as though she were a feather, her weight nothing to him.

Clinging to his hard, bulging biceps, she stared into his face, her head swimming as she sat astride his lap now, not over it.

"I have missed you," he said. "My cock has missed you." He was fumbling with his breeches, pushing them aside as he freed his erection.

She saw it and her cunny clenched in eagerness to feel it

filling her. "Yes. Oh, yes…" She rose up, her gown around her waist.

"Sit on me," he said, holding his erection upright. "Take me."

She nodded and bit on her bottom lip as she hovered her entrance over his cock tip.

His hands circled her waist and he pulled her down, forcing her to take him.

She let her head fall back and groaned as his width stretched her and his length filled her. She kept on going until she was fully seated on him and her smarting buttocks rested on his thighs.

"Joanna." He gasped, spearing one hand into her tousled hair. "You're all I need."

"And I you." She caught his mouth in a kiss, driving her tongue in to find his.

He kissed her back with an urgent fervor that had her hips grinding against him, working her clit on his body as she hugged his cock into hers.

He was tense and trembling. A surge of power went through her. She might have just received a spanking from her husband, but now she was in control. He needed her like he needed to take his next breath.

"Don't stop." He gasped, breaking the kiss. "This is incredible. You are incredible. Oh, Lord above, don't stop."

She flung back her head and he kissed her neck, holding her close, urging her on. But riding him was easy, as if she were made for it, and the pressure on her nub was growing. Soon she'd find pleasure. It was so close. And hearing Philip groaning, pleading, desperate for release only pushed her on and heightened every sensation.

Her big, strong, powerful husband was once again at her mercy.

"Oh, oh…Philip…my love." She gripped him harder, digging her fingernails into his flesh. "I am… I need… I…oh…"

It was as if another force had taken over her. The wildness of her grinding hips and the need in her body for climax had removed all other thoughts from her mind. She let her inhibitions go and took herself to an awe-inspiring climax. One for which she had waited in solitary confinement for so long. And now it was here and she cried out her pleasure, extending every moment of it. Bliss sung around her body. It pulled her muscles then squeezed them tight. Her cunny did the same, hugging and releasing his cock.

Breathing hard, she allowed the ecstasy to continue.

"You're so beautiful," he murmured, pulling her to him for a kiss.

But it lasted barely a second because then she was on her back and he was over her, his cock ramming into her puffy, spasming cunny.

"Oh, yes…" he said, locking his arms and looking down at where they joined. "This is what I've missed so much." He screwed up his eyes and thrust his hips over and over, pounding into her and extending her bliss as he found his. "I love you. I love you, wife of mine."

"And I love you." She clasped his face and stared into his eyes as pleasure gripped him. It seared through his soul, stealing his body for long, beautiful moments as he pulsed his seed deep inside her. "I will always love you."

He collapsed onto her, pushing the breath from her lungs.

"In the name of the Lord," he said, quickly withdrawing and rolling to his side. "If that didn't create another child, I don't know what will." He pulled her close.

"The child will have a sore behind," she said, plucking at one of his chest hairs.

He caught her hand. "The child will know to behave when his, or her, father is around." He paused and kissed her head. "Just as you should."

Chapter Twenty-Three

Philip opened his eyes to the cool light of dawn and the first thing he saw was his wife's face.

She was sleeping peacefully, her long lashes casting shadows on her cheeks and her lips slightly parted. How he'd missed her pretty features, her soft skin, and her sweet, welcoming body. She was thinner than he remembered, though he hadn't been surprised. Many of her letters to him during pregnancy spoke of her lack of appetite and her abject misery at being confined to her room—even though he'd been assured by Queen Isabella that it had been a self-imposed confinement.

He moved a strand of hair from her brow. She didn't stir. In fact, she couldn't be more different to the wild and frenzied, jealousy-stricken woman he'd been faced with the day before. How she'd lashed out with her tongue. How she'd slashed at poor Carolyne's hair. It was as if a demon had possessed her, taken over her. The only thing he could think to do was upend her and spank the devil out of her.

And it had worked.

At least he hoped that was the case.

A rook cawed outside, no doubt sitting on the roof, and the brittle sound echoed into the room.

Joanna frowned and turned toward him, as though escaping wakefulness and the day beyond.

He held her closer. How he wished his sister, Margaret, were in residence. She'd always been a good friend to his wife, able to speak to her when she was being stubborn about things.

Yes, that was it… stubborn. His wife was the most stubborn creature he'd ever come across. Just look at her behavior at French court. Nothing could sway her from acting out her Spanish roots. She'd been both determined and stubborn.

But Margaret wasn't in Flanders. Their father, Maximilian, had organized her second marriage to the Duke of Savoy and she'd been gone for some time. All was well, very well, and she'd made progress with the duke's rightful claim to his lands and possessions over that of his bastard brother by getting Maximilian to nullify the letters that gave René legitimacy. Her husband was now a powerful man in a strategic position in the Western Alps who could be useful to the Habsburgs.

Margaret was an intelligent, indomitable woman, just like her mother.

And just like his wife. Clever, educated, full of thoughts and ideas the way a man was. But combined with a woman's disposition, that made her volatile and unpredictable, as she'd proven yesterday. It scared him to a degree. Not that he believed she'd do anyone actual harm, but her fast temper and quick words could get them into hot water politically if she were let loose in a man's world of governing and policymaking. And a man's world, it was. Traditions stated that rulers be exclusively male. History proved it. It was the way it should be.

How would she handle being queen one day? Her people would love her—he was sure of it. But were she to make a spectacle of herself, fly into rages, or make unreasonable demands, she'd be a laughingstock and not taken seriously. She needed him at her side, as king, as ruler, as pacifier. That was the only way she'd be a good and noble queen, with him as her king.

"You are awake, my love," she whispered quietly.

"Yes."

"I am glad to be waking up at your side." She yawned then stretched.

The sheet slipped, exposing her dark nipples, and his cock stirred. "And I yours." He sat up. Much as he'd like to spend the day naked with his wife, there were issues to address. "Though I have much to do. The Estates General are meeting and—"

"Oh, *Philip*, today? Really? Surely, we can have but a few hours together. To go and see the children together."

He was quiet for a moment. "It is true." He smiled. "I am aching to meet my new son, Ferdinand."

She looked away and dipped her head.

"Joanna?" Terror gripped him. "What has happened?"

She shook her head and her shoulders tensed.

Oh, dear Lord. Had his new baby son not survived the journey? Had sweating fever taken him before he'd even had a chance to know his face? "Tell me." He rushed around the bed and flung open the curtains so he could better see her expression. "Tell me. What has happened to him? What has happened to Ferdinand?"

"I am so sorry," she said, a tear escaping her left eye and rolling down her face. "I am so sorry."

"What are you sorry for?" He clenched his fists, tight balls of worry.

"He is not here."

"Not here? What do you mean, not here? On this Earth?"

"Oh, yes, he is on this Earth. As far as I know." She swallowed and clasped her hands in her lap. "I mean he is not here at Coudenberg. He is still in Spain, with his grandparents."

"I don't understand." His heart squeezed with disappointment and the need to ride, this moment, through the fields and mountains and grab his son was almost overwhelming.

"My mother, she said he had to stay there. As an heir to their crown, they wished him to remain at Spanish court, as they have never met Charles."

"But…But he is *our* child. He belongs with us." The urge to stamp his foot was too much and he did just that, thumping it down onto an oriental rug.

"I should have written to tell you," she said, pushing back the covers and standing. "But I thought it should be done face to face."

"But at least I would have been prepared. I'd presumed he'd arrived with you yesterday at dusk and had been sleeping in his crib with a wet nurse tending him."

She shook her head and took his hands in hers, squeezed them gently. "That was my dream, my wish, but I was stopped. My mother is a cantankerous woman who is stubborn beyond belief when she has made her mind up about something."

He stared into her face and saw her mother's eyes and the same straight line of her mother's mouth.

He sighed. "I am bitterly disappointed. I believed we would all be together as a family. Finally, after all of this time."

"I feel the same." She slipped her arms around him and rested her head beneath his chin. "You know I do."

He held her close, her slim body delicate in his embrace. "We will go to him as soon as it is possible. I will speak to the king and queen and assure them he is safe with us, and remind them that he is not their heir presumptive—that is Charles. It is he who will reign after them."

"You mean after me…and you."

He laughed softly. "Of course that is what I mean, my love."

She relaxed against him and he kissed the top of her head. "We will proceed shortly to see the children. You will be amazed at how they have grown and how well they are coming on with their education. Eleanor is already becoming quite proficient on the harpsichord."

"Oh, how lovely. I am excited to hear her play."

⇉⇇

SUMMER SLIPPED TO autumn and with it, the days shortened and cooled. Geese were fattened. The truffle hunters busied and a Yule log was chopped in preparation for the twelve days of

Christmas.

Philip had relaxed into being a husband again after being parted from Joanna for so long and enjoyed indulging his desires most nights. Her willing, nimble body was always so tempting and she appeared to enjoy their joining every bit as much as he did. At least that was what he presumed from her cries of delight and the moans for more.

Right now, he was studying the long banqueting table that had been set up for the first day of festivities after advent. A boar's head, gaping mouth stuffed with an apple, took center stage, and around it aglow beneath the candlelight sat pots of pickles and fresh loaves of bread, cheese, figs, pies, and walnuts.

"Papa." Charles tugged at his breeches. "Can I have an apple?"

"Please."

"Please." Charles, three now, dashed to the table and came worryingly close to pulling an entire roasted chicken on himself.

"Be careful." Philip scooped him into his arms then passed him an apple. "Where is your mother? Your nursemaid?"

Charles bit into his apple, juice dripping down his chin.

Philip smiled indulgently. His eldest son was going to be a powerful man with a vast empire, or at least that was Philip's plan. With a marriage into France and his great-grandfather and grandfather and himself potentially passing down the role of Holy Roman Emperor, Charles would command great swathes of Europe and beyond.

Which meant it was nice to see him playing carefree with his siblings. Because one day in the future, he'd have a colossal weight upon his shoulders. Being a monarch gave luxury in the form of splendid palaces, feasts, and bejeweled possessions, it was true, but it also came with responsibility and the constant need to look behind and around, work out who was friend or foe, who was plotting.

"Ah, there you are, Charles." Joanna walked into the Aula Magna, her scarlet gown skimming the floor and light from the candle's flames dancing on her face. "Your nursemaid has been searching all over for you."

"I wanted to see Papa," Charles said through a mouthful of apple.

Philip kissed the child's cheek then set him down. "I will see you later."

"Yes, Papa." Charles raced past Joanna to his nursemaid.

Joanna laughed. "He knows that it's story time. He loves that so."

"And I love you." He pulled her to him and stepped closer to the fire. The mantel was decorated with holly and ivy and flames licked upward, reaching for the chimney.

She smiled and kissed him. "I look forward to the feasts and the celebrations of this time of year, but mostly, I look forward to you not having any meetings."

"It is good to relax."

"Indeed, and what is there to do when the nights are so long?"

"I think we entertain ourselves well, wife of mine."

She giggled, a light, little sound that made him smile and want her all the more. "I agree."

"And as our guests are not due to arrive for another hour, I suggest we retreat to our bedchamber to await them."

"But…" Her eyes widened. "I have just prepared myself for the—"

"You can prepare yourself again." He dipped his head and kissed her. She tasted of honey and temptation. "Do not deny me, for I want you. My body wants yours."

"I would never deny you. I am whole when we are together." She slipped her arms around his neck and kissed him deeply.

He moaned as blood rushed to his groin. He pressed against her, letting her know how much he wanted her. Would always want her. He was under her spell.

Chapter Twenty-Four

Joanna sat back and rubbed her belly. She smiled across the room at Philip. He was busy writing to his father.

"Have you noticed anything about me?" she said coyly.

"I can't say I have." He frowned and dipped his pen tip into ink.

"You must have," she said. For days, she'd been waiting for him to notice her swelling abdomen. "Take another look."

He finished a word then set down his pen and looked at her. As his eyes skimmed her body, they widened. "You are with child again?"

"Yes." She laughed. "You have put yet another son into my womb."

"I do love our daughters," he said, standing. "But another son would be a blessing from God." He walked to her, knelt, and then clasped her hands in his. "My wonderful wife, you give me such joy."

"As you do I."

He kissed her knuckles.

Knock. Knock.

Philip frowned. "It is late."

Joanna nodded worriedly. "Maybe one of the children is sick. Eleanor complained of a sore stomach earlier." She pulled her hands from Philip's and clasped the cross around her neck. "Please, Lord, protect our children."

"Do not jump to conclusions." Philip stood. "Your mind always goes to the worst. It is like a sense of doom lives within you."

"I cannot help it." She watched him stride to the door. "The doom...I think it is there."

He opened the door to Belmonte.

"I come with urgent news," Belmonte said. "From Castile." He handed forward a scroll. "Arrived this very minute by envoy." He was breathing hard, as though it had been he who'd galloped over the mountains.

"Oh, dear." Joanna stood, her heart pounding. "My little Ferdinand. Sweet, little baby Ferdinand. What has happened to him?"

Philip said nothing. He snatched the scroll and tore it open, flakes of red wax fluttering to the floor. He read in silence, his eyes flying over the words.

"What is it? Tell me. What is it?" Joanna rushed to him. She thought she might be sick, or faint—or maybe even die with worry.

"It is your mother, Queen Isabella of Castile."

"Heavenly Father." Belmonte crossed himself. "Not our beautiful queen." His face turned ashen.

"My mother. My mother. What has happened?" Joanna strained to see the words on the scroll.

"I am afraid," Philip said, passing the scroll to Belmonte then taking her by the shoulders. "She has died. She is with the Holy Father."

It felt to Joanna like all of her insides had turned to lead and dropped into her feet. Her chest squeezed and her stomach lurched. "No. No. Take that back. Don't say it. There must be a mistake."

"It says so in the scroll," Philip said, his face twisting as if reflecting her pain. "I am so sorry."

"No, not true. Not true." Her eyes stung as a wave of tears crested then fell. "My mother...no...please." She looked at

Belmonte. "This is not true. My mother is fit and strong...so strong."

"It is true she was in fine health last we saw her," Belmonte said, his bottom lip quivering. "But illness can be a terrible, swift thing."

"Illness. What took her? What could possibly be strong enough to take the Queen of Spain?"

"The letter reports that she stepped away from duties several weeks before her death," Philip said.

"What else does it say?" Joanna looked up at him, dashing away the tears. "Please, tell me."

"It says, naturally..." He paused and a single frown line crossed his brow. "That you are now Queen of Castile. Queen Regnant."

She stepped backward, staring at him. "That is not what I want to know. What were her last words? Did she ask for me? Did she suffer awfully?"

"There is no mention of such details," Philip said. His jaw tightened, a small muscle flexing beneath the skin.

"My queen," Belmonte said, bobbing his head. "I am here to serve you now and always. It is my honor to be at your side. Whatever you need, I will get for you and I will lay down my life for you and yours."

She looked at her loyal and faithful servant. "I thank you, Belmonte." She tipped her chin and bit back a sob that threatened to shake her ribs from her body. "But I need to be alone with my husband." Her head felt like it was bursting and her heart breaking. She swayed to the left, the room suddenly spinning.

"My love." Philip's arms were around her. "Please...I beg you...do not be unwell at this news. Not when you are with child."

Words stacked up on her tongue but wouldn't come out. Darkness was coming and she clung to her husband as she lost the battle to stand.

"Quickly, get her onto the bed," Belmonte said, also rushing to her side.

Philip swung her into his arms, holding her close. Her head felt so heavy, she couldn't hold it up and so let it drop to his warm, solid shoulder.

Her dear mother. Oh, what a loss. How would she go on?

Every bitter word said between them twisted inside of her. Every sharp look and mean thought stung her skin like a swarm of wasps. They should have been better to each other. Much better.

And now it was too late.

"Here, rest," Philip said, gently laying her on the bed. "I will fetch the sal ammoniac to revive you."

Joanna shook her head. The smell of the ammoniac was vile. But in an instant, it was there and she breathed in the acrid, salty vapor without meaning to.

She coughed, her eyes flying open as she sat upright, gasping at the shock of the scent.

"Be calm." Philip sat on the bed and took her hand in his. "It is natural that you would be distraught at the loss of your mother."

"I... We..."

"I know. But all will be well. She is with her beloved Holy Father now."

Fresh tears fell on her still-damp cheeks and she held Philip's hand in both of hers, gaining strength from him.

He kissed her brow tenderly then turned to Belmonte. "Take this to Thomas. He needs to be informed so that he can take the necessary steps at court today. There is much to be done."

Belmonte studied Joanna as though deciding whether or not to leave her.

"Go," Philip said a little sharply. "This minute, Belmonte."

"I will be quite all right," Joanna said. "My husband will care for me."

Belmonte hesitated, then, "Yes, Your Majesty." He took the script then crossed the room, the heels of his boots clipping when he reached the wooden flooring. He left and closed the door.

A silence stretched, broken only by the sound of her pulse thudding in her ears.

"You must rest," Philip said eventually.

"I *am* resting," she said. "But tell me all the news that came from Castile." She rubbed her belly. "I need to know."

He released her hand and walked to the fire, clasped the mantel, and stared into the smoldering logs.

For a moment, Joanna studied his long, lean back, pert buttocks enclosed in new dark breeches, and wondered what else he had to tell her. There was clearly something. His knuckles had paled, he was gripping the mantel so tightly.

Still, he didn't speak.

She reached for a kerchief to blot her wet cheeks and the loss of her mother gaped dark and hollow again. How would she be able to live without her? It was true they'd had their differences, but she loved her with all of her heart. She sniffed and a sob caught in her throat as she flopped back against the stack of pillows. "If I am queen, you…you are now…King of Castile," she managed. Surely, that would take the tension from his stiff shoulders.

"No!" He turned, his eyes narrow and his arms rod straight at his side. "Once again, I have not been afforded my true title, my rightful title." He gritted his teeth.

"What do you mean?"

"It seems your mother, the queen, in her will has not even mentioned me or my title. Only that you will act as Queen Regnant, to reign *suo jure* over the kingdom. Independently of me."

"What? No, I don't believe it, Philip. Why wouldn't she name you as king?"

"Because she never liked me, despite her choosing me for you."

"Please, do not say that. She was very fond of you. I know she was."

He huffed. "Then why not pronounce me king? Am I to forever walk in your shadow?"

Joanna said nothing. She didn't understand her mother's decision, either.

"It makes a mockery of me, does nothing to take into account my years of experience ruling, governing, decision-making." He paced the room and ran his hand through his hair, looking more stressed with each step. "And my loyalty to Castile, Aragon, all of the kingdom of Spain and its new western territories."

"I am sorry. I am truly sorry."

"Are you?"

"Yes, of course. I wish us to rule Castile together as king and queen." She paused. "We will go and speak to my father. He can revoke the will, I'm sure. Make you king."

"Huh, Ferdinand will never do that. He is still angry about my meetings with Louis." He laughed bitterly. "Plus, he enjoys being king way too much to give up anything to me. He will claim Castile for himself."

"I'm sure he will if I ask him." She paused. "And I am queen now. Can't I make the changes?"

He sighed and closed his eyes. "I do not know, but what I do know is we cannot travel while you are with child again. We are locked here for many months, and during that time, I have a feeling Ferdinand will meddle and conspire and make those plans to grab Castile for himself when it should be ours. Aragon alone is not enough for him in this new kingdom."

"Please, do not think so badly of my father."

Philip walked to the desk and sat. He picked up his pen once more.

"What are you doing? Can't you leave letter-writing until later?" Joanna wiped at her eyes. The black hole inside of her was growing, grief taking her into its bitter grip.

"I must write to *my* father," he said. "There is much to tell him and I know he will give sound and sane advice."

"WHAT IS THIS?" Joanna studied a shiny, Spanish coin, the sun glinting off its polished surface.

"You do not recognize the faces?" Belmonte asked as he stood before her in the rose garden.

Beatriz, holding baby Mary and seated on a bench beside Joanna, peered at it too. "He has a very big nose," she said.

"Indeed." Joanna peered closer. "And her chin is small." She turned it over and read the embossed lettering. "Oh, my goodness. This can't be... This is my father and me, isn't it?"

"I am sorry to say it is." Belmonte hooked his fingers in the waistband of his black, leather belt. "Delivered today to antagonize your husband, I'd say."

"And in turn antagonize me. How could he?" Anger bloomed. "How could my father do this? It is petty and underhand."

"What is it?" Beatriz asked, jiggling the baby, who was stirring. "I do not understand."

"My father"—Joanna seethed—"has had coins minted with *Ferdinand and Joanna, King and Queen of Castile, León, and Aragon* emblazoned upon them. These are our images."

Beatriz gasped. "With no mention of Philip?"

"No." She tightened her lips, anger at her father rising further. "And Philip will not be pleased that my father believes himself and me to be the true and legitimate rulers of Castile and beyond."

"Only himself, Your Majesty." Belmonte grimaced, as though holding in knowledge that was akin to barbed wire. "Himself only as ruler."

"Himself? But I am on this coin," Joanna said.

"Yes. Please explain, Belmonte," Beatriz demanded.

"Ferdinand has spread rumors that you are unfit to rule, my queen."

"*Unfit?* But I am as strong as an ox. I have just given birth for the fifth time to a healthy child. Who could be stronger? What could be more proof?"

"I agree." Belmonte pressed his hand upon his chest, over his heart. "I admire your strength and give thanks to God for it."

"Yet my father sees me as unfit?" She shook her head in bemusement.

"I believe…" Belmonte cleared his throat and looked down at his feet.

"You believe what?" Beatriz asked.

"Please tell us what you know." Joanna tipped her head, hardly believing that there was more to her father's desperate power grab.

"It pains me to say this, but he is claiming you are of unfit mind and that is why you are unfit to rule."

"Unfit mind." Joanna jumped up. "But that is ridiculous. He raised me to be an educated and thinking woman, and now that I think and speak with knowledge, I am of unfit mind?"

"The night at the castle gate in Castile, when you wanted to go to Philip, that won't have helped the situation." Beatriz shrugged.

Joanna glared at her. "I was simply missing my husband."

"And all the villagers saw the…incident," Beatriz said. "That is how your father will have added fuel to his rumors. He will have reminded them of that night and your banshee wails."

"*Banshee wails.*" She tore her glare from Beatriz to Belmonte. "I was upset and with child and my mother was being most unreasonable."

Neither Belmonte nor Beatriz spoke.

She huffed. "I need to speak to Philip. The sooner he knows of this underhand plot, the better."

JOANNA FOUND PHILIP in the stables with Thomas, discussing the merits of a new foal his favorite mare had produced.

"My love," he said when he saw her holding the hem of her gown away from the dusty ground. "You are here to see the foal?" He smiled. "Come, she is beautiful."

She nodded a greeting at Thomas and then stepped up to the stable door and peered in.

A pretty, chestnut foal on gangly legs suckled from its mother.

"She is but two days old," Thomas said. "And strong too."

"It is amazing how quickly they stand when it takes our young an entire year to master the skill." She smiled. "Quite something."

"She needs a name," Philip said, resting his hand on the small of her back. "Why don't you name her?"

"May I?" She smiled.

"Of course."

She thought for a moment. "Gianna. I believe it will be good luck for her."

"Gianna. Perfect name," Thomas said, picking up a brush and letting himself into the stable.

"Philip," she said. "I must speak to you on a matter of great urgency."

He frowned.

"Come, this way." She led him to a shaded corner of the courtyard and pressed the coin into his hand. "My father...he has minted these coins to circulate far and wide in our kingdom."

Philip's expression changed from one of calm to fury as he read the inscription. He had no need for it to be explained. It was as clear as day to him.

"Of all the... deceitful, sly, scheming, cheating, devious..." He sucked in a breath. "How has this...this thing... come to be here?"

"It was sent to Belmonte and presumably meant to be shown to us."

"Your father has gone too far. I had planned for us to travel there in only a matter of months to correct this situation, but he has made it impossible for civil conversation." He turned and strode ten paces to the left then ten paces to the right. Suddenly, he stopped and held up his hand. "I know how to respond. Yes!"

"What? What are you going to do?"

"I will mint my own coins."

"You will do *what*?"

"I will mint my own coins, with both mine and your heads upon them and stating that we are the true rulers of the Crown of Castile." He smacked his fist into his palm. "In fact...I will declare myself heir to the Kingdom of Spain if he will not. It is only right. And what is more, it is time."

CHAPTER TWENTY-FIVE

Two months later

"WE WILL MAKE plans to leave for Spain when the weather cools," Philip said, pouring Joanna a goblet of wine as they sat on chairs placed in the shade of an oak tree on the far side of the lawn. "You will not enjoy a journey in the heat as much as you would not enjoy a journey in the snow. Autumn will suit us well."

She nodded.

He sighed. "Why are you so quiet today?" He plucked a grape from a bunch that sat in his hand, threw it into the air, and caught it in his mouth.

She shrugged and looked at the horizon. The sky was white blue, the August day blazing the scorched earth.

"Joanna, talk to me. I know you have not left the house and grounds for weeks, but I cannot abide this silent treatment."

"Then you know how I feel to be denied." She didn't take the wine he offered and instead folded her arms.

"I swear on the Holy Bible I have no idea what you are talking about." He sat on the chair beside hers and took a slug of his drink. "Honestly, I am dumbfounded by your mood of late."

"'Dumbfounded by my mood of late'?"

"Yes. It is not becoming and most unsettling for myself and the children. You have been withdrawn and snappish."

"'*Snappish*'?" She turned to him.

"Yes, I feel like you do not love me anymore." He raised his eyebrows in challenge.

"Of course I love you. I love you *too* much. That is why I am…"

"Substantiating rumors that you are unfit of mind."

"How dare you?" Her temper flared. "That is not kind, Philip. I am not *loca*." She swirled her finger beside her temple. "And you know I am not."

"So tell me. There is clearly something wrong and if it isn't that you've fallen out of love with me or that you are mad, what is it?"

"Are you having affairs with the courtiers?" There, she'd said it.

"What? No." He slammed his drink down on the small, walnut table set between them. "Why would you say that?"

"You know why. Don't pretend that you don't."

"I have no idea why you think that." He held out his hands. "I promised to be faithful to you on our wedding day and I have been, no matter what your imagination thinks."

"And can you blame my imagination when you have not been in my bed since Mary's birth?"

He closed his eyes and rubbed them with his knuckles, sighing. "You know why."

"I do not. All I know…" She stood and rammed her hands on her hips. The feelings of rejection were all-consuming, and jealousy had tormented her each night she spent alone. Imagining him with Carolyne and her courtier sluts tortured her until the dawn broke. "All I know is that you are not with me, and you are a man, a man with a ferocious appetite for coupling, so I cannot believe you have not satisfied your urges all of these months."

"Please, sit down." He glanced at the house in the distance. The windows glinted in the sunshine. "I beg you."

"Not until you tell me the truth."

"The truth?"

"Yes, who is she? Who has been satisfying you? Which woman at court?"

He sighed.

"Her name," Joanna demanded. "*Now.*"

"So you can cut off her hair?" He tipped his head and studied her. "You know they say you slashed Carolyne's cheeks too. Until blood covered her white dress, turning it completely scarlet."

"They do not!" She was aghast at the lie.

"They do." He shrugged. "Gossips love to embellish a story."

Joanna wanted to slap his face in frustration at this news but contained herself. "I learned that what I did was wrong."

"You did." An infuriating smile tipped his lips. "As did your rump."

Her eyes stung. "Philip. I can't bear it. I only want you and knowing you want others breaks my soul."

"I do not want others!" He stood and held out his right hand, palm up. "And this is your answer."

"My answer?" She frowned, confused. "What do you mean?"

"Your answer as to how I have…"

"I don't understand."

'You demand to know who *she* is. Well, *she* is this…" He shook his hand at her, fingertips curled into his palm.

"Philip?"

"This." He paused. "Is how I've satisfied my ferocious appetite for coupling of late."

Her eyes widened and she swallowed thickly. "You mean…?" Was he saying what she thought he was?

He bit on his bottom lip as though holding in a grin. His hand still held forward.

"You mean, you…yourself…that you…?" The words wouldn't come out. It wasn't something she'd ever thought he'd do. Him. Her husband touching himself. Bringing himself pleasure.

"My hand is not the same as your wet cunny." He stepped close, so close, she could see the dots of his stubble over his top lip. "But it scratches the itch."

"When you...?" She could hardly believe they were talking this way in the broad light of day...that he was telling her such intimate secrets. Things he did alone, in the dead of night, in complete privacy. But oh, it was arousing to hear it said. So deliciously sinful, it stirred her immensely.

"When I take my cock in my hand and work it until my seed drips from the end, yes, it is pleasurable," he murmured, "but it doesn't give the same satisfaction as being with you. Being *inside* you."

"So be inside me again." She cupped his cheeks. "Please, I beg of you."

"You cannot fall with child again, not until we have been to Castile and claimed our rightful titles."

"So that is why...?"

"Yes, my love. That is why I haven't come to you, or brought you to my bedchamber. We have a duty to fulfill and you need to be fit and well to travel."

"But, Philip, it hurts me, physically *hurts* me, not to be with you." Her eyes prickled with tears. "I can't bear it."

"I am sorry, my love. I am so sorry." He frowned, his eyes darkening, as though it pained him too.

"But all you had to do was ask and I could have..." She held his hand between their faces. "I could have done it for you." She swallowed tightly, imagining the act and how thrilling it would be.

"And do you think I would have the willpower to not spread your legs and enter you when the pleasure reached boiling point?"

"You are a king, master of lands and peoples. I am sure you can master your own desires."

"I'm not sure if I could, not with you." He groaned softly and kissed her palm. "I have missed you, your sweet body, your taste. Please, never doubt that."

"So don't deny yourself for another moment. Take me."

"We have the bigger picture to think of. We must travel and you cannot with a babe in your belly. I fear it would be too much strain for both of you and I would never forgive myself if something were to happen."

"I understand, and I thank you for your concern." Her body was reacting to the closeness of his, her nipples tingling and need flooding her veins. Plus, the relief that he hadn't been unfaithful was like a weight had lifted from her. "But we need not deny ourselves entirely as we have been doing." She slipped her hand down his body, tracing that hard outline of his sternum and abdomen beneath his linen tunic. "For that is just foolish."

"Joanna," he murmured. "What are you doing?"

"What I should have been doing these last months." She cupped his groin and her heart skipped a beat when she felt his growing hardness.

"We are outdoors... The house is—"

"A long way off, Philip, which is perfect."

"But...the bedchamber."

"Do not speak of bedchambers when we own this land, this tree, the air we breathe." She swept her lips over his and squeezed him through his breeches. "You banished the courtiers, remember, claiming you wanted us to be alone for the afternoon."

"That is true." His voice was deep, husky, the way it always was when he was thinking of coupling. "My plan had been to cheer you from the melancholies brought on by grief."

"Grief, yes, but also abstinence." She untied his waistband and pushed at his pants. "Tell me, when you took your cock in hand, like this, did you think of me? Did you think of being naked, hot, aroused and inside me?"

A gasp caught in his throat. He was hard and solid, his flesh warm and smooth. "Joanna."

"Tell me," she whispered against his lips. "Did you think of me when you touched yourself?"

"Yes. Yes. Always." He slipped his arms around her waist. "Only you." He kissed her.

She melted against him and worked his cock in the space between their bodies. His breaths quickened, huffing into her mouth as his kisses became less controlled.

It was thrilling to be touching him this way and feeling his cock solidify as he drew closer to climax. His cock tip rubbed on her gown and her arm ached, but she kept on pleasuring him. Excited for the moment of release.

"Oh, dear Lord, I'm…I'm…"

"Find your satisfaction, dear husband."

He looked down at her hand. It was almost a blur, she was going so fast.

"Like this." Breathlessly, he took her other hand and tucked it between his thighs. "Hold them. Hold them tight."

His balls sat in her palm.

"Stroke them too."

She caressed them firmly.

"Oh…yes." He closed his eyes and gritted his teeth. "Don't stop. Please don't stop."

Joanna had no intention of stopping. If only she'd been allowed to do this to him every night of her confinement, she'd have had no worries about him straying. She'd have known he was hers, and hers alone.

He moaned long and low, appearing to brace himself, as though standing was requiring too much concentration. His knees locked.

A slick of moisture seeped from his tip and onto her palm. She used it as lubrication as she upped the pace.

"Ah…yes." He said, clasping her shoulders and pressing his brow to hers. "I'm going to release my…seed…oh…"

She stared into his eyes as he filled his lungs with breath and was held hostage to pleasure. And then his cock was throbbing and her fingers coated in warm liquid.

On and on she went, working through his groans of bliss and storing every moment in her memory. Her sweet, passionate husband was at her mercy, vulnerable and owned by her and the ecstasy only she could give him.

His mouth hit down on hers in a wild, primitive kiss and he cupped her face, holding her to him. His tongue sought hers in a frenzied dance.

Clinging to him, she stilled but kept hold of his cock and his balls.

After a moment, he pulled back and stared into her face. "I hope we have a kerchief to hand."

She giggled, a bubble of emotion that burst up from her chest.

"Joanna?" He smiled.

"Don't you think we are brazen?" she asked. "And isn't it fun?"

He also laughed. "It is you who is brazen, for it is you who put your hand into my breeches, Joanna." He stepped back and she released him.

Her hand was glistening with his seed and a sticky stripe hung on her pale-blue gown. "It is my right to touch you," she said, raising her eyebrows. "For you are mine, as I am yours."

"That is true enough." He looked around with a frown and then plucked a square of linen from the side of the basket that contained their luncheon. "Here, let me..." He carefully wiped her gown and then her hand.

"I like the evidence of your pleasure," she said.

"And you would set tongues wagging if you were not thoroughly decent when we return." He glanced at the house and then frowned.

"What is it?" She followed his gaze.

"I believe someone is heading toward us on horseback. Look, they've just left the stable block and are coming this way instead of the main track to the road."

"So they are." She sat, feeling hot and self-satisfied. She had performed her wifely duties again, at last. And she had a feeling Philip would be coming to her for gratification, now she'd proven she was up for the job. She reached for her wine and took a sip. It was warm and sweet and filled her mouth like sugared fruit.

Philip righted his breeches then tucked the kerchief away. He, too, sat. He crossed his legs and let out a long exhale. "Who it could be?"

"Thank goodness he or she didn't appear a few moments ago. They'd have had quite the show."

"Joanna." He shook his head. "We need to be careful about what we do and say. You are a woman whose reputation must remain scrupulously intact."

Holding out her arms to the sides, she tipped her head and stared up at the branches of the oak tree. Shadows peppered their way through the leaves, which lifted in the gentle breeze. "Why? We are monarchs. We rule lands and seas, so we can do what we want. And if that includes acts of pleasure, then so be it."

Philip chuckled but then stopped abruptly and stood again. His arms hung at his sides and his shoulders tensed.

"Is it an envoy?" she asked, dropping her hands to her lap. "More bad news? Perhaps my father is dead too."

"You should not speak ill of him."

"Even though I know it would please you if he died?"

Philip said nothing.

"Do you know who it is?" she asked, standing and sensing something was amiss. "Is it not an envoy?"

"No." He paused. "It is not."

"So who is it?"

The figure atop the galloping horse wore a billowing, black cloak, hood up, and was stooped forward as he gained ground. Clearly, he was determined on reaching his destination. Them.

"I think..." Philip said. "It is my father approaching."

Chapter Twenty-Six

The gleaming, black horse came to a grinding halt just to the right of the oak tree. It snorted and pawed the ground. Its coat held a sheen of sweat highlighting the dips and rises of its strong, muscular body.

The rider dropped his black, velvet hood from his head and grinned down. He was clean-shaven, his strong-featured face lined by weather and sun, and his blue eyes sparkled as though full of joy. "Greetings!" He beamed. "Are you not surprised to see me?" He laughed and flung his hand in the air in a flamboyant, curling wave.

Philip stared at the man he hadn't seen in the flesh for over a decade. A cascade of emotions rushed through him like boulders crashing down a mountain. Shock. Joy. Anger. What was Maximilian doing here?

"Your Majesty," Joanna said, bobbing her head. "A surprise, indeed. And your timing is impeccable."

"It is?" Maximilian raised his eyebrows.

"Yes." Philip cleared his throat. "Not a moment too soon."

Maximilian swung his leg over his horse's rump and landed on the ground as nimbly as a man half his age would. "Joanna. At last, I meet my new daughter, and Castile's new queen." He strode up to Joanna and wrapped her slight body in his wide arms, pulling her close and exuberantly kissing each of her cheeks. "What a joy to see you. I hope you'll forgive my rather covert appearance." He pulled back and relieved himself of the heavy cloak, dropping it to the ground with a flourish. "I'm attempting to travel incognito."

"It is truly a surprise. A wonderful surprise," Joanna said, beaming. "To see you here at Coudenberg Palace. Isn't it, Philip?"

Philip watched the greeting as though he were in a dream. What was the King of the Romans doing here? Maximilian had always had a firm dislike of Coudenberg. Never once had he visited after his departure from it, even when Philip had asked him for help.

Except this time, after his last letter, a true and heartfelt plea for advice, here he stood. His father.

"My son. You are looking well." Maximilian reached for Philip and drew him into the same wide, enthusiastic hug he'd given Joanna. He slapped him several times on the back.

Philip felt the affection from his father, the genuine pleasure he got from hugging him, and his anger at being deserted for so long, mostly slipping away.

"Your eyes are just like your mother's," Maximilian said, holding Philip at arm's length and studying him. "So like hers."

"Grandmother often told me that."

Maximilian smiled and released him. He looked at the basket of food. "Enough for three? It has been a long journey. I did not wish to show myself at the house—couldn't stand the fanfare—and went only to the stable yard to seek out a groom. He told me where you were."

"Please, help yourself." Joanna picked up another goblet and filled it with dark, red wine. "Be our guest."

Maximilian laughed. "How strange to be a guest when I used to live here."

"That was a long time ago." Philip tipped his chin. "You have no claim on Coudenberg now." Was that why his father had appeared? He wanted land? Territories?

Maximilian clasped Philip's shoulder and after taking a slug of wine, he said, "I do not wish to take Coudenberg from you, son.

It makes me melancholy, but I will not bore you with those memories."

"Melancholy?" Joanna asked.

Maximilian nodded and glanced away, his eyes misting. He stared at the horizon.

Philip hated to see pain on his father's face and he knew exactly why it was there. He also understood now, more than ever, why Maximilian had stayed away. "Father, there are pheasant pies in here, your favorite—or at least they were."

"Ah, yes, I thank you." Maximilian took an offered pie. "Excellent." He smiled, the sadness lifting with what appeared to be well-practiced effort.

"Here, Father, sit. You have had a long journey." Philip pointed at his seat.

"No, no, son, I have sat for too long in the saddle. My legs will forget what they are for if I do not stand."

Joanna sat.

Philip hesitated then did the same. The horse ducked its head to graze in the shade.

"So…" Maximilian took a bite of pie, crumbs scattering. "Tell me, Joanna, how it feels to be Queen of the Crown of Castile."

"I am not there, with my people, so it's almost as if nothing has changed."

"Everything has changed." Philip frowned.

"I know my mother will not be there when we visit. That is a change."

"I am sorry for your loss," Maximilian said. "I hear your mother was a beautiful and pious woman with an indomitable spirit."

"That sums her up well," Joanna said. "I take comfort knowing that she is with her beloved John and my sister now, in heaven. In the arms of the Holy Father."

"It is indeed a comfort," Maximilian said, crossing himself.

"You received my letter," Philip said, unable to hold the question in any longer.

Maximilian nodded and continued to eat his pie.

"Is that why you came?" Philip asked. Could it be? Would Maximilian have made this long and unusual journey because of the situation Philip now found himself in with his wife's father?

"There is much to discuss," Maximilian said. "My son." He smiled.

"I will leave you to your discussion." Joanna stood. "And depart back to the house. It is getting too warm here."

"My love." Philip stood. "I will walk with you."

She laughed and squeezed his hand. "I am quite capable of walking that distance alone, and from your vantage point here, you will be able to see that I am still on two feet when I arrive. You stay, please. Talk to your father. It has been a long time since you were together."

Philip hesitated.

"I am more capable than you give me credit for." She laughed and kissed his cheek, then turned to Maximilian. "We will feast in your honor tonight."

"That will blow my discreet visit somewhat, but..." Maximilian gave an elaborate bow. "I could never refuse a queen, and a beautiful one at that."

"You flatter me so." Joanna smiled at him, her eyes sparkling. "I am glad to have you here. Truly. And I know my husband is too." She turned and walked away, her gown brushing the grass and the sun glinting off the golden threads in her headdress.

"She is quite the woman," Maximilian said, taking Joanna's seat. "I made a good match for you, am I right?"

"Yes." Philip poured them each more wine, then he too sat in the shade next to his father.

"Yes, but...?"

"I beg your pardon?" Philip said.

"I suppose there's a *but*." Maximilian raised his thick eyebrows. "There always is."

"There is no 'but' as long as I..." Philip thought of her hacking off poor Carolyn's hair. Of how only last week Joanna had insisted there be no female staff allowed in his bedchamber, not even for cleaning and fire duties. And how only minutes ago, she'd asked him if he'd been having an affair. "As long as her jealousy is kept under control. Then she is the perfect wife."

"Ah." Maximilian nodded. "And do you give her reason to be jealous?"

"No." Philip scowled. "I have been faithful. She just gets it into her head that I have not been."

"Then you mustn't give her reason to suspect."

Philip frowned.

"I mean, my son, go out of your way to ensure nothing even looks suspicious between you and another woman," Maximilian went on. "You clearly have an intelligent wife who can read people, including pretty girls who may have their sights set on you. Ensure you give her nothing to read with her clever eyes."

"So I cannot *speak* to another woman?"

"Not unnecessarily, no."

"But that…is…?"

"Preposterous? No, it is what a man must do, on occasion, for a quiet life and a happy wife."

Philip's attention was drawn again to Joanna, who was shrinking as she got closer to the house. "I do want her to be happy."

"I am glad to hear it. I am also glad to be here to meet her, and my grandchildren."

"Are you glad to see me?" Philip couldn't help the sharpness of his tone. "Or am I an extra?"

"My son." Maximilian reached across the seats and squeezed his forearm. "Of course I am glad to see you. You are not the extra. It is you with whom I have come to spend time."

Philip swallowed, not realizing how much he'd needed to hear those words.

"I received your letter," Maximilian said, his tone a little gruffer as he sat back. "King Ferdinand of Aragon is out of control."

"I agree. You know he is trying to say Joanna is of unfit mind in order to seize control."

"Yes, I had heard that, though she seems perfectly sane to me." From his pocket, he withdrew a coin. On it were Philip's and Joanna's faces with the inscription *Philip and Joanna, King and Queen of Castile, Léon, and Archdukes of Austria and Burgundy.* "I am not so sure I can say the same about you. What is this?"

Philip clenched his fists and his belly tightened. "I am the rightful king. They are the coins that should be in circulation...and clearly, they are, since I had them minted in Antwerp and Bruges."

"Do you not think it was a little petty to stoop as low as your enemy?"

"'Enemy'?" Philip paused. "Yes, he is my enemy and no, I don't think it was low at all. The people of Asturias need to know who the rightful monarchs are. Myself and Joanna."

"Joanna, for sure."

Philip jumped up. "Do not question my right to that throne!"

"I am not, but many are." Maximilian paused. "Or should I say *were*."

"What are you talking about?" Philip scowled down at Maximilian, who reached for another pie and bit into it.

After he'd swallowed, he said, "Am I right in saying Ferdinand lost his monarchical status in Castile after Queen Isabella's death?"

"Yes, you are correct."

"Although his wife's will permitted Ferdinand to govern in Joanna's absence or, if Joanna was unwilling to rule herself, until Joanna's heir reaches the age of twenty."

"Yes. Those are the details which I dispute. As Joanna's husband, I should be king if she is queen, which she is." Philip flicked his hand impatiently. "Go on. You said *were*. The people *were* questioning my right."

"The tide is turning." Maximilian nodded slowly.

"Please, do not talk in riddles." Irritation gnawed at Philip.

"I believe Ferdinand has sorely misjudged the mood of the people, for he is planning on remarrying."

"Remarrying? I had not heard this."

"Yes, Germaine de Foix." He studied Philip.

Philip racked his memories. "Oh! She is Louis's young niece. We met her at French court."

"Yes. Exactly, my son, so we can presume he has embarked on a pro-French policy after all of these years of animosity."

"More than animosity. It was outright *war*. If it weren't for my treaty and the future marriage of Charles to Claude, they still would be at war." Philip shook his head at this news. What a turnaround of Ferdinand's attitude to the French.

"You did a bold thing with Louis, intelligent and inventive too." Maximilian nodded. "And though it made you many allies, it made Ferdinand your enemy."

"He will not live forever. He is aging fast."

"His popularity is also dying fast," Maximilian said with a smiling huff. "The people of Castile and Aragon are incensed. They have lost fathers, brothers, and sons in the war with France and now Ferdinand is to be in bed with a French bride. Showing her off at court, dining out, visiting Cathedrals. Oh, no, they are not happy about what is coming."

"I am not surprised. They loved Queen Isabella, almost to goddess status."

"Indeed, and now her widower is rebounding with a French woman, a potential French heir on the horizon. There have been riots, death threats, considerable unrest."

Philip sat and gripped the arms of the chair. He stared at a blackbird pecking in the grass nearby. If Ferdinand was out of favor, this could be his moment to swoop in and take the crown with the support of the people. An act that would make Ferdinand look smaller, weaker, more pathetic than he would surely be able to cope with.

"So you see, Ferdinand's upcoming wedding has had the opposite effect to what he wanted," Maximilian said. "People are not drawn to him as king now—they are repelled. Joanna has never been more popular, more loved, or wanted at home. Her home."

"We should go sooner than planned. To Castile."

"Yes." Maximilian sipped his wine. "You really should."

"And I can claim my title as king. My rightful title."

"Yes." Maximilian clasped his shoulder. "You should do that too. It is yours, my son."

Philip felt a surge of energy rush through him. This was good news his father had delivered. Very good news. He jumped up. "We should not delay."

Maximilian laughed, a deep rumble of a sound that reminded Philip of his very young years. "I agree you should go soon, but please, let me enjoy being here for a few weeks. It would make me very happy."

"Of course you can stay at Coudenberg, for as long as you wish, but...?" Surely, the sooner they left, the better. And Philip had much to do. Letters to send in order to harness support from Castilian nobles, bishops, and prelates. Decisions to make, plans to plot.

"Son," Maximilian said firmly. "What I'm saying is I want to spend time with *you*."

Philip sat again, this time with a bump. All thoughts of letters, plots, and plans disappearing. "You do?"

"Naturally. You are my son and I love you."

"You do?"

"Very much."

For a few minutes, they sat in silence. Philip was warmed by his father's words, then Maximilian spoke again. "Joanna is an intelligent woman. I can see it in her eyes."

"She was well-educated, yes."

"It is more than that. If she is anything like her mother, she is canny, passionate, and determined."

"I dare say she *is* like her mother."

"And her mother was a successful queen...with Ferdinand at

her side."

"What are you trying to say?" Philip asked.

"*Una cosa medesima.*"

Latin. "One and the same?"

"Yes, one and the same, the same crown." Maximilian pressed his lips together for a moment, then, "I know it goes against your Burgundian instinct, what you have always known, but you must both wear the crown as equals. It is the only way both your marriage and the governance of your country will be successful."

"But I will be king." Philip stabbed his finger on his chest. "And she my queen. I will rule with her at my side."

"No." Maximilian shook his head. "If you only ever take one bit of advice from me, my dearest son, then you must co-rule, side by side. Give Joanna a voice, let her use her mind, her clever mind. I am sure she will serve you and her country well."

"She has no understanding of politics. Politics is for men exclusively."

"I think you'll find she has a very good understanding of politics and will forge a very good political identity for herself if you let her."

"But why would I?"

"Philip." Maximilian sighed. "You have not married a milk maid, or a tanner's daughter. You have married a woman who has been raised by a queen. She has learned canon and civil law, genealogy and heraldry, grammar, history, languages, mathematics, and philosophy—if I was told correctly, that is."

Philip said nothing, thinking of the times his wife had indeed spoken knowledgeably on all of those subjects. "You were correctly informed."

"So you must let her put her mind to use. You must be equals in all aspects of your lives." He closed his eyes and tipped his head back. "Trust me. I know it brings the most happiness, the most fulfillment, to be together as one."

Philip stared at his father's profile. What his father said was true, but it did go against his instincts to give Joanna a rein in the handling of politics. He'd only ever known men governing here in his homeland. Men making all the important decisions and policies.

"Please, tell me you will try," Maximilian said. "She might be feisty and sharp-tongued, but that means she's quick-thinking, likely with an ability to preempt, and like all women, sense another's mood and motive with sometimes scary speed and accuracy."

"It is true. She is all of those things."

"Then let us consider it a plan that you will co-rule with Joanna, Queen of Castile, and let us consider it a plan, also, that in a few weeks, you will go and claim your lands and your rightful title."

"To cheers and celebrations if all goes well."

"The people will be ecstatic to have their queen home," Maximilian said firmly, "and to see her with her capable, handsome husband, they will be ready to accept you as king and cast Ferdinand even further into the gutter."

Philip could see it now. The adoring crowds, the waves, and smiles, all for him and Joanna. Ferdinand forgotten. An outcast, now that he'd made the disastrous decision to take a French bride.

Chapter Twenty-Seven

Joanna studied the faces around her. It wasn't often she saw bishops, ambassadors, and the courtiers struck as though watching a storm of shooting stars.

But that was the effect Maximilian had on them. It was as if he were some kind of deity who was blessing them with his presence.

And it was Joanna next to whom he'd wanted to sit at the head of the table with Philip on his opposite side. He'd only had one other request for the banquet in his honor, stating there must be no blueberries of any kind, claiming to have had a very bad experience on one occasion.

"The Venetian ambassador is quite taken with you," Maximilian said, giving Joanna a lopsided smile.

"I am pleased. We spoke at length this afternoon." She brushed bread crumbs from her lap, her black, velvet dress smooth beneath her palms.

"He considers you to be a wise and prudent queen."

Joanna thought about his words for a moment. "It is my intention to rule with wisdom and always put the good of my people first when making decisions. I have faith that God will be at my side."

"And what of the last few months?"

"I do not know what you mean." She popped an almond into her mouth.

"The ambassador said that he was quite taken with your beauty and with your healthy complexion, considering your illness of late."

"My illness?" She paused. "Surely, he means 'pregnancy' and 'confinement.'"

"That is what I hoped." Maximilian paused. "But unfortunately, I believe your father is still spreading rumors that you are *loca* and that is what the ambassador was referring to."

"They are but rumors. There is no truth."

"There is no truth to the contrary when you have not been seen in your homeland for so long. In fact, Ferdinand, your father, put out a statement saying…" He paused, as though recollecting. "The illness is such that the said Queen Doña Joanna, our lady, cannot govern."

Anger welled inside of her.

Maximilian went on. "What is worse is the Cortes believe him and are happy to let him rule in your absence due to your state of mind."

"He is wrong. You sit beside me now. Do I appear sane or crazy? Tell me. Which?"

"Perfectly and unequivocally sane." Maximilian bit into an apple and smiled as he chewed. "And educated and astute and quite honestly, to use another of the ambassador's words, sublime."

"Good. For I *am* sublime." She tipped her chin. Her father was certainly managing to cause her trouble across the miles. "It is just as well we will journey to Castile soon so I can quash these untruths and set the Cortes straight."

"Indeed."

She pursed her lips and pushed her plate aside.

"Do not be downcast, my dearest."

"It is hard not to be gloomy when one's mind is questioned by the masses."

"I have learned many things over the years." Maximilian set a stuffed fig on her plate and drew it back in front of her. "And one of them is that your mind is one of the few things you do actually have control over."

"Go on."

He sipped his wine. "When something happens, good or bad, you get to choose how to react to it. For example, if you disagree with someone—a friend, a husband or wife—you can choose whether to fly into a rage or sit and discuss it."

She pursed her lips. What had Philip been saying to him?

"Personally," he went on, "I prefer rational thinking, though I have found, and this is just me, that I often need to step away, calm down, and then go back to the conversation."

"Why do you say these things?"

"Because I can see that you have a quick and brilliant mind, the way my dear wife had." He paused, sucking in a breath. "And that can scare people, make them unkind to you because they fear you are more intelligent than them. Just look at your father. He is trying to take control of what is yours by saying you are unfit of mind when in actual fact he is scared of your mind."

"He is wrong that I am unfit."

"I know that. Philip knows that. Everyone around you, in this grand banqueting room, knows that, but do not give the gossips any grains to grind." He set his big, warm hand over hers and squeezed. "Maintain dignity and grace, even when you want to scream and shout and smash things to pieces."

Her heart was pounding, her dress suddenly hot and itchy. "I was raised to display dignity and grace." Oh, but it was hard to quash the need to scream and shout when she feared her husband was unfaithful or her lucidity was questioned.

"You were raised as a princess, an *infanta*, yes, but now you have a much bigger weight upon your shoulders."

"It is true I had not expected to become queen. With a brother and sister older than I, the crown was a distant prospect."

"And I didn't expect that, either, when your parents approached me with a suggestion of marriage to my son. I didn't think for one moment that you would be queen."

"And had I been the eldest daughter? My chances of taking the crown greater, then what would you have said?"

"Still a most definite *yes*." He touched his chest, his fingers skimming the Habsburg crest elaborately embroidered on his tunic. "It is clear you were meant to be with my son, no matter what."

"My love," Philip said, leaning forward. "We should do something to cheer you, and something fun for the children. What do you suggest?"

"Jousting!" Maximilian said quickly. "By moonlight."

"By moonlight?" Joanna laughed at the idea.

"I do not wish a spectacle for the masses when I knock my son from his horse." Maximilian chuckled.

Philip laughed. "You think you can, huh?"

"Hey!"

"The children sleep when the sun sets," Joanna said with a smile. "They are resting now. If they don't, tomorrow will be unbearable for the nursemaid."

"Then it will be a festival solely for you, my dearest," Maximilian said. "To wipe the gloom from your face in preparation for your journey to Castile, where your people eagerly await their queen."

※

TWO NIGHTS LATER, under a full moon and a sky alive with tiny bats, Joanna sat next to Beatriz with a blanket over her lap. Lanterns were lit around the arena, casting shadows on the sandy floor. The central fence was draped in flags bearing the sawtoothed red cross of Burgundy.

At either end, horses in armor stood pawing the ground, as though keen to get the secret event started. Atop a bay was Philip, his suit of armor glinting, and at the opposite end, his father, Maximilian, on a gray horse with armor heavily decorated with the Habsburg crest. He was being tended by Belmonte, while Thomas adjusted Philip's stirrups.

"What if they kill each other?" Beatriz worried.

"Oh, it is only a bit of fun." Joanna flapped her hand in the air. She'd seen Philip joust at festivals. His strength and skill was obvious. "To cheer me up, apparently."

"I've heard that Maximilian is quite the expert in the saddle," Beatriz said.

"Do not doubt my husband." Joanna sipped from a goblet of wine. "He is younger and stronger, remember, and equally skilled."

"That is true." Beatriz fiddled with her rosary, the beads softly tapping together. "But I do hope they don't get hurt."

Excitement gripped Joanna. She didn't think Maximilian would endanger Philip—he loved him. That was clear to see in the way he spoke to him, clasped him into rough hugs, and admired the way Philip spoke of his plans for the future and the way he'd managed disputes in the past.

"It is so good that Maximilian visited," Joanna said. "He has boosted Philip's mood. He was so depressed about not being named king."

Beatriz nodded. "It displeased him very much. And now I see him smiling and his determination to right the situation resolute. His confidence has grown with his father's attention."

"He was confident and capable before Maximilian arrived." Joanna rubbed her hands together. "Look, they are starting. It is so exciting."

The two men had picked up their lances, the weight of them evident in the way they lurched until they settled into place. Philip's bay snorted and flicked his head impatiently. Maximilian's horse hopped on the spot, as though struggling to contain its own excitement.

Belmonte and Thomas stepped away from the horses to take a seat behind a rope. Belmonte was tense. She could tell by the way he held his shoulders.

"Are you ready?" Maximilian shouted.

"I am ready for anything!" Philip called back.

"Joanna," Maximilian called. "Give us your applause and cheers, for this show is for you."

Joanna stood and clapped. "And what a show it is."

"And... begin!" Thomas shouted.

It was as if the two horses understood the command because they accelerated from standstill to gallop in a few paces, each tearing down opposite sides of the rail so that they were going to pass in only a matter of seconds.

Each man held his lance forward, the tip aimed over the rail, ready to unseat the other.

She held her breath and knotted her fingers. Her heart was thudding as the horses drew closer, closer, closer.

And then they passed, the lances not making contact at all.

"Oh, that was very nearly a hit," Beatriz said as the horses slowed.

"Go again!" Philip called, spinning around, his lance still held out like a long needle.

Maximilian didn't answer, but he too turned his horse. Within seconds, they were racing toward one another.

Joanna clapped and hopped on the spot. "Go on, Philip! You can do it."

A sharp clang sung through the night air. Contact. Philip's lance had grazed Maximilian's side.

Beatriz gasped and clasped her hand over her mouth.

Maximilian wobbled to the left, the weight of his armor clearly making it hard to right himself. But he did and was soon straight again and his lance forward.

Philip was laughing as he once again turned on the dusty ground. "Have you had enough, old man?"

"Who are you calling 'old'?" Maximilian shouted back.

"And go!" Thomas shouted, holding both arms in the air. "Best out of three."

The horses were off, dirt flicking up behind them. Lances

were at the ready, the riders tipped forward determinedly.

This time, the noise of metal on metal was near deafening. Each lance delivered a brutal blow that knocked the other rider from his horse.

Philip was first to land on the hard ground, his armor clanking as he rolled to a halt on his belly.

Maximilian landed a split second after him, flat on his back, his lance landing over his legs.

Belmonte and Thomas raced forward. Two stablehands grabbed the horses.

Beatriz let out a yelp. "Oh, dear Lord. Whatever damage has been done?"

"They are wearing the finest armor," Joanna said, watching as Philip was helped to roll over and sit. "They will be unharmed."

Maximilian sat, removed his helmet, and passed it to Belmonte. "Son?"

"Father." Philip coughed. "You had a lucky aim that time."

"As did you." Maximilian chuckled and stood stiffly, metal tapping on metal. He made his way to Philip.

"Anything broken?" he asked as Philip got to his feet.

"Only my winning streak."

"Ah, son." Maximilian play-punched his chest. "We will call it a tie. Then there will be no breaking of any streak."

"Yes, it was a tie," Joanna said. "And a very good contest at that."

"Did you enjoy it, our queen?" Maximilian called.

"Oh, yes, very much, didn't we, Beatriz?"

"Mmm, yes, I suppose."

Joanna signaled to the sky. "The night is young. What next to entertain me?"

Philip shook his head and smiled. "Do you not think the King of the Romans, and myself, Archduke of Austria, Duke of Burgundy and King—"

"I know. I know you are very busy during the day, but not right now." She grinned "How about some falconry?"

"At night?" Maximilian removed his heavy gloves. "I am not sure that is wise."

"Mm, okay, how about archery?"

"My love, sensible suggestions only," Philip said. "How would we see the target?"

Joanna laughed; she was indeed having fun. "Perhaps a tug-of-war. Thomas and Belmonte can join in."

"Oh, yes, that's a good idea—safe too." Beatriz nodded enthusiastically. "Yes, let's do that."

"Excellent." Maximilian flung up his arms. "Let us begin. Let us entertain the queen. Where is the rope?"

Chapter Twenty-Eight

"But, Philip, why must we journey by ship? It makes no sense. Certainly not this time of year."

"It makes perfect sense. It is much quicker."

"I am not convinced of that, and besides, the Bay of Biscay is a watery hell. You will see. You will be so sick, to the very base of your stomach, that you'll wish you were dead."

"You are being dramatic." Philip tucked in his linen shirt then fastened the leather belt on his breeches. "Now come on. We have discussed this before. It is time to leave. The carriage awaits."

"I should say goodbye to the children one more time."

"No." His tone was firm. "We have done that already and there were enough tears. I won't go through it again or put them through it again."

She glanced down at her gloved hands. It was so hard to leave her babies behind. They were her heartbeat, the air she breathed.

"And besides," Philip said, picking up her Bible and passing it to her, "we are soon going to see young Ferdinand. I am so very excited to meet my second son for the first time."

"He will not know us."

"All the more reason for us to go to Spain."

"There are many reasons." She stood and took the Bible, studying her husband. "Not least because my people want me there."

"Which is why we must get there swiftly, before your father meddles any more with your rightful lands."

Joanna sighed. "I will agree to traveling on water on one condition."

"Anything, my love."

"Other than Beatriz, there will be no other females on the ship."

His brow creased into several lines. "I do not understand."

"Really?" She stared into his eyes, eyes she knew so well, eyes that were the window to his soul. A soul she loved with every shred of hers.

"Really, I do not understand."

"Dear husband of mine, when I am bedridden with sea vomiting and if you are not, I do not want the added misery of other women planning illicit relations with you."

"But? Joanna…" He took her hand. "That won't be—"

"That is the only way you will get me to walk up that gangplank. No other women on board."

He rubbed his chin. "Your mind works in mysterious ways, Joanna, but yes, if that is what you wish, you and Beatriz will be the only women."

"It is what I wish." She smiled and kissed his cheek. It was warm and soft, not a stray bit of bristle. "Come, let's go, or we'll be late."

"OH, DEAR LORD, have mercy." Joanna gasped as she was rolled to the left and then the right. It was impossible to stay still on the roiling bed.

"The sky has turned as black as night." Philip looked out of the porthole of their cabin. "A storm as malevolent as the devil himself has laid itself in our path."

"And we have only been sailing a day. We're not even near

the worst of the seas." She held her churning stomach and closed her eyes. This was exactly as she'd feared, only worse.

"My love." He staggered back to the bed, sat, and clutched her hand. "What can I do to help you?"

"There is nothing you can do." She squeezed her eyes closed. The waves were whipping against the side of the boat, spitefully tossing it this way and that.

"But I hate to see you like this. It pains me."

"I told you the sea made me sick."

He kissed her hand. "I will tell the captain to make haste to land. I cannot let you suffer this way."

She nodded feebly and braced as the ship lurched upward as though about to take to the sky.

"I will give my instruction immediately. Stay here."

"I cannot go anywhere."

He left the cabin and Joanna grabbed a pillow, pressing it over her face.

The hull creaked as though the strain of the storm were testing its strength. A thud of water hit the porthole and a crash of thunder rang through her ears.

Fear crept up her spine and mixed with her gripping nausea. What if the boat couldn't survive the storm? What if her timbers were snapped? What if the sea won this contest?

The ship lurched again, dipping its aft this time.

Another creak and a bang as a trunk skittered along the floor and hit a wall.

She sat, pressing her lips together. Lightning filled the cabin, white-hot and dazzling.

"Philip," she gasped, placing her feet on the decked floor and standing.

She had to grip the paneled wall to move at all, but after a few moments made it to the door. The breath was pushed from her as the ship tipped to the portside and she slammed up against the wood.

Suddenly, the door opened.

Philip.

His face was wet with sea spray and his hair flattened to his head. His tunic was dripping and his cheeks flushed.

"What is it?" she asked, seeing the fear in his eyes.

"Come quickly. This way." He grabbed her hand.

"But why…" He dragged her along the corridor, then slipped his arm around her waist to help her up several steps to the outdoor deck.

"What are we doing? Surely, we should stay below."

"No." He cupped her face and dipped his close. "We have to get off the ship."

"What? That's crazy."

"The captain says there is water leaking in on the starboard side, and the timbers have given way, weakened—I don't know. But I can't have you in such danger. This leaking vessel will go down."

"Oh, dear Lord, have mercy." Her fear turned to panic. The westerly wind whipped her hair against her cheeks and she could taste the salt in the air. "Philip, what can we do? Where is Beatriz?"

"My men are getting a raft ready and I have sent Belmonte for Beatriz."

"A raft?" She looked out at the tossing, violent ocean, the waves colliding and slapping together sending great plumes of spray in to the dark sky. "How can a raft survive this storm? We will all surely perish."

"That is true." A deep, stern voice. "You will have no chance on a raft."

"Captain?" Joanna turned to see the captain. His hat was pulled low and rain sliced off his broad shoulders. "Please, tell me, are we all to die?"

"No, Your Majesty. Land is not far away, less than half a mile. There will be no need to use the raft. The ship can get there, I am sure of it."

"Are you?" Philip demanded, holding Joanna tighter as the

ship pitched once more. "I need your word that the ship is safe for my wife."

"You have my word," the captain said, wincing as a streak of lightning forked overhead. "I can get the ship to…" His words were cut off by yet more drumming thunder claps.

"Where can you get us to?" Joanna shouted. "France?"

"No. I can get you to England."

JOANNA STEPPED ONTO the pier at Falmouth, England on shaky legs. Her knees were weak, much like the ship's timbers, and her muscles tired from staggering around.

"We must let the King of England know that we are on his land," Joanna said. "We are monarchs, after all."

"Yes. I agree," Philip said. "Though the people here seem friendly."

"Indeed." Joanna smiled at the curious faces around her. Weatherworn fishermen and their wives. Small children peeking around skirts and older people in chairs stitching colorful nets. The village was quaint with brightly painted houses and slate roofs. A high, stone wall protected it from the harbor. A clock tower showed the time and behind it, green and pleasant hills led up to a now-blue sky.

"Thomas," Philip said, turning. "Send Pedro de Anchemont to let King Henry know we are here."

"Perhaps I can see my sister." Joanna clasped her hands beneath her chin. "Little Catherine. She is all alone here since her husband, Arthur, died."

"I will do everything in my power to ensure you see her." Philip turned again to Thomas. "Please, find out where she is."

"Yes, Your Majesty." Thomas turned.

"Now, if we can figure out how to communicate, we will find somewhere on dry land to rest." Philip surveyed the pier. "Ah, there. That gentleman looks like a dignitary. Perhaps he will speak a familiar language."

⇶⇷

A FEW HOURS later, Joanna and Philip were feasting on smoked fish, bread, pastries, and ale. A juggler was performing, throwing numerous batons in the air and catching them with great skill. A sackbut played a jingling melody in the corner.

"It is so wonderful to be off the boat," Joanna said, smiling. "And this small dwelling is so charming, even if the food is rather salty."

"My anxieties are certainly eased now you have color on your cheeks." Philip took a swig of ale. "And these people are clearly impressed to have a king and queen pay them a visit."

Joanna had been used to her husband referring to himself as "king" as opposed to "consort." And it seemed he believed it now, he'd said it so often. And with Maximilian reaffirming the belief, it was set in stone…as far as Philip was concerned.

The music stopped. Conversation quieted. All heads turned to the door.

Philip instinctively put his hand on the dagger attached to his belt. Thomas did the same with his own dagger, as did the other guards.

"Greetings!" a deep voice bellowed. "In the name of King Henry VII of England, a warm welcome is extended to our esteemed guests."

Philip stood, his chin tipped and his chest puffed up. "I thank you."

From the crowd, a tall man with a wispy, gray beard and a flattened hat emerged. His attention fell on Philip and he beamed. "Ah, Your Majesties, what a pleasure it is to have you both in England." He bowed low. "The king is most anxious to make your acquaintance at the earliest opportunity. In the meantime, he has asked me, and these good lords and noblemen, to ensure you have everything you need and are properly entertained."

Joanna's heart filled with warmth. What a welcome, indeed. The English people were most congenial.

"As you can see." Philip held out his hands. "We are being looked after most wonderfully. And I thank you and the king for such an extension of hospitality. We, too, are keen to make his acquaintance."

"And my sister Catherine," Joanna said. "I should very much like to see her."

The earl hesitated for a moment, then said, "I am sure that will be possible."

SEVERAL DAYS LATER, Joanna stood at the entrance to Windsor Castle with such an air of anticipation, she couldn't stop fidgeting with her black, embroidered headdress, her heavy necklace and her long, scarlet sleeves. But it wasn't the King of England she was excited to see, it was her dear little sister. Not so little now, but all grown up. Joanna knew instinctively that she wouldn't have changed much, not inside. She'd still be the sweet, inquisitive little soul she'd always loved.

Behind her stood Beatriz and Belmonte and the Earl of Arundel. The earl had urged her to arrive at the castle in secret. Philip had already been with the king for a few days, making his acquaintance, hunting, feasting, and talking politics. Joanna had wanted to arrive sooner, but Philip had been keen to make sure all was safe for her.

But now the time had come.

They walked across the cobbled courtyard to the New Tower. The earl nodded to two courtiers, who opened a vast, oak door with iron hinges.

And then, through the shadows, Joanna saw first Philip and

then King Henry.

A hat that looked much like a beret sat atop the old king's head and it held a large ruby set in decorative gold. His fair hair was wispy and his face long, cheeks sunken. His robes were heavy, covering what appeared to be a slight frame. Certainly, he appeared small standing next to her tall husband.

The king's eyes sparkled and his mouth stretched into a smile showing darkened teeth. "Joanna, Queen of Castile, what a pleasure it is to finally meet you." He stepped forward, kissed each of her cheeks, and then embraced her in a firm hug.

"It is a pleasure," she managed.

"And you are every bit as beautiful as your husband told me."

"I thank you. And I thank you for such wonderful hospitality."

"The delight is all mine. And to have your husband's company has been an exceptional treat. Most agreeable and joyful. He is a man with many great ideas and plans for the future. Our countries are indeed special allies."

She smiled at Philip. "Is my sister here?"

"Yes, my love. Up these very steps."

Her heart picked up and she clasped her hands together. "Please, do not think me rude if I go to her. My arms ache to hold her. My heart beats faster at the thought of seeing her dear, sweet face."

The king laughed. "I understand. It has been many years since you have seen her."

"It has, and I am thankful to you and the good Lord for keeping her out of harm's way all of this time." She gathered up her hem. "Up the stairs, you said?"

"Yes, the last door." The king gestured flamboyantly. "Go. Go. And I will look forward to speaking with you later. Perhaps at dinner, if you would join your husband and me? Cook is preparing swan."

"I would like that very much." She didn't wait around a moment longer. She practically ran up the stairs, Beatriz hot on her heels.

When they reached the corridor Beatriz said, "Do you think she has changed much?"

"Taller and wiser. She has been through a lot since the death of her young husband, Arthur."

Beatriz said nothing. They rushed past richly decorated tapestries and arrived at the door. For a moment, Joanna hesitated, then she pulled in a deep breath and opened it.

Standing in milky winter light drifting in from a lead-paned window was Catherine of Aragon.

Her pretty face was framed with a pale-brown headdress dotted with pearls, and a matching gown was ruched at the shoulders, gathered at the waist and frilly around the white cuffs, which were also studded with pearls.

"My baby sister." Joanna rushed forward, arms spread. She scooped Catherine into her arms and held her close. Her frame was stronger yet still slight and she smelled of roses. "Oh, how I have longed for this moment but didn't believe it would happen." She pulled back, tears dampening her cheeks.

Catherine's complexion was delicate, her eyes glistening with emotion, and she swallowed tightly. "The Lord works in mysterious ways, dearest, beloved sister."

"He certainly does. We were nearly lost at sea, and now...now I am in the King of England's court with you." Joanna laughed, a sudden, jubilant burst of emotion. "How wonderful. I hope we can spend many days together."

Catherine took her hand and smiled. Her eyes were also tear-filled. "That is what I hope too. There is much to tell you." Her attention strayed over Joanna's shoulder. Her eyes widened. "Beatriz! Is that you?"

"My dear child." Beatriz stepped up and gathered Catherine into her arms. "Oh, how grown you are. How very beautiful you are."

CHAPTER TWENTY-NINE

JOANNA SAT IN the window seat of the top room of the tower and sipped sweet peppermint tea. She couldn't tear her eyes from her beautiful sister. Becoming a widow at the tender age of just sixteen hadn't faded the sparkle in her eyes, though her smile was not as quick to tip her mouth as it had been.

"Please, tell us more," Joanna said. "Tell us everything."

"I am afraid there is no way to add roses and perfume to the full truth." Catherine scowled.

"I am sorry for that and I will help in any way I can." Joanna took her sister's hand. "As will Beatriz."

"Of course," Beatriz said, "you have been in my prayers every night. I am so relieved that the sickness that took your husband did not steal you away from the Earth too."

"It would have been God's will if that had been the case." Catherine touched the cross at her neck, one that their mother had given her when she'd been born. Joanna remembered it.

"My father by law, whom you have just met, aged quickly after the death of Arthur and then with the loss of his wife too…"

"Yes, he does look rather…disheveled." Joanna's mouth downturned. "For a king, that is."

"He is thin, it is true," Beatriz added.

"He worries about the Tudor dynasty," Catherine went on. "It hangs precariously by a thread now that he has only one son, Henry, who is still young, five years younger than I."

"Unless he has more heirs now," Joanna said.

Catherine's lips tightened.

"What is it?" Beatriz asked, setting down her cup.

"For a time…" Catherine looked between the two women. "He talked of marriage to me."

"What? No…you can't," Joanna said.

"It was not for me to have a say in it," Catherine said. "King Henry didn't want to pay back my dowry to Mother and Father and he knew me to be young and believed me to be fertile."

"So why didn't he marry you?" Beatriz asked.

"For that, I have our parents to thank." She smiled at Joanna. "For all they were stern at times, they have our best interests at heart, really."

Joanna bit on her bottom lip. Now was not the time to share with Catherine how their father was spreading rumors about her sanity.

"I wrote to Mother," Catherine was saying, "telling her of my distaste for the marriage and she replied…" Catherine paused. "I want to get this right. She replied with 'That is an evil abomination that offends my ears.'" She laughed.

Joanna and Beatriz laughed too.

"She had a point," Joanna said. "And no doubt a plan to distract him."

"Indeed, you know…or rather, *knew* her well," Catherine said, "for she sent him news of her niece, Joanna of Naples, newly widowed and quite beautiful."

"And what did Henry do?" Joanna asked.

"Almost immediately, he sent a delegation to Italy to discover more about Joanna. He also instructed his envoy John Stile to find out about Joanna's appearance."

"This doesn't surprise me," Joanna said.

"Yes, I agree. He wished to know the color of her hair. The condition of her teeth and the shape and size of her nose and eyes."

"That is a great many details," Beatriz said.

"That is not all. From what I heard, he also demanded to know the state of her skin and complexion and whether she had hair on her face. He instructed Stiles to pay particular attention to her breasts…"

"How very improper." Beatriz gasped and pressed her hand to her chest.

Catherine leaned forward and lowered her voice. "He wanted to know whether they be big or small and was apparently delighted to find out that they be somewhat great and full, comely and not misshapen." She giggled.

"Oh, my." Joanna laughed and shook her head. "What a relief you did not have to marry him. He is a brute."

"Indeed." Beatriz wiped away a tear of mirth. "And what of you? Will he repay your dowry and send you back to Spain?"

"No." Catherine shook her head. "My fate has been sealed here, in England."

"It is a fine land," Joanna said.

"Not so much in the winter." Catherine shuddered. "It is bleak and cold with many days of rain. You would like it much better if you were here in the summertime"

"Rain is good for the crops."

"There are no olives."

"I shall ensure many barrels are sent to you, dear sister." Joanna kissed the back of Catherine's knuckles. "For I hate the thought of you not having olives to nibble."

"I thank you."

"You said your fate was sealed," Beatriz said. "Why do you think that?"

"Because…" Catherine glanced out of the window. "Upon hearing of our mother's death, I became quite unwell. Sickness in my stomach—even the Spanish physician could not heal me. His final suggestion was that I needed to marry and resume sexual activity." She rolled her eyes. "I mean, really! If not having sex made a woman ill, then don't you think every nun in the land would be mortally sick?"

"I dare say." Joanna nodded.

"Good point," Beatriz added.

"I am to marry the young Prince Henry, when he is of age," she said. "Pope Julius has given special dispensation."

"That was needed?" Joanna asked.

"Yes, because I was married to Henry's brother. And the Bible forbids a man to marry his brother's wife, but as our marriage was unconsummated, we never lay together, so the Pope has given us his blessing."

Joanna was quiet, as was Beatriz.

"And he's a pleasing person, young Henry," Catherine said, a smile suddenly lifting her mouth. "Clever and witty. I enjoy his company and he enjoys mine. Certainly, he seems to have eyes only for me, even though he is young."

"And I can see why." Beatriz tucked a strand of hair behind Catherine's ear, the way she used to do when Catherine had been an infant. "You are a sight to behold."

"I thank you, dear Beatriz." Catherine took her hand.

"And a man who has eyes only for you is a gem, indeed," Joanna said. "One you should keep tight hold of and never let go."

"I would agree with that wholeheartedly," Catherine said. Her expression suddenly lifted. "How excited you must be to return to Castile."

"Yes, indeed I am." Joanna had dreamed of the fanfare, the adoring crowds, the cheers and adulation for both her and Philip. It would be a wondrous occasion and one her father could not ignore. There was no way Philip could be denied his crown when she had an entire population and army on her side. "It will be a joyous occasion and what will please me the most is being invested alongside my dear husband. He will look so handsome wearing a Castile crown and one day the Spanish Crown."

"Indeed, he will," Beatriz said.

"I cannot wait to meet him." Catherine poured more tea. "But perhaps tomorrow. Today, I am indulging myself with your company alone, for I have missed you so much, dear, kind, brave Joanna."

"How did you find your sister?" Philip asked from a plush chair. He wore just his breeches—his broad chest bare—and held a leatherbound book.

"Physically, she is well, but life has been hard here in England for her since her husband's untimely death." Joanna set her headdress to one side and looked around the room. "We have much to discuss, she and I."

"And you will have time. We will stay awhile. It is good for future relations between our countries." He paused. "What do you think of our host?"

"He is most hospitable and what a lovely room he has given us. Much better than a cabin on a storm-battered ship. The floor doesn't move, for one thing."

He laughed. "I agree."

They had been lodged in a very grand section of Windsor Castle. The walls were adorned with silk tapestries and heavily framed paintings of landscapes. Above which was a border of crimson velvet stenciled with the king's devices: roses, portcullis, and shields.

The bed was a mahogany four-poster, the deep-green curtains thick with golden thread. The solid furniture gleamed with polish and was set with trays of goblets and wine, as well as apples, dates, and walnuts. A large window, set forward in a squared section of the room, offered views of the wintery landscape with its bare-boned trees and copiously clouded sky.

"The fire has not long been lit," Philip said, standing and striding toward it. He threw on another log then held his palms to the warmth.

"That is good. It is deep winter here." Joanna lit a fat candle on a bookshelf."

"It will do us good to rest up after our awful experience."

"I thank the Lord we survived." She touched the cross at her neck. "At one point, I believed we were taking our last breaths."

Philip stepped up to her and wrapped his arms around her. "I too give thanks. What a loss it would have been for Castile if we had drowned."

"And for our children."

He smiled and touched his lips to hers. "That goes without saying, though I must say we have left Charles a great inheritance of land and titles."

"He will be a powerful man one day, but not for a great many years, I hope." She set her hands on his warm chest. "Make love to me, Philip. What will it matter now if I become with child? We will be in Castile before I even know it."

"You tempt me so." He groaned softly and kissed her deeper. "Another child would indeed be a blessing and a great gift."

"So give in to temptation," she whispered as she tugged at the front lace of her gown.

He studied her movements and when her breasts were exposed swiped his tongue over his bottom lip. "My sweet Joanna, you drive me *loco* with desire for you."

"As do you."

"So I suppose we are crazy for each other." He cupped her right breast and kissed her again.

She melted into his hard, strong body. He was so alive, so vibrant and powerful. With him at her side, she could do anything, even defeat her father.

Within a minute, they were both naked and falling onto the bed. A log crackled in the grate and a hunting horn sounded in the distance. Joanna ignored it all as her husband settled between her thighs and found her entrance.

"I wish for you to find pleasure many times," he murmured, easing inside her. "So that you truly forget all of your worries and your tumultuous time on the ship."

"I have forgotten it already." She gripped his shoulders and stared into his eyes. "You are all I think of."

He smiled then clamped his lips together as he drove in deep.

She gasped. His cock's entry was always a blissful stretching that bordered on discomfort before becoming absolute pleasure.

He moaned, deep and guttural, and his body connected with hers.

She bucked up to meet him, grinding against him as she wrapped her legs around his hips. She knew his body the way she knew her own and ran her hands down his long, lean back to cup his firm buttocks.

Within minutes, he was skillfully driving her to her first orgasm. She didn't shy from it. She reached for it, then claimed it, and as she spasmed around his cock, lost to ecstasy, she thought her heart would overflow with love.

A love that was so profound, so weaved into the fabric of her soul, that without her one and true love, she was sure she'd unravel, her threads would be laid bare, and there would be nothing left of her but madness.

THE END

Don't miss EMBRACED BY THE EMPEROR and find out how Philip and Joanna's children fare in sixteenth-century life and love.

Book Club Questions
Adored by the Archduke

1. Women's lives in the Middle Ages were very much determined by their fertility. How do you think that compares to modern day around the globe?
2. What did you think of the bedroom scenes in *Adored by the Archduke*? Were they believable? What do you think about Philip spanking his wife for her bad behavior?
3. How do you see Joanna's state of mind develop throughout the story and are her moods and paranoias justified?
4. Queen Isabella of Castile is a powerful character. How do you see her as a mother to her children?
5. The Spanish Inquisition was launched during this time period. What do you know about it?
6. What did you think of the pace of Joanna and Philip's relationship?
7. To whom would you recommend this book?
8. What emotions did Joanna's situation invoke in you?
9. What emotions did Philip's situation evoke in you? Would you date him?
10. If *Adored by the Archduke* were a Netflix series, who would play Philip and Joanna?

Character Interview
Adored by the Archduke

Hop on over to Lily Harlem's website to enjoy an exclusive interview with Philip and Joanna.
www.lilyharlem.com/philip-and-juana.html

Suggested Playlist for
Adored by the Archduke

"Song of Kings" – Clamavi De Profundis

"everything i wanted" – Billie Eilish

"Daylight" – David Kushner

"The Lasty" – Santigold

"Falling" – Harry Styles

"Fuel to Fire" – Agnes Obel

"Didn't You Know" – Delara

"Breathe Me" – Sia

"Poison & Wine" – The Civil Wars

"Look What You Made Me Do" – Taylor Swift

"Love The Way You Lie" – Eminem, Rihanna

"Fade" – Lewis Capaldi

"Would I Lie to You?" – Charles & Eddie

"Vampire" – Olivia Rodrigo

"Forgiven" – Within Temptation

"I'll Be Good" – Jaymes Young

"Woman in Chains" – Tears For Fears, Oleta Adams

"My Immortal" – Evanescence

About the Author

Lily Harlem wears many colorful, feather-adorned hats but being an author is one of her very favorites.

Since leaving an adrenaline-packed eighteen-year career in acute nursing and picking up a pen she hasn't looked back. With industry awards and bestsellers, she has over one hundred novels to her name and many short stories. She's an indecisive butterfly when it comes to genres and pairings though historical romance has become a firm favorite in the last few years – dashing dukes, dominant Vikings and surly Highlanders, what's not to love?

She's British through and through with a Scottish father and English mother. Lily has lived in England, Scotland and presently resides in rural Wales with a desk overlooking rolling hills. Mr Harlem is a constant source of inspiration, and his family are Irish so a great deal of time is spent on the Emerald Isle too.

Her characters' love stories may span the centuries, but they all have a few things in common—passion, romance, adventure, a happily ever after…oh and the bedroom door is always left wide open. If you've fallen for the hero in a Lily Harlem book you'll get to know him intimately and discover all of his skills, and his kinks. Enjoy!

Website – www.lilyharlem.com
Facebook – facebook.com/groups/188731774881774
Amazon – amazon.com/stores/Lily-Harlem/author/B004MHRTQK
BookBub – bookbub.com/profile/lily-harlem
Twitter – @lily_harlem

www.ingramcontent.com/pod-product-compliance
Lightning Source LLC
LaVergne TN
LVHW011930070526
838202LV00054B/4570